GLORY DAYS

GLORY DAYS

ROSIE SCOTT

THE SEAL PRESS

Copyright © 1988 by Rosie Scott

This U.S. edition first published by The Seal Press, 3131 Western Avenue #410, Seattle, Washington 98121. Published by arrangement with Penguin New Zealand.

Library of Congress Cataloging-in-Publication Data
Scott, Rosie, 1948-
    Glory days / by Rosie Scott.
        p.   cm. — (International women's crime)
    ISBN 0-931188-72-5 : $8.95
    I. Title.   II. Series.
PR9639.3.S39055   1989
823—dc19   88-37561
                                                                      CIP

Cover illustration: Clare Conrad
Printed in the United States of America
First edition, March 1988
10 9 8 7 6 5 4 3 2 1
The Seal Press
P.O. Box 13
Seattle, Washington 98111

To Danny, Josie and Bella

1

After I did my last number I went out back for a while to talk to the band, have a smoke and relax.

The audience tonight had been really sludgy, they were against us right from the start. They drank and talked all the way through the set, waves of sodden hostility came off them. It looked as if fights would break out later on. One guy yelled to me to get my gear off and when I told him to get stuffed he made as if to come up on stage. Drunks didn't usually worry me, but it seemed serious. There was a look of drunken hate in his eyes and he stumbled hard against the table, crashing cans off all over the floor as he lunged. The bouncer moved over in his direction so I finished the song and got off quickly.

Out in the dressing-room I just sat, I couldn't be bothered moving. It was quite comfortable. There were huge holes punched out of the plaster walls and the foulest graffiti I've ever read scrawled over every surface. For me, the place always vibrated crude energy, the ghosts of a thousand bands, the night life, the buzz, being wasted, shooting up and being sodden drunk, the groupies.

I'd always liked playing at Mainstreet, there was none of that white-lit razzle-dazzle you got in some venues, or the TV middle-New Zealand tinsel feeling with middle-aged punks talking real tough to the kids. In those places any passion or guts was obliterated by the plastic. There was history in Mainstreet, another dimension made up of seedy events, and music was part of the air you breathed there. The dressing-rooms, the band stage, the dance floor were awash with it. It was the closest you could get in Auckland to something so urban and personal.

Sometimes though, like tonight, I was glad I only did an

occasional gig with the band for the under-the-counter extra. They had to drag around the pubs in Auckland every night, hassling with the brewery management, getting paid nothing, lugging all that endless gear up and down backstairs. It was Cash, the leading guitarist, who kept them going with his megalomaniac dreams of fame and money. The band was down to three members, and almost skint through Cash's mismanagement, but he always had an answer if someone wanted to give up.

'Think of Split Enz,' he'd say, his manic eyes flashing. 'Lived on the bones of their arse for years before they got a break. Now look at them!' There was never a trace of humour in the man, and not only that, he could never leave well alone. Here we were that night, sitting quietly, trying to forget all the little humiliations, and he had to start in on his favourite paranoia, managers. As soon as he was well into it, Simon just got up and left without a word. He never said much, but he always made his presence known.

'Then the bastard just told me — sorry there was nothing in writing. There wasn't nothing in bloody writing either. I told him straight, listen to me, mate, I said . . .'

Jeff winked at me. They had a kind of Laurel and Hardy act going which was boring for anyone around them. They were like a married couple.

'Which manager?' I asked, not really interested. It was nice to sit there a minute, I felt like being social.

'Bob.'

'Him? Come on, Cash, you never open your fucking mouth whenever we're having a hassle with him.' Wink, wink.

'I fucking did. I told him where to get off and I said I wanted that hundred bucks or he'd hear from my lawyer.'

We all shifted around in the little plastic chairs, making ourselves more comfortable, helping ourselves to the cashew nuts the last band had left. It was very late and the place smelt like an old sad party in a boarding-house room. The grime was centuries old, no one could ever clean it again, even if they wanted to. The dust was like gas in the air.

'You still want to sing for us Friday? Glory?' Cash was a little, intense, thin guy with a very complicated mental life. You could hear his brain buzzing like a computer. He was like my second husband — always on the make — but not nearly so brutish.

'I don't know.' I'd had a run of nights like tonight, the smell of stale beer and hung-up jerks in the audience. I probably needed a break from it for a while. I had a lot of work to do with my new exhibition coming up.

'No kidding? You going to ask for more money?' Cash was always super respectful with me. We had separate contracts with Bob and I realised he was going to do something with that information.

'Look, old mate, don't go telling the manager either, because I'll know who it was.'

'Come on, man, what do you take me for?'

Jeff doubled over with laughter, wheezing and panting.

'Just don't,' I said.

'She's got your number.'

Jeff was snorting like a madman. His face was so ghastly pale he looked like he was having a fit.

'What's so funny?' Cash asked, but he couldn't help smiling, watching me shiftily and trying to hide it.

'You!' shouted Jeff. 'You should have seen your face.'

They were both laughing that endless inane stoned laugh which could go on for hours. A kind of erch erch from the stomach.

'You buggers are nuts,' I said. I got up to put my fur coat on. I really fancied myself in it even though it was a second-hand one from the Mission shop off Dominion Road. This started a further wave of hysteria from them.

'Look at her in her coat. She's like a huge cuddly polar bear, num num. Look at those tiger eyes.' Con-man that he was, he had already forgotten his faux pas. I advanced on him holding my furry arms out, and enveloped him in.

'Like it?' I asked, hugging him a bit too hard. His body felt like wire. I could glimpse his scared pale eyes.

'You're squashing me, you bitch,' he said. I picked him up like a baby and started cradling him.

I sang, 'Hush little baby don't you cry,' in my breathiest voice. He squirmed away like a small boy. When I put him down he got quite sulky, huffing and puffing and lighting a cigarette. Jeff nearly wet himself.

'Feel better, diddums?' I asked kindly. I suddenly felt good again — full of the milk of human kindness.

'A polar bear,' and Jeff went off again. He looked as if he was going to be sick. Cash was too pissed off to say anything. I knew he wouldn't say anything to the manager though, that's why Jeff was laughing so much. We both knew Cash was really a wimp for all his big-noting.

'Bye,' I said. I liked the feel of his frail little body in my arms — it was like holding a child. It made me feel like a queen, a great massive island, a holder and sustainer. I'd always wanted to do something to Cash like that. He'd probably secretly enjoyed it.

I walked past the stage door, my eye out for the obstreperous prick who shouted at me. Going past those mumbly old tables in the semi-dark, with the heaps of cans underfoot and mangled cigarette packets twisted into the ashtrays, I thought of yet another drawing of this place. It was like a rococo dream with its balconies and tropical seediness, its great fans moving sluggishly above the dance floor.

'Hey, Glory!'

It was Patrick, an art student I knew, waiting for me at a table at the back. He looked out of place with his fashionable punk clothes and razor-short bleached hair. It was all too shiny to be the real thing. There was a girl at his table who was completely comatose. She was only young, maybe fourteen, still a schoolgirl, with cropped, henna-ed hair, soft and ripe as a plum. Her eyes were closed and she didn't look too good. She was holding a lighted cigarette in her numb hands and as I watched, it tilted dangerously close to her thin child's wrist. I had to take it off her, in her state she probably wouldn't even feel the burn.

I'd seen her before. She seemed out of her depth, she was always hanging around with drug-world people. She looked like a rich schoolgirl out on a self-destruction course, as if she was sleepwalking. Tonight she was just sick and vulnerable. Patrick didn't seem to be taking any notice of her. He said to me, 'It's hard to track you down, Glory. You never answer your phone.' He gave me a cigarette.

'Oh. I'm very busy.' I sat down out of politeness, took the cigarette and even a drink from the can.

'I just wanted to invite you to my opening,' he said. 'I mean, only if you want to come. I'd really like you to.' He smiled at me, full of high spirits, black-eyed as a robin through the smoke.

'When is it?' I asked.

'Couple of weeks. I'll send you the thing. It's being printed.'

I didn't go to many openings now, I never learnt anything valuable there except for the art-world gossip — who was getting which grant, the various feuds going on, the movements of the dealers and gallery owners. I had an uneasy feeling about gatherings like that, they made me anxious and aggressive as if all my shortcomings had come to a head. Places like that made me feel as if I was moving underwater. I kept every gesture very slow so as not to provoke the attackers ready to spring at my throat. But I felt a certain amount of obligation towards Patrick. He had attached himself to me with the ferocity of a limpet, something I normally wouldn't tolerate. He had saving graces — he was brilliantly talented and he always knew when he'd gone too far with me. I liked him and I wanted to help him.

Patrick inhabited a strange world, his friends were all high-powered decadent super-rich students. Kids who would do anything for a buzz, bored malcontents straight from the hothouse of Dio and Kings with skin like cream, and hard eyes. I'd even done a couple of sittings with him on the strength of that peculiar whiff, but I soon got tired of it. His face was too ordinary to attract me for long. He didn't take any offence though, he was a really professional painter for such a young kid. He knew where my interests lay.

'I'll try. It's very close to my opening.'

'Oh. Can I come to that?' He had the easy cheek of his class, that instinctive opportunism. It was a real barrier.

'Yes,' I said.

Another band was starting up, very desultory, the drummer was falling over himself, obviously half cut. There were only a few drunks left in the audience, mumbling to themselves in the gloom. When the loud bad music suddenly started up it was like a blow to the head. I didn't feel like talking any more, so I got up to go.

He said quickly, 'You want a lift, Glory?'

'No. I've got my own car.' He stood up with me, gathering his bag and knocking over the half-empty beer can.

'What about your mate?'

The girl with Patrick had slowly slumped forward onto the table, her soft bare childish arms right in the slowly spreading beer puddle. Her breathing was stertorous and she was motionless except for the huff of her chest. I put my arm under her shoulder and her skin was dry and unpleasantly cold to the touch. There was something so touching about her little bird bones under my hand.

'She's nothing to do with me. She just came and sat here. She's a fucking junkie.'

We both stood looking at her. He didn't care about wetting the kid with his beer.

'I gotta go,' said Patrick finally. 'Steve's waiting outside.' He paused, wanting a cue. 'You want to do something with her? She'll sleep it off. She's alright.' He peered over at the child's face pretending concern. 'Good colour,' he said.

I knew he'd help me if asked, for his own reasons entirely, but I decided against it.

'You go on,' I said.

'See you later, Glor,' he said. He knew there was a beat in there somewhere that he'd missed and he was anxious to gloss it over. He needed to be on side with me.

'You sure?'

'See you,' I said, thinking about what I should do. The kid looked awful, but I knew from experience that walking her around could start off circulation again and raise her blood pressure. I could just tell Bob the manager and leave it to him, but I didn't want to. The kid was probably a runaway.

I sat down again looking at her. The place was just about to close down for the night and I wanted to leave.

I said to her, 'Listen, can you walk with me? I'm taking you for a walk.' She fluttered her eyelids and suddenly gave me a sloppy trusting baby smile. From somewhere in her poor old zonked-out mind she'd heard me. She moved her hands slightly, all the nails were bitten to the quick. That was enough.

I said, 'OK. Let's go.'

I pulled her up and she came easily, balanced for a moment, then her soft body fell against me and I had to take all her weight. It was like carrying a dangling floppy doll. She wasn't very heavy and she let her head fall on my shoulder, so trusting. She was still a child and I wondered how she had ended up like this alone in a sleazy nightclub at three o'clock in the morning, not a friend in the world, and all that poison clogging up her heart.

We managed to get along through the tables and down the stairs but I needed a breather once I'd hauled her down into the foyer. The two of us leaned against the wall like drunken companions. There was a sick smell coming from the dirty, can-strewn carpet, and in the greenish light the whole place looked really scabrous. It was deserted except for Shorty the doorman, in his little box. His collapsed face leered up at me like a dream, he was like a sad old reptile guarding his filthy cave.

Shorty sat there night after night cracking his knuckles, drinking cokes and trying to force conversations on people. Whenever there was a fight he was nowhere to be seen. He reckoned he was bantamweight boxing champion of New Zealand in 1942, but like most of his stories that was only part of it. His mate said he'd never got past the provincial titles, he'd ruined his chances with the booze. He was a garrulous old bastard, punch-drunk, aggressive with loneliness. He lived up the road in one of those old boarding-houses in Upper Queen Street, and drank himself to sleep each night with sweet sherry. He was nearly at the end of the line. We all went past him fast, but I knew when I was trapped.

'Hello, Glory! How's tricks?'

Gidday, Shorty.'

'Know that guy? In the audience? The one what was abusing you?'

'No. How did you know about that?'

'Scum, · that's what they are. Needs his head pushed in. Wanted to take all your clothes off. A great big tall girl like you. Hee, hee, hee. With all that meat on your bones.'

I sat there, getting my breath back, the girl leaning comfortably against me as if she was only sleeping.

'What's wrong with the girlie? I've seen her before too. Sick, is she?'

'Can you give me a hand with the door?' I got her up again and we started off.

He stood there in his little box trying to detain me somehow. casting around in his rusty old brain for something to say, to keep me there. He'd taken a shine to me when I first started, he considered me a cut above the rest for some reason. I could almost hear the click of the tape as it started winding up. For an old bugger he still had ferocious needs.

'Did Cash tell you, Glory?'

'What.'

'Bob's trying to kick me out? Reckons he doesn't need me? I said to Cash, I was here when the little shit was still sucking his mother's tit. You know what I mean? Twenty bloody years. It was a bloody better class of clientele in those days as well. Not like the riff-raff you get now. Peter Pan it was. I wore a uniform, the whole caboodle.' His rheumy old sherry-soaked eyes looked at me craftily every now and again to see if I was responding right.

'This lot. They'd do anything to turn a buck. Not you, Glory. You're class.'

I'd heard it all before.

'I've got to go. She's heavy. Come on, give us a hand will you.'

'Any more parties, Glory?' he asked recklessly, throwing away his last card.

14

Once he had come to a party we had next door and ended up out cold in the bathroom all night so no one else could use it. To hear him talking it was a really big deal, with him the star turn of the night.

'Nah,' I lied. I wouldn't have told him anyway.

'How's your flatmate? The one without the hair? Doing alright?' It was years ago now, that party, but he still asked after everyone with the casualness of an intimate friend.

'Shorty. Come on, will ya.' His brand of pathos was a real winner.

'Alright, alright.' He came out of the box. It was a big concession.

'I'll walk you to the door. There's a few roughs around tonight. Scum of the earth.' He puffed out his puny asthmatic chest as he held the swing door open for us.

Out on the street, the blast of cold air revived the girl slightly. She staggered, shook her head as if to clear it and started to mutter.

I said, 'It's OK. We're going up to my car. The walk'll do you good.'

Her eyelids fluttered open for a split second and she put her head clumsily against me. Her gesture was so trusting I had no choice but to hitch my arms around her narrow little shoulders and start off again slowly and painfully. She even smiled slightly with a flash of intense sweetness before her face became inhuman again. This was such a murky struggle for a child to be immersed in; she had the puffy greenish skin of someone drowning, she kept moving her head from side to side, her eyes closed with the preoccupation of it.

I thought of the car, away up on K. Road, as she hung against me, her body defenceless against the cold tide of heroin. The intimacy of our bodies was almost unbearable as we laboured up the road. I could smell her sick sweat and sour breath — and feel the sucking noises she made against my cheek. I carried her like a doll or a baby against my hip, lurching up the road like a grotesque mother. There was no doubt I'd made a mistake and she was worse than I thought, but I reckoned it was quicker to keep going now that I was halfway up. Casualty was only a few minutes across Grafton Bridge as long as the car didn't play up.

We went up past a group of queens gathered in the shadows of the wild west verandahs out from the junk shops and crank religion fronts just opposite the park. They were sitting on a *Herald* box, drinking and jeering in their throaty exotic voices as cruising customers lost their nerve and picked up speed. Every time a car sped off they all laughed and catcalled mockingly. They didn't seem to care about losing business. Me carrying the kid past them was cramping their style, anything that looked like trouble scared business off straight away. I could just glimpse the hard masculine jut of their painted faces, the painful sheen on their skin, their outlandish beauty as we toiled past. The air smelt of petrol and I could taste the sickness of it in my mouth.

A siren started up in the distance and then another joined in, caterwauling some spine-chilling warning on the other side of the city somewhere. The sound came through the late night mist like something tangible, the night seemed full of ghosts. You could hear calls and screams and the screak of the old swings echoing up from the dark bowl of the children's playground in the jungle of Myers Park. Kids were sitting on the swings down there, sniffing glue most likely, or fighting, or just huddling together in the cold. A young girl was tortured there once, by her zonked out playmates, right through a long summer night. I was singing at Mainstreet that Saturday and she must have died just after my last song.

All the night people wandered in up from the park and the spacies arcades, kids blanked out with glue like zombie animals, queens, crims, streetwalkers, all the street people who worked at night and did their trade and deals. It was a place alive with shadows. Now it was just me and the queens and the heavy child — I could hear the rasp of my own breath and the clink of the bottle the queens were passing round.

In the end I had to stop for a rest, leaning up against a ledge outside the antique gun shop. I wedged the kid between my thighs and gave myself up to catching my breath. My heart was thumping and I felt the sweat on my face drying in the cold air. One of the queens drifted over to see what was wrong. I could smell her musk.

'What's the problem, dear? Had a few too many?'

'She's OD'd I think,' I said shortly.

'You have to keep them walking. Better get her to hospital, dear.'

She was genuinely concerned, she came close and peered into the kid's face, whistled and her voice dropped.

'She's not too good, honey. Got a car?' The queen was wearing a blue sequinned dress which caught the streetlight, and cruel stilettoes. Her leg muscles were thrown upwards and out with the strain. She looked stunning.

'Yes. It's miles away. I'm trying to get her to walk.'

There was no real need for explanation, she had a very experienced eye, obviously.

'I'd better take you to Casualty. You look stuffed. Girls, keep my patch warm!'

She was embarrassed, roughly gesturing towards a great shiny Ford Fairlane parked up the alleyway from the Rembrandt. Forgetting herself for a minute she spat into the gutter.

'That would be a help. Thanks'. My shoulders were aching and couldn't believe how much my heart was racing. It felt as if I'd been staggering for miles.

'Nothing much going here anyway. They're all nervous tonight. The cops must be round.'

We both got in and slung the kid's body awkwardly in the back seat.

'Smack?' The car was really powerful even though it was such an early model, and she drove with masculine style, one muscular elbow out the window, Radio Hauraki all-night show on full bore on the car radio. The car stank of perfume, there were rugs and pillows and leopard skin upholstery. Two furry little things jiggled up and down in the back window. I felt warm and safe, luxury at last.

'It looks a little under-age if you ask me,' she said, jerking her head backwards.

'I don't know. I don't even know who she is. I found her at Mainstreet.'

The queen drove very fast with her dress crushed up between her beautiful thighs — and I could feel the flex of her muscles on the seat as she manoeuvred the big car. She had huge sad bloodshot eyes and brown teeth.

'She looks like she could snuff it.' A heavy sideways flick of a look from her glitter-strewn eyelids.

'You sing down there, don't you?'

'Yeah.'

'I'm Grace. Pleased to meet you.'

The receptionist at casualty didn't even glance up when we dragged our body into the brightly lit hospital-green waiting room. Stains all over the walls, peeling paint, a drunk snoring on the bench. Old blood stains, sweat and tears in this place — all the stabbings and bashings and mangled city-crushed bodies had already passed through on their macabre Friday night procession, there was no one left.

'Long to wait, dear?' sang out Grace to the receptionist. She offered me a smoke. She looked wonderfully bizarre with her sequins flashing and her scarlet mouth. She seemed to be enjoying the break from routine.

The receptionist looked over at the child.

'No. Rush is over. I'll take some particulars if you like. Doctor's just ducked out for a cuppa.'

She looked absolutely incongruous in that bleak city morgue — a large pleasant motherly woman, she was like a South Islander with her wide unsuspicious country gaze. She was being talkative, lonely now that the rush was over.

'I don't know anything about this,' I said. 'I just found her.'

'Well good on you for bringing her up. Poor little mite. Give me the particulars in case anyone needs to contact you. It's nice to see we're still not as bad as America.'

America?' I didn't know what she meant.

'She means the violence,' said Grace in her poisonous contralto. 'You know, people stamping over bodies in L.A.? We're still a caring, sharing place, dear. She should meet some of my clients. Then she'd change her tune. The only thing they like to share is their great big cocks.' She crossed her legs taking a huge drag of the cigarette. Grace was a real queen, quick on her feet as a boxer, her eyes shrewd behind all the glitter. Whenever she stopped talking her expression became dreamy, off-centre, as if she was listening to something else. We sat down trying to prop up the kid. She kept rolling off the bench.

'Nearly time, dear,' the receptionist said.

As we shuffled into the little cubicle with the tatty old white curtain, the doctor nearly collided with us. He was young and pale with fatigue, puffy skin under his eyes. He looked nearly as bad as our kid. His ginger hair curled down his neck and in my sensitive state the freckled white neck and coarse crinkly hairs made my flesh creep. From his manner I could see he took us both for whores.

'She needs to be admitted,' he said after a cursory examination.

'OK. You won't need us any more will you?'

'Receptionist got your particulars?'

'Yes.'

'Thanks for bringing her in. We'll pull her round.' He gave me the briefest of pleasant smiles.

The girl lay there as if finally letting go after what must have been a nightmarish journey for her in her jumbly half-waking state. We all turned to look at the pathetic little body on the narrow plinth. She was stretched out on her back, her mouth open, snoring harshly, completely lost. Her blind foetal face was impervious to our stares, the sordid room, her own body. In the harsh white light of the examination room I saw her extraordinary beauty for the first time. Even with the junkie skin and her shaved head she had the faintly amused sly ease of a Botticelli angel, her closed face was perfect.

I felt bad seeing her there — it was like a physical pain in my chest. Her trust, her beauty, her childishness were such a fragile defence against the forces she'd let into her life. Whatever reasons she had for shooting up were irrelevant in the face of the strength of poison on her veins. I was surprised at how disturbed

I was. She was like someone I'd already made a connection with from years back and I wanted to look after her, carry her into the light. She was like me years ago, she was my daughter and flesh of my flesh.

'She's only a kid,' Grace said. 'Pathetic isn't it.'

'We're getting 'em younger every day,' the doctor said.

He turned back to the body and we got out quickly. I didn't want to stay. An icy wind had sprung up and as we walked to the car-park it was already starting to rain. I wondered how she'd feel, waking in the hospital with no one she knew, her tender brain eaten out, alone in the ward with the nurses and the white beds. It felt miraculously light to be walking without the weight of her sick little body.

'I hope she pulls through,' I said, almost to myself. 'I appreciate the lift,' I said to Grace as she opened the door.

She shrugged her shoulders, genuinely casual.

'She's only a kid,' she said again.

'Thanks,' I said. 'My car's just outside St Kevins Arcade.' Grace drove in silence and dropped me without a word. The brief spark was over. She was back to work.

I drove home quietly, carefully. I knew that the thin rain was death on the motorway.

At home Al and the kids were watching the tail end of a Friday night horror movie on TV. All the lights in the house were on and the TV music was really brassy, some kind of schmaltz Hollywood orchestra working up for the kill.

'Jeez. It's late for you two. You have to go in the morning, remember. What are you doing up so late?'

'Watching the movie. It's neat,' said John.

Rina said nothing at all. Looking closer, I saw she'd gone to sleep, her little white lashes firmly on her pale cheek.

Al said, 'I'll take her to bed in the next commercial. How'd it go, Glor?'

'Bad. There was a real aggro atmosphere.'

'What does atmosphere mean?' asked John, his eyes not moving from the screen. A question from him was still a rare gift.

'Surroundings, feeling, ambience,' I said gladly, sinking back into the sofa. Al made a cup of coffee for us after he'd lumped Rina off to bed, and some mushrooms on toast. The house rattled with the wind and lurched, and I could smell the rubbish in the Kleensak from where I was sitting. There were mangled cold chips on the carpet from Rina's traditional Friday night tea. It smelt like home and I let my whole body slump into the ease of it.

'Roxy rang,' Al said.

'Oh yeah,' I said not interested, drinking my coffee. I didn't feel like talking.

'She reckoned it was urgent.'

'Oh yeah. Al, can you help me move that big painting in the hall?' We went out and moved the painting down into my studio. I said goodnight to Al and Johnny and went off to my room. The coffee and food had woken me up again and I felt like having a look at a couple of paintings before I went to bed. The thought of the coming exhibition was starting to worry me.

I switched the little bedside lamp on and there was my model, Roxy, sitting on the bed staring at me, hardly even blinking at the light. My heart sank at the sight of her. She was up to her usual trick of lying in wait for me. It always made me feel pushed, taken by surprise, to have her hanging round when I got home.

'You gave me a fright,' she said. 'Where've you been?'

She handed me a cigarette as I stood over her.

'Jesus, Glory, this room really pongs. I reckon the kitten's been pissing under the bed again. It stinks in here.'

I said nothing. I could see at a glance she was in a bad way and I didn't feel like some fraught emotional scene at this time of night. I was drained enough from the little junkie without anyone else.

I hadn't known Roxy very long, but she'd already assumed an intense intimacy with me, ringing me up all the time and coming round at odd hours. Sometimes she waited silently in the house for me till Al had to get her to leave. She made him nervous. When I was painting her she used to talk endlessly, long tales of people who'd done the dirty on her, complicated deals which always ended in some outrage done to her. She was full of the injustices of the world. Her life as she described it always seemed to be teetering on the edge of some apocalyptic unmasking, a continual reel of dramas playing out to their inevitable end, with her, innocent, wronged, fighting to the last.

She had that blankness, the love of conspiracies, the utter self-absorption that a lot of junkies I knew had. She was the sort of person I felt a guilty fascination for — as if her blood on the floor somehow justified my own careful stance against the world. There was something glittering and driven about her that I was drawn to in spite of my best instincts. Or maybe because of them. I was never sure.

She was such an exceptional model I tried to stay on reasonable terms with her, at least until I could finish the series, and she'd probably already picked up on the weakness of that. She had a face which exactly caught the quality of some images I'd been mulling over for a long time, the basis for the series of paintings I was doing. Extravagantly, heartbreakingly beautiful, it was a full-blown soft blurred look as if someone had just called her and she was waiting guiltily for them to call again. The proportions of her face were stretched to the utmost limits of decency — the mouth, the eyes, the cheekbones were all heavy, and blooming, and riotously extreme. I loved painting her because her face could change so spectacularly. Sometimes her face could shrivel and shrink suddenly, her eyes go depthless with cruelty, the planes of her face jutting fiercely as she turned on the point of her torments. At times like this she could become an old woman right in front of my eyes, the junk emptying out of the cells of her face like water out of a sponge.

Her heart-stopping beauty, the softness of her skin were incongruous if you believed half of what she said about herself — the hoodlums, small-time dealers and thugs she mixed with, the violent scenes those bleak eyes of hers witnessed every day. She was a princess, that tough baby, with her chaotic moods, her vulnerability, that kind high-strung power which appeared out of nowhere sometimes and hit you between the eyes. You couldn't fully relax around her, you were always waiting for the next bite. It was a job that suited her exactly, modelling, she lay there chain-smoking while the junk wore off, talking, her soft comely body draped like a queen, the sole focus of someone's attention at last.

'Where've you been?' she asked again.

'Usual places,' I said politely, meaning none of your business. I had to watch myself with her at the best of times and I had never seen her as troubled as tonight. She was between shots too which was unusual because she generally took great care to see me when her eyes were dilated up to twice the size, full to the brim with the confidence and gaiety of smack. She smoked the cigarette and eyed what she could see of the room with distaste.

'I'm going to come in and give this studio a real once-over.' she said. 'It's embarrassing. You're supposed to be this big-time painter and look at this room. You need a minder. I'd do.'

She moved in and out of personae with nightmarish ease, that kid. Sometimes she gave the impression she was working off some unseen cues, from a tape winding up in her head. She hardly ever responded to what was in front of her.

'OK, Roxy. What do you want?' I asked, hearty, knowing full well it wasn't going to be that easy.

'I wanted to talk to you.'

'Yeah?' I nearly said, so what's new but decided against it in the interests of diplomacy. 'Want some wine?' I always kept a little store in the studio for late-night sessions and for friends — wine and sweet things to eat, chocolates, peppermints and potato crisps.

'I'm having a hard time,' she said.

'That so?' I leaned back against the wall, waiting.

'You're the only one who can save me,' she said, fixing me with her mournful eyes. She was really jittery. I didn't know what to say. She'd never said anything so personal to me before, she didn't usually stray so far from the conventions. She was really giving off a panic heat.

'What about Jesus?' I said, and then felt sorry.

'Don't fucking joke. It's not a joke,' she said, drinking her wine. Her hands were shaking. 'I'm in trouble.'

I said, 'OK. What's the matter?'

'It's all getting me down,' she said. 'I need a holiday. This modelling is bloody tiring. You don't seem to realise what it takes out of me.'

'Well it's nearly finished. I've nearly finished,' I said, hoping to call her bluff.

'That's not it, Glory. You're really thick sometimes.' She was twitching with unexpressed grievances, little rages, the strange forces of her personality moving like water under her fine skin. She was trying to get some mysterious affirmation from me, a fight, anything. She wanted the full range of my attention and I didn't want to give it to her.

'What then?' I knew she wouldn't tell me the real reason, but I couldn't help it, she always sucked me in in the end.

'You're the only one who's ever understood me,' she said. 'Sometimes I think we were sisters in another life.'

There was a silence. I poured myself some wine, resigned to it.

'Sisters,' I said. 'Jesus, Roxy.' It was hard to keep the disgust out of my voice.

She suddenly laughed, genuinely amused. 'Glory, you've got to learn to take affection,' she said. 'You're too frightened of emotion.' She touched me on the arm with her soft hand.

'It depends on the person,' I said, which was the nearest I got. I didn't have the motivation to keep up with hours of this for just the one half second of truth I'd get.

'What do you mean by that?' she asked.

'I've got to go to bed,' I said. 'I can't think anyway. I'd be no help to you tonight.'

'Where've you been that you're so tired?' she asked.

'Mainstreet. I've been to fucking Mainstreet. OK?'

'OK, OK, if that's how you feel. I was only asking.'

'Nagging,' I said. 'You were nagging.'

'You're just trying to kick me out aren't you? You were alright to listen when you wanted something,' she said. 'Eh? Then it was great. Now you don't need me for modelling any more it's all suddenly changed. It's all so very different.'

'Who said I didn't need you for modelling?' I asked, confused. I decided she had probably taken speed or something.

'You did. You know you did, Glory. See contacts of mine have already told me that I'm doing you a favour. With looks like mine I could name the price. According to my contacts, you're paying me nothing. They reckon I'm being soft, just because I believe in you as a painter.'

'You agreed on the fucking pay, Roxy. You said you needed the money. We talked about it and I told you I couldn't afford any more. It was a straight business deal. You said nothing like that when we were talking about it before.' I was getting really aggravated by her. 'Anyway it's late. I don't want to sit here talking all night.'

'I thought you were supposed to be my friend,' she said huffily. 'Where'd you get that shit coat? You look like a hippy-dippy. Dah, dah.' She pulled on her lower lip, trying to annoy me.

'OK. Fuck off, Roxy,' I said. 'I've had enough. Go on.' I shooed at her.

'Listen,' she said. 'Just listen for once.'

'Oh Jesus.' I almost felt like laughing. It was hysteria. Luckily the wine had softened the edges or I would have thrown her out. 'I've been listening. You've got nothing to say except insults.'

'You're so patronising,' she said, narrowing her eyes. 'You're so fucking superior. Don't think I don't know. You may be the greatest painter living, but you can't act superior with me. You came from the scum of the earth. At least my parents weren't fucking scumbags.'

'You said we were sisters, Roxy,' I said. 'Sisters under the skin. That was only a few minutes ago. How can such a lovely thing have changed so quick?'

'Yeah, laugh at me. That's right,' she said. 'I say something nice to you and you just throw it back in my face. You just think I'm a fucked-up beauty queen don't you? A dodo drug freak. I know what's going on in your head. Queen of the night come to lift your paintings from the dead. That's me.'

'Fair enough,' I said, genuinely hurt.

'Alright, Glory, that was a shitty thing to say. You know I was only bullshitting. I wouldn't model for you if I didn't think you were something. That's the truth. I don't even know what I'm saying. I'm in a state, that's all. I'm upset.' She grabbed hold of my hand and kissed it. Her mouth was hot and wet and I pulled back from the repellent feeling of it.

'I'm just so insecure,' she said. 'When I'm with you I feel inferior. It makes me want to get at you. I feel as if you've had all the chances I never had.'

She was working herself up inexorably into one of her mysterious grievances and it made me desperate to head her off. I had heard it all before, her near-genius IQ, the jealous headmistress who had her expelled, all the talent and beauty of her down the drain because of the callousness of the world. Roxy was haunted by the lack of recognition, she carried round a painful itch for fame and money and love and never seemed to understand why it wasn't hers. According to Cash, she was the spoilt only daughter of elderly parents, always had things her way, but it was often hard to separate fact from fiction with him. He even told me that he'd been to afternoon tea there once and they had served it in delicate china cups. He said there were pictures of Roxy all over the piano. And she conned fifty bucks off them right there in front of his eyes. Her father was a wharfie and they told him proudly how they'd scrimped and saved to get her into a private school.

But whatever the reasons, family or not, Roxy was used to getting what she wanted, so she saw success only as a trick formula, a con, that she could pick up by being with people like me. You could see her struggle between jealousy of me and an almost hysterical desire to be my disciple, my friend, muscle in on my fame and somehow, anyhow, go down with me to posterity. Tonight especially, the whole fevered tone of it was exhausting.

'OK. See you tomorrow,' I said, trying to sound wonderfully matter of fact. 'We'll talk tomorrow.'

'Oh you'll talk will you? Big deal. I'm trying to tell you a few important things for your own good, but you won't even listen.'

'Get out will you, Roxy. I'm tired.'

'Yeah sure I will. But don't you ever think of anything else but yourself?' Roxy said. There was sweat glistening on her face, on the upper lip.

'You won't tell me what's wrong,' I said, sucked in again in spite of myself. She had the rare gift of involving people in her life and general vulnerabilities whether they wanted it or not, even someone like me who'd made the Roxys of the world my lifetime study.

She said, leaning back on the bed, her eyes closed, as beautiful as I'd ever seen her, 'I sometimes feel like just slitting my throat. Just before I met you I tried to do it. Cut my wrists. I was completely out of it. I thought there was no fucking point in living. I've got nothing, people only want me for what they get, sex, scoring, smack, Roxy's always there for them. I've been moving round a lot recently because I start to feel sick if I stay in a place too long. Sick, as if someone was poisoning me. And so I got a razor blade and gave myself a shot to make it easier. But once I was smacked out of my head with it I couldn't do it. I kept sawing away, and not even a bit of blood. It was really blunt. I just gave up and went to sleep.'

'Roxy, I've told you before. There are some good clinics here. You have to get off heroin before you can do something.'

'What can a clinic do that I can't do? They're just a bunch of social workers, completely removed from life. I'm not a junkie anyway, Glory. You know that. I can still take it or leave it.'

'Sure, Roxy.' This was another conversation I was tired of.

'You don't believe me do you? You don't think I could do it?'

I said, 'If you say so. You know yourself about that. I can't say.'

We were silent again. She said, 'Alright I'll go. I know when I'm not wanted, Glory. You can give me that credit at least.' She got up. I didn't answer.

'Can I see your last painting?' she asked, still playing for time. She knew I could never resist that.

'Yeah, yeah.' I switched on the main light and pointed to the one of the young woman lying dead on the lino.

'Do you like it?' I asked her. I suddenly wanted to know for some reason. She turned and watched me with her huge empty eyes. When you looked closely at Roxy's face, she had interesting skin — it was faintly yellowish with a tired dirt texture. Almost reptilian. That was really close. Away from her it looked as soft and blooming as a rose.

'Who is it?' she asked. 'The woman?'

'I don't know,' I said. 'I wasn't using you as a model if that's what you mean.'

She moved away. 'Who is it?' she said again.

'What are you going on about now?' I asked.

She was looking really yellow in the harsh light. She said, 'What's the story? What do you think you're doing?' She took out another cigarette.

'Painting,' I said defeated. 'Painting my life.'

'See, people have always warned me about you. They said you were a loony. I never listened, out of blind loyalty. Never. But you're trying to throw a jinx on me.' Her voice rose to a wail.

'Look, shut it, Roxy. You'll wake everyone,' I said to her fiercely. The conversation was getting beyond me.

'Fucking curse me. But don't think I don't know,' she said. 'I'm awake to it.' Her face took on the crafty expression of total paranoia. 'Don't think I'm not awake to you.'

'Don't you like it or something?' I asked, irritated, putting it back, choosing to ignore a lot of her messages.

'Like it?' She laughed her hoarse chuckle. 'What do you think, Glory Day? Sell-out queen?'

'Well, I don't fucking know,' I said irritably. 'That's why I'm asking you.'

'Who is it?' she said again.

'Well, it could be you, it could be me, it could be Patrick,' I said driven.

'Patrick? That little cunt? The rich twit. The one who sucks up to you? He's more your style isn't he?' She smiled at me. 'Since when have you been into betrayal in such a big way?'

'Since never,' I said. 'It's one of the few things I know for sure

---

28

if you must know. I want to go to bed, Roxy. You're too full of bullshit for me,' I told her.

'I can see it a mile off,' she said. 'You want to get rid of me.' She was shaking so badly she had to put the cigarette down.

'Yes. That's it. You've said it.'

She got up, keeping her head down. Even her hair looked unusually ratty and dried out tonight. She was a mess.

'Well thanks for nothing,' she said. 'See you around.'

I said nothing. When she was like that, all I ever wanted was for her to go. Starting an argument was her favourite trick, she craved that kind of sharp attention, especially from me. Most people she could bend to her will, no trouble, then withdraw her deadly charm and leave them squirming, ready to do anything to appease her.

I walked with her out into the cold air of the backyard, just to show her I had no hard feelings. There was nothing stirring, not even a car down in the motorway below. It was almost as quiet as a country night, with that same immensity, that fresh chill in the air. There was even the smell of freshly cut grass wafting up from some garden to remind me of old times. I could feel the rain blowing up again from the south.

'I've always been a good friend to you, Glory. You'll never know how much,' she suddenly said through the darkness. It sounded like a promise. She even reached over and gave me a dry little kiss on the cheek. It was these little tendernesses, the unexpected tokens of her strange affections after her rages which kept me patient, relaxed me. Without them, and that face, she would have burnt me out months ago with her wearying attentions and unpredictability.

'See you,' I said.

She went silently down the back through a hole in the fence, pretty as a panther. Knowing Roxy, there was probably some faithful sucker waiting for her in a car, happy to play a part in whatever drama she'd concocted to get him to take her to my place at four in the morning. He would be just as much in the dark about what was really going on as I was.

As I went back in, I knew with irritation that my train of

thought about the painting had been completely broken by her radioactive presence. It wasn't just her, either. I was thinking about the little junkie, I had even remembered her name while I was talking to Roxy in the studio. It was Marianne. Marianne Someone. Roxy's car went off down the road and I turned back into the house.

I had a sudden urge to go and sit by my Rina in the dark. I hadn't seen her all day and my head was too buzzy for sleep. I went in and sat on her creaking bed, listening to her breathing and trying to make out her drawings on the wall, the lovely bizarre shapes she made, cheeky looking people with gashes for mouths and artless innocent limbs. Mum from Rina with big shakey xxxx's. Posters of Bruce Springsteen smiled down at me, ghostly in the darkness.

I wondered if Rina had any notion at all of the nature of the disturbances that lithe hoony delinquent excited in her. Probably not. His white smile was like a shark's. He looked as if he had everything well in hand in spite of the rough Asbury Park edges he still kept up for argument's sake.

As I sat there, my mind still slowly humming down, I gradually became aware of a sickish sweet smell permeating the room. It was horrific, and insidious, and it took me a while of knocking around in the dark to find the source of it. In the rats' nest under the bed there was a plastic bag full of decayed lunch and other unnamable substances. She'd jammed it craftily with all her mother's cunning right up behind the dress-ups box. Al came in as I was scuffling round under the bed trying to pull it out.

'Shit you gave me a fright,' he whispered. 'I thought you were a burglar. What the fuck are you doing? You'll wake her.' He was disgusted. He hated being taken unawares.

'She takes after her father. He's into decayed vegetable matter as well,' I said walking past with the reeking bag at arm's length. It was just for something to say. As I went past I could smell the nervous sweat on him. He'd always been terrified of burglars.

He said, 'Stuff it,' and stumped off murderously, so we almost collided in the hall.

'I'll bury it tomorrow,' I said, more to myself as I dumped it into the already overflowing Kleensak.

I came back into her room still restless. I couldn't keep the junkie out of my mind. I kept seeing her face and the ravages of heroin on her childish skin. Just sitting beside Rina in the dark was the only thing that seemed to soothe me.

She slept so soundly, her head fluffed down amidst the softness of the pillow, her breath quiet and regular as a cat's. One wrinkled hand was thrown free of the blankets, occasionally her mouth made soft kissing noises in the intimate dark. It was like a picture book kid's room with its clean lines, so strongly there, her child's spirit hanging so fragile in the air, the plain window opening out into the immeasurability of the night. There was something comforting and soft and true about it, but otherworld as well — the child's body with its peaceful breath, and that calm window opening out into a limitless universe with nothing to keep her from floating out.

I sat there in the dark thinking of different things and listening for her breathing before I went to bed.

2

There were too many undercurrents going on in the house that morning. We all woke to the sound of Al and Sue fighting in the kitchen. The wind had sprung up again at dawn, creaking and whistling round the house, scraping at the loose sheets on the roof. On Saturday mornings the traffic always started early and it was really rocking the house, the stretch of Mt Wellington highway below us was whooping and howling like a machine. Everything was grey and scratchy, there was no rest in the house anywhere. I myself woke up headachey but intact, full of energy and murderous intent.

Rina and I could hear the two of them whining and snarling all through the house. I heard John get up and kick at the door, muttering sleepy curses at them, but the brief silence didn't last long.

'I get sick of them two fighting,' Rina told me, sitting on my knee.

It was the May holidays and John was up for a few days. His visits were so rare I wanted to make it nice for him, but events were conspiring against me, and there was nothing much for them to do except watch TV and listen to the quarrelling. John didn't say much out of politeness.

The lawn at the back was awash with slush and mud, next door the guys hadn't turned up to their broken down workshop and all the rusted cars in the lank grass looked even more useless than usual. It was the sort of day when you saw people straggling up the road to the dairy against the rain to buy fags, cars whooshing past, spraying up the water at them in a thin drizzle.

All morning I was tossing around in my mind about Marianne, I couldn't stop thinking of her. I even rang the hospital but the woman just said she'd take my number. I was feeling edgy anyway because I had a lot of work to do and I couldn't get started again. I needed a charge just to finish the last lap. There was too much going on for me to concentrate.

'I've got to get these paintings done. I'll throw them out,' I said.

'Don't throw Al out,' begged Rina, stroking my chin and gazing in my eyes. She loved him dearly. He was always comfortable with her. The other day I heard him singing 'You are my sunshine' to her in the kitchen.

'You used to fight with your boyfriends,' said Johnny, his eyes on the TV.

'Me? Never. You're joking. Since when?'

'Rina's dad. That Weasel,' he said with a reminiscent smile. 'You gave him a hiding when youse came back from the pub.'

I hadn't given my second husband a thought for years, he was such a fleeting ghost in my life and John mentioning his name like that out of the blue gave me a shock. I wondered what other memories he had stored away. He wasn't a hard boy, my John, but he'd learnt a few things out of necessity. At fifteen he was dark and confident like his father, with a helpless laugh which went straight to my heart. His grandmother had brought him up with a lot of style.

He was more Maori than Pakeha, my son, and sometimes I envied him his childhood. He swam in the warm water of his pond with a lot of natural confidence. He had found his place effortlessly in the family gatherings, the old country ways. When I was younger, I used to imagine him sleeping on the marae in the darkness with the breathing and whispering of his own people around him, and how safe he was from me. He never liked staying long in the city, I suspected it was Nettie who forced him to come in the first place. She had a lively sense of family duties.

'You've got a memory, Johnny. You remember bloody everything,' I said, hearty. I tried to be close to him, but his heart was elsewhere. It was a matter of plowing through until we both reached adulthood. So I kept trying with him though I knew the mistakes of a sixteen-year-old mother were often irreparable. In those days I used to hit him, and worse, till his kind Nettie rescued him. I comforted myself that at least I'd given him over gracefully, that even in my childish cruelty I knew enough to do what was best for him. But it wasn't much of a consolation.

'I don't want you to go and do painting,' whinged Rina, tugging at my skirt. At eleven she had the alert old-monkey eyes of the Down's Syndrome child, with the strange flaky skin around them, which was another mark of her race. Like John she had been brought up with certain expectations of affection, but there their backgrounds diverged sharply. Rina's only experience was city, and very seedy city at that. It was probably why she had such a passion for Bruce Springsteen, his poor white trash, working-man songs all corresponded to her own knowledge of the world.

She started snivelling and dragging herself onto the sofa as if she was wounded, limping and flopping in a way she instinctively knew drove me nuts.

'No, I've got to work, for shit's sake,' I said.

'You're mean,' she whined.

'Look, watch telly with Johnny. He's going home today so you won't see him again,' I said, trying to sound reasonable. I was on my best behaviour for Johnny, and Rina knew me like the back of her hand.

'No, don't want to,' she said through her nose.

'I can't entertain you all day. I've got to work,' I said.

'I don't want you to tain me,' she said. 'You've got a stain all down your front. You're a big mean bastard and you've got a fat bum.' She made a terrible face. John had always thought his half-sister was a bit of a freak, but they were distant enough for him to appreciate her. He was trying not to laugh.

'You'll get a thick ear. You're getting too bloody cheeky,' I roared and made my escape. We were almost even, but Rina knew from long experience how to fight dirty. It always surprised me that a kid could be so unrelenting. She sometimes got into a certain mood when she came out with outrageous insults — staring you straight in the face, unblinking, hard as nails. It was funny coming from such a mild little body as her.

Insulting people was only a sideline with Rina though, her main preoccupations centred around affection. For instance, I always imagined her tagging along with the older kids at school loving them with all her heart, never suspecting for a moment that they didn't love her — scuttling around the city playgrounds looking for crumbs, with her crumpled face, like an alien dropped out of the sky. Interested in affection and the ritzy charms of rock musicians, wearing tatty bracelets on her grubby little wrists, her hair already middle-aged thin, she was so unlike her comely half-brother it was comical to see them together.

Just as I was going out the door Al came out of the kitchen.

'I don't know what to do.' He looked so tired I felt sorry. He wasn't used to this quarrelling any more than I was. Roxy sometimes asked me in her pleasant poisonous way what a spunky young guy like Al was doing with me and Rina in a dump like ours. The truth was, Al had been safe up here till he met Sue. He was a man so beautiful that people stopped and stared at him in the street, and Al's constant preoccupation was to hide himself from that wicked admiration. The whole sex war, with its energies and secrets, had completely freaked him out at an early age, and he'd taken refuge with us. He'd get nervous, his face would go shifty and mean, he'd lock himself in his room and mutter so loud we could all hear him in the kitchen.

He always wore mirror glasses to hide his eyes, his hair shaved off in a vain attempt to disfigure himself. In point of fact he was a quiet man, prone to thinking, watching the world, fixing his bike and drinking with the boys next door. We'd been mates for years, Al and I. He reminded me of my first heartbreaking love when I was ten. A graceful bodgie, sharp and streetwise with a pointed Italiano face. Too smart for his own good, but his sensitivity remained.

It was Al's physical ease that made him so desperately attractive, his grace, the way he moved through the world comfortable in his body that made women want him. He'd roll up his sleeves to the elbow and fix the bike, squatting on his haunches, a cigarette in his mouth, his eyes squinted against the smoke,

35

absolutely absorbed. It was the titillating knowledge that that was the way he screwed — with the same absorption, the same precision, the same relentless power.

Al was an unusual man. Over-burdened with guilts and sensitivities he was a masochist deep down, and Sue had cottoned on to all that in a flash. She was like me when I was younger, hard and fast and mean, but there was not a lot of love to her. She held onto Al keeping him there half delirious with pleasure, half horrified, but the price they paid for their pleasures was pretty high and the going was always rough in between times.

'That's alright,' I said. I felt awkward in the face of his unhappiness. He gave me some letters and disappeared round the back as quietly as he had come, droopy and hangdog. I heard him in the shed outside, tinkering with his bike, the radio on.

In the mail there was an electricity bill, the official invitation to Patrick's opening and a letter from Nigel, my agent, confirming arrangements for my exhibition. As a rider he had written: 'Those Australian dealers, Harveys, are interested apparently, which of course is a great coup. Trans-Tasman art deals are one in a million usually. You've become quite a figure. The jaded Auckland art world is obviously into *nostalgie de la boue* in a big way. Will be coming out sometime this week for a quality control check.'

Nigel wasn't too sold on me as a person, though he always exuded intimacy and tried to make ironic old mate jokes, but he knew when he was onto a good thing financially and held onto me like grim death. For all that, he genuinely liked my paintings, and I had a certain amount of respect for his taste, if not his ability to steer me round the jungle of deals and dealers. He never tried to rip me off. The trouble was our relationship had started off on a bad foot. The first time he ever came around Rina was really playing up and kept paddling at him with her dirty hands. She had a cold and never worried about wiping her nose at the best of times. Not only that, but Al was doing his bike in the living-room because it was raining at the time and the next-doors, all wearing their patches because they had just been to court, were sitting around watching TV and making offensive comments about a group of anti-Springbok protesters occasionally glimpsed at the edge of the field.

I said to someone in passing, 'You're fucking brown, haven't you got any feeling for your black brothers?' They've suspended a lot of protocol for me, though of course Nigel wasn't to know that — and it certainly seemed like a provocative remark in the circumstances. They were only small time anyway, a pack of homeless kids with three bikes between them, but he wasn't to know that either.

Nigel sat on the sofa in his canvas jacket and designer jeans with an untouched beer can in his hand, listening to all of this with stunned disbelief. It was a small sitting-room, and there were five of them not counting me and Rina. I could tell he was nervous. He kept trying to ward Rina off, secretly, in the same way as you kick a fawning dog and don't want its owners to know. He had a look of real revulsion on his face. I had to admit Rina certainly didn't look her best that morning, nor did any of us. No one talked to him after they'd taken one look at him, but they had fallen silent. I didn't feel like talking either, and he kept trying to start the conversation the way nervous middle-class people have. Every time he said something the silence got more intense though no one was looking at him.

'Could I see your studio?' he said at last.

'Watch out for him, Glory. He looks like a real goer,' called out Moe as we left and they all laughed raucously.

Of course now that I know Nigel better I see it was sheer fastidiousness. He'd just stumbled into a roomful of people he'd consider pure scum — men with tattoos, long hair, leathers, patches and greasy stink. And not only that, but me, the 'find' he was so excited about, the talented painter, was no better. Here I was, sitting around in a man's dressing-gown, my hair wet from the bath, joking and drinking. He was used to bohemian, working class even, but genuine underclass was going too far. The studio was a bit of a shock as well. It was tacked onto the back of the house. I'd just ripped out the outside wall and added a few feet into the back, and put in some demolition windows. But it was still small because I slept in there as well and the bed took up most of the space.

That first visit he looked at the paintings in record time and left like the wind. It was all a bit overwhelming with the unmade bed and the smell of cat piss where Rina's scabby little kitten had been hiding under the bed. I was definitely short with him as well because I didn't like his attitude to Rina. He told a friend of mine after that first visit, a dealer of another gallery, that I was the most wonderfully sordid person he'd ever met. But I knew what side my bread was buttered on and I was quite happy to start up a business partnership with him. He actually seemed to be quite titillated by my life, most of his partners were men, over forty, and pretty well burnt out.

The series I was working on that he had such high hopes for was called 'Senseless Violets'. It was mostly to do with smashed bodies — road accidents, murders, domestics, pub fights, gang violence. It was very lairy, in heartless skin colours, dark pinks, haemorrhage browns, and I was using enamel because I liked that shiny repellent surface. By stripping the images down to almost clinical representation I wanted them to convey point-blank the pity of violence without any unnecessary comment from me.

It was a very tricky position, because I've never been interested in straight proselytising, however strongly I felt, and I didn't want to do it easy with a lot of cloudy indignation. For instance I knew the brutal pleasures of violence from my own experience — the graceless, clumsy, almost sensuous way men move in their slow-motion dance, the loverlike moving in for the kill, the release of it, the sexual rage and fear behind the death dealing. I wanted to use that hard-earned knowledge of mine to give another texture to the paintings, to pay attention to the motives of the killer, usually a man, as well as the pain of the victim, usually a woman. Dangerous ground — veering between merely cheap, banal sentiment on the one side, and voyeurism on the other, when even a hint of either would have been outright failure from my point of view.

Painting violence like that in all its muddy depths, poking my finger into the festering boil of it, was a way I saw of forever stripping it of its false glamour. It was like looking into a medical textbook, Al said when he saw the first few paintings, which was greatly cheering at the time. Technically I'd been trying for the same feeling as those dark-grained sleazy cop photos of murder victims. You saw them sometimes in American doco art photography books. The blood like ink on the floor, remote distaste on the faces of the cops, their twenties homburgs throwing a shadow over one eye, a door left half open, the sense of intrusion into something unbearably pathetic and private. And the body, with its tenderness and dignity, sprawled heavily against the wall, so touchingly vulnerable to the voyeuristic eye of the camera.

It was the connection between the act of violence and the total stillness of the dead body that I wanted to establish, the pity and finality of it. I wanted to bind the violent act to the pain of the victim forever. For a while earlier I had been doing sculptures with chicken mesh and barbed wire and great swathes of polythene on the same theme. But I found I preferred flat surfaces for the sheer murderous grief of the image. I was just finishing off a young woman folded in on herself, her legs and body heavy with death. She was lying on a fake brick-patterned lino floor. It was the painting Roxy had thrown such a tantrum about. It was detailed, almost hallucinogenic, much more so than the others, but the ultimate impression was the sadness of it. Painting it was like being involved in a ritual. I wanted to celebrate the moment when her death became eternal, by paying loving attention to every detail. I wanted the body, so still and pulpy and dead, to exist in its space with full consequence, to show once and for all how final this particular woman's death was, and how cruel — that she stayed there, dead for ever, even if you turned your fickle attentions elsewhere. That the shape, the disposition, the new form death took had its own dignity. It was the feeling I had for the dead woman that gave such power to the picture.

I knew there was even more at stake than usual in this series. I'd been feeling the slide into something nearer the bone for me all the way through. I was painting from my past, from my own experiences as always, but for the first time since I had started I felt the easy rush of ten years of groundwork helping me through.

For nearly ten years I'd been working on my technique the hard way, doing the slog of forcing everything into my own grinder, but this time it was different. My other series, the one on families, on Rina, had been twice as painful because of my technical struggles — this time I was on a plateau, I didn't have to stuff around with basics. It was all pure form and my preference unmistakable.

For months now I'd been working late into the night, happy as any obsessive with this new ease of mine. It was obvious the paintings themselves were a quantum leap ahead. I never started any painting without total commitment, but this time there was a lightness that came from confidence, a certain heady feeling of success in spite of the surly subject. The series set a new high for me in following my own bent, giving out some strong statements to the world, painting away past sorrows. 'Senseless Violets' was more comprehensive than anything I'd done before, and a lot more electric, especially with a model like Roxy.

But all the months of work had caught up with me and I'd been feeling jumpy in the last week. The incident at Mainstreet had suddenly brought my brooding to a head. I wasn't used to all the introspection the kid had plunged me into. And in spite of all the advantages Nigel had for me as a painter, dealing with him when I was slightly off-key made me worse. I always found it hard to believe that people like that could be so on the level all the time. They went on living so cosy, it amazed me. I'd always preferred my own kind as genuine company. Nigel's wit gave him a certain edge, but mostly he was hard rock Kohi right from the cradle, clean as a whistle day and night and full to the back teeth with disapprovals. I hoped he wasn't really coming today.

In the studio Rina's kitten had been pissing again where generations of cats always went. I knew because it came screaming out from under my bed the minute I walked in, and there was a pungent sour stink in the air. I sat on the bed for a while, just looking out the back, collecting myself ready for the last stretch on my lino woman. Outside in the backyard the corrugated iron fence was half down and flapping in the wind. It had rusted dramatically over the winter, and the graffiti on it had faded and blurred into corrosion. Weeds like wandering Jew, dandelions, onion flowers grew up against it and over the pile of beer bottles stacked there. I kept meaning to collect the deposit on them when I got round to borrowing Sarah's trailer but already they were so covered with greenery and earth it seemed a hassle to disturb them. I noticed that a couple of trees I'd planted a while back were both dead, still tied pathetically to their stakes, killed by Al's habit of pissing on the lawn when he was drunk, most probably.

Al had left bits of old cars and bikes rusting in the long sodden grass, ready for when he wanted them. We used to sit out there on warm days with the next-doors and drink beer under the shade of the grapefruit tree, listening to the roar of the traffic on the highway below.

I got out the paint brushes and just as I was nudging the painting into the light Rina came screaming in.

'Roxy's coming up the path! I'm gonna hide, man!'

Roxy was in fact right behind her, dressed like a rock star, all bracelets and wreaths of tack, a pink tulle bow in her teased out red hair. She looked like a big doll. She was even carrying some purple carnations. She had obviously had a taste at the exact right time — she wasn't gaga, nor was she strung out. I felt the irritation in me to see her, I'd already decided that if she threw another scene, that'd be it, model or no model. She gave me the carnations.

'Look, I'm dropping in to say I'm sorry, Glory,' she said. She sat down and lit a cigarette. 'I really am. I was having that many hassles, I was just taking it out on you. It's unforgivable when you've been such a special lady in my life. I was a real bitch.'

'Oh, that's OK.' She smelt beautiful, some kind of exotic perfume was coming off her in waves. Amidst the startling beauty of her face her eyes were sliding around a lot.

'That's OK,' I said again, hoping she wouldn't stay.

'You've got a cup of coffee for a thirsty friend?' she asked.

'I've just started work,' I said. 'I've got to finish this for the exhibition.'

'Oh, I know. Busy, busy, busy Glory,' she said. 'Genius at work.' She started humming. 'Just one cup of coffee? To prove we're still soul sisters?'

'It's OK,' I said. 'We can forget it. I understand.'

'I mean I could tell at the time,' she said. 'Both of us had had a hard day. Even the best of friends have their moments.'

'Sure do,' I said, continuing to work.

She said, 'I mean that picture. I realise you didn't mean to fuck me off or anything. It was just a mistake. It was a coincidence.'

'I don't know what you mean, Roxy,' I said. 'What picture?'

'You know what I mean. You know what picture.' Too late I realised there was still a storm raging in her head about something. I didn't like people coming into the room talking to me when I was trying to work at the best of times, and Roxy, when she wasn't modelling, trailed her crisscross auras, her poisonous heat into my room like a leaking nuclear powerplant.

'Roxy, I want to work. I don't know what picture you're talking about.'

She said, 'But I thought you understood. I thought we were friends again.'

'But we are,' I said. 'I don't know what you're so upset about. You wouldn't tell me last night, and now you're starting up all this shit again.'

'I was going to tell you last night but you seemed so strung out I thought I'd wait till the morning. Can't you see, I was just thinking of you?'

'Well tell me now for Chrissake,' I said, giving her my full aggravated attention. 'I'm tired of it.'

'You're tired of it! Tired of it! Well fuck me. I just don't believe this. Glory, I thought you'd be so pleased to see me, I thought you'd welcome me with open arms. I wanted to give you the chance, the benefit of the doubt. The flowers — I wanted them for you!'

'Roxy, I don't know what you're —' She wasn't even listening, she was so enmeshed in the grief playing out in her poor head.

'I've tried to give you one last chance,' she said. I'd never seen her so mysterious and manic. She was standing in the middle of the room, wringing her hands like a goddess.

'Are you talking about this fucking picture or the money I'm paying you or what?' I asked, pointing at the picture dramatically. I felt really harassed, her emotion was hard to take. Roxy's weasel remarks, however unjust, had a trick of winding themselves into my brain and permanently altering the way I looked at something, and I didn't want to hear any more.

'One last chance,' she said. Her eyes were misted over with genuine tears. 'After all the things I've done for you, you treat me like this.'

'Is it the picture?' I screamed at the end of my tether. 'Or what?'

Al came to the door looking startled at my raised voice.

'Phone for you, Glory,' he said as Roxy pushed past him. We could hear her running down the path to the road. 'What's the matter with her?'

'Don't ask me,' I said. 'I'm sick to death of all these fucking interruptions. Tell them I'm not in.'

'It's the hospital. They reckon you left your phone number.'

The woman on the other end of the line hesitated after I answered. Then she said, 'I'm afraid the patient you inquired after is deceased. She died last night in fact.'

I stood there holding the phone, feeling sick. I had such a bad feeling that I couldn't move or put the phone down. She died last night then, just after we took her to hospital. The pity of it turned me to stone. She must have given up the ghost on that hospital bed, even with that ginger-haired doctor there beside her to massage her heart. I thought if only I'd moved quicker — it must have been all of three-quarters of an hour from when I first saw her till I got her to hospital. There was that crapping around with Shorty. And those two rests. And the eternal crawl up the hill. I could have saved her maybe. I thought of her trusting body leaning against mine and her bitten fingernails, as she sat dying at Mainstreet.

Her death had been the worst scenario and the most unlikely. I'd always assumed deep down she'd recover, I'd half made plans to go and see her in the afternoon, offer her a place to stay when she got out. It was as nonchalant as that. And here I was with her dead on my hands. Even as I thought of that, the immediate implications swamped other considerations. The cops would be involved for sure, the name Marianne was a warning that she came from a well-off family somewhere — she looked like that anyway. I thought of Grace and how pissed off she'd be by a sudden visit from the cops. I felt instinctively that we were both too involved. We'd done something so out of line it was sure to be seen as sus. Even the woman at the receptionist desk had commented. We must have seemed such unlikely samaritans — Grace with her sequins and me the size of a house in my glittery thirties number from a junk shop. It would seem all too strange once the cops heard about it. I pulled on my raincoat and yelled out to Al who had disappeared out the back again.

'Look after the kids, will you? I've got to go out for a while.'

It was raining outside, and the car was really dead, so I had to crash start it, jerking and bucking all the way down the road. When I finally got going I realised I'd forgotten to say goodbye to John. He was off back home. It seemed to be our fate, try as I might to make it right. There was no way I could turn back by then. I decided to try the Bridgeway first, that was where a lot of queens drank in the mornings, and I thought there was bound to be some connection somewhere. I didn't want to spend hours chasing around Auckland. As it turned out I was lucky straight away. It was still only eleven but there were already a few drinkers there, sitting comatose over their morning beers and smokes. I asked the nearest queen.

'Oh. Grace? That one there's her mate. Who are you, dear? A butch or a big D?'

I went over to the corner of the bar where Grace's mate was. She was past caring about the impression she made, she had that moody gross big-nosed beauty that I really appreciated.

'No, dear. I don't do women,' she said. 'If you are a woman.'

'Take it easy,' I said half-heartedly. The ride in had been very fast and my heart was still racing.

'Grace? Grace's home. She's got her period. It's alright, dear. I know you. You were carrying that kid up the road. You looked like the Cookie Monster. You don't forget a sight like that.' She smiled at me, too world weary to be seriously vicious.

'That's what I want to see her about,' I said. I knew she wouldn't tell me anything unless I made myself clear.

'I told the silly bitch to leave well alone. Trouble with cops, eh? I could have fucking told her. But no. She always knows better, does our Grace.'

'I hope not. I just want to see her before the cops do.'

She looked at me consideringly. She had false eyelashes on even at this time of the morning and they looked painful, clotted, like insects clinging to her eyelids. 'Here's the address.' She wrote slowly with a snazzy gold pen, her long blood-red fingernails scritching on the paper. She smelt of old perfume and nicotine and night sweats.

'You look after Gracie.' It was a warning.

I said, 'Thanks,' and raced out again.

The address was Newton. It was an old boarding-house on the main road next to a car yard right in the bowels of the city. There were hundreds of mangled cars rotting in tiers there, in an oil-stained yard. The traffic going past it was murderous. It was car land up round there and the boarding-house looked as if it was ready to self-destruct with the sheer weight of traffic. The little well of the front garden was way down below the road, piled with sodden cartons and beer cans and junkfood wrappings. There was one ragged half-dead tobacco tree against a basement window.

The sheer tonnage of traffic shook the walls continually, it was like a storm raging outside. An old man shuffling round in the hallway pointed out her room, down the stairs, obviously the basement one. When I knocked on the door, I felt a small shock of surprise in the room, as if a visit hardly ever happened. Grace opened it. She was wrapped up in a beautiful red silk Japanese housecoat, with embroidery all along the sleeves. It glowed in the mean darkness.

45

'Who is it?' she asked testily holding the door open and blinking against the light. Without make-up her features looked strongly masculine. She needed a shave and there were violet shadows under her eyes.

'Me. Glory. You helped me last night with that junkie.'

'Oh. I thought I hadn't seen the last of you,' she said. It was obvious we already had an agreement between us, which confirmed my creepy instincts.

'How did you find me?'

'Your mate at the Bridgeway.'

It was such a tiny room and so dark it was like being in a closet. She switched the light on.

'I was dozing. I need my beauty sleep. Sit down. Don't mind me, dear.' She was still flustered by the visit, but not intending to show it. She made instant coffee. The room was terribly tidy. There was a two-plate stove on a table by the wall, shelves of plates and cans and even a bowl of apples gleaming on the shelf by the bed. There were posters all over the walls and a Tretchikoff with those white horses by the sea in pride of place.

It was like a child's pretend hut, with lines drawn into the earth dividing up the rooms — the block of wood for a stove, plastic doll plates piled up with hydrangea leaves for dinner. It was the life a child might imagine for herself, everything she ever wanted in the smallest area possible. The world outside triumphantly annulled forever.

'I've even got some bikkies. It's your lucky day. What's the drama? Kid dead?' The cup of coffee was lukewarm, with undissolved coffee powder still floating in it.

'Yes,' I said. 'I think the cops are going to be involved and I just wanted to warn you.'

She was amused for some reason. She pulled across the curtain and peered out dramatically. 'Well the boys in blue aren't here yet. Not that I can see anything from here. What's the weather like?'

'I just wanted to tell you that I've never met the kid before and I know nothing about it in case you're wondering. That's what I'm telling the cops as well.'

'Well, Glory, that's very nice of you. In that case I'd better hide a few things.' She fished around in her robe and zipped out a flick knife. 'Some of them get really tacky. You wouldn't believe. Last night I had to go round on all fours with a sheep-skin over me so he could pretend he was fucking a bear. I mean for God's sake.' She threw the knife out the window and peered out to see where it landed. 'Oh shit. Now I can't see where it went. I'll have to climb out and get it later. You can't see a bloody thing out there.

'Very well known of course. I always keep things confidential, part of the service, but I'll give you a little clue. He's a religious chappy? Interviewed on "Top Half" the other night. Top Half's right. That's why I'm so shagged out today. He must have weighed a bloody ton.'

'A bear?' I said temporarily diverted. 'Why should he want to fuck a bear?'

'His mother probably changed his naps on a bear skin,' she said absently.

I could see she was preoccupied and merely chatting as a social gesture.

'They have all these hang-ups from childhood — you wouldn't believe. The fetishes they come up with. It's tragic, and exhausting. It's such a relief to have a young one just straight gay. There were two of them last night and after I'd worked the old magic I told them, I said, now don't youse two boys turn into a tragical old queen like me.'

'Come round some time if you're passing,' I said.

'I don't know where you live, dear. It's very annoying, the demons coming round now. I haven't had my morning smoke, I haven't got my make-up on —'

It was a polite way of telling me to go, she was thrown into a panic and obviously didn't want me there.

It was much later that I realised that I shouldn't have gone. It gave a lot more weight to things in the eyes of the cops. It was a dumb kind of protective gesture, but it was wrong. Grace might have looked tough, but she was as vulnerable as a bird, she was like an endangered exotic species and I had caused her harm by blundering onto her territory.

Driving home that morning I felt uneasy, as if there was a whole lot of unfinished business somewhere. I felt very bad about Marianne, for one.

Not only that, but Nigel was waiting in the lounge for me when I got home. He had a real shitty look in his eye and launched straight in the minute I walked in. At least Al had remembered to take John off to the train.

'I mean, Glory, it's not as if you're completely established or anything. You simply can't afford not to — you of all people can't get into some kind of bullshit artist wank. Do you follow me? I've been working my ring off for this, sweetheart — and what have you got? Enough to cover one wall if we're lucky. I'm not saying they're not marvellous. They are marvellous, Glory. Stunning. It's just volume we're talking now, dearie. I mean in some ways this opening is the crucial one. If you fuck up you'll just slip into second-rate ville — the good mediocre painter who'll never do anything startling. Formula stuff. Good formula, but formula.'

He had never gone so far before — he was obviously panicking. I knew anyway from a mate of mine that his gallery was going into a slight decline. The pickings not being that rich in the first place, I could tell the dropped margin was worrying him. Younger more dynamic painters had started to desert for a racy little gallery which was more into cooperatives and had a less hierarchical set up for the whole marketing deal. Some of those painters he'd helped establish and he was bitter about what he called disloyalty. Of course some people would say he'd been milking them for years and they were just taking more financial control. I knew for a fact anyway that I was Nigel's great hope, so I didn't intend to give in.

'Nigel. Want a beer?' I went into the kitchen and opened a bottle with a vulgar blurt sound.

'It's eleven-forty in the morning, Glory.' His mouth was working with distaste.

'Where's everyone?' I asked sitting down, my head throbbing from the morning's emotions. I was drinking straight out of the bottle, which was childish I admit.

'There's no one here. I arrived and the door was wide open. Not a soul.'

There was an awkward silence.

'When's the opening?' I asked, just to stir.

'Too soon, dear. Relax, Glory dear, relax. I have a great deal on my mind. When you've finished your beer we'll go and have another considered look. Considered. I may be exaggerating of course.'

He took the bottle from me resignedly and drank. He wanted to make it up to me.

'Sometimes I wonder if it's all worth it. He looked around mournfully. Lapsing into self-parody was his only way of expressing his rage at me. 'Searching for beauty amidst the broken debris of a clapped-out society. Hassling some huge dyke for her meagre collection of bric-a-brac.'

I didn't say anything. There were some things I needed to sort out before I could even start painting and Nigel had about as much idea of them as a child. For all his panache and worldliness he was also a sneaky ignorant little boy with his round bottom and sleazy charm. I wanted to get rid of him.

'Have a really quick look,' I said. He looked critically at the paintings again, his face crumpled with total absorption.

'Alright. We'll see what we can manage,' Nigel said at last. 'But there's not enough for the main gallery. Well you know that anyway. You've got a bit of time I suppose. A few days. You'll do wonders won't you?' Then he said in such a quiet voice I could hardly pick it up, 'There are two cops at the back door, Glory. Is there no end to this?'

'Shit,' I said. 'I'd forgotten they might be coming.'

It was awkward with Nigel there because cops always related to me in a disrespectful way. It was the house, the way I looked, those subtle indications of class that cops were so strong at picking up. They knew instinctively what kind I came from and they were certainly not interested in any spurious art status. They'd see Nigel as a poofter, nothing more. If Nigel saw all this it would really lower all my bargaining power. In my war of

nerves with the bastard, the slightest sign of weakness and he'd
be in for the kill.

'You may as well go home. It's probably for Al.'

'Oh for sure,' he said. He probably knew more than he
was letting on, though how he found out was completely
beyond me.

'They're not going to bloody arrest you are they? This bloody
opening's doomed isn't it?' But to his credit he went quietly out
the side door. I saw him walking round the side of the house,
head down, trying to calm himself down, his body rigid with
suppressed rage.

'You Glory Day?' the cop asked in an over-friendly way. He
had a middle-New Zealand look about him and years of respect-
ability and judgements had taken their toll. The other one
looked like a small-town respectable gay basher, the kind who
rides round the streets in his father's Toyota after rugby club
piss-ups, looking for some soft flesh to tear into. Handsome,
closed, with that secret exuberant violence, a great whiff of
danger coming off him in a sour wave. They had both delved
and dived into so much human foulness their faces and hearts
had turned to stone.

'We're making a few inquiries, Glory. There's been a recent
death, suspicious circumstances, and we think you could help
us.'

I could see my Moe like a huge bear ambling up from next
door. He always turned up at my place when cops came. Just to
keep an eye.

'Watch out for Rina,' I asked him.

'They taking you in?' Moe asked.

'We'll go up to the station, Glory,' said the other. He had a
breathy sort of loony voice I didn't like.

'Fucked if I know,' I said to Moe.

'Watch your language,' he said friendly. It was just a warning.

'Is this an arrest?' I asked.

'No of course not. Something on your conscience?'

Grace was in the back seat of the cop car. I was pleased to see
her, but I felt responsible for her again. She smiled beautifully,

unperturbed. She was all made up and tarty again, she had her confidence back.

The boys were all out in force now, standing on the verandah. Even though cops were a common occurrence in our two houses, they all used to come out as a gesture. It was a silent send-off, no one waved or called abuse. The rain started up again as we set off.

'Are we going to the Otahuhu station?' I asked Grace as the car sped into the north-bound motorway. She made a face. 'This seems to be the big time.'

The car reeked of warm plastic and Grace's strong perfume, the big bodies of the cops filled the spaces and we drove in the electric silence that kind of journey has. It all seemed an over-reaction on their part — a young junkie had overdosed, and it was usually no big deal, but I knew from experience it was no good us being righteous. They were so used to injured innocence it was just a sour joke to them.

The big tower of Central looked military, in a Mad Max world it would be the eye of authority beaming down on the city. It was designed to intimidate, destroy, crush, the ultimate in siege mentality. There were those spooky concrete car-parks underneath — like climbing down into the bottom of a well.

'They both look terribly rough trade,' Grace hissed at me as we got out.

She was resigned to a thumping already, and I felt jumpy for her sake. Queens were even lower in the scale than street kids and they always rated a couple of smacks at least. It was hard to know where I stood in the scale of things.

In the little room the two cops stayed. I couldn't quite get a fix on all this. It seemed definitely excessive. They started getting into Grace in front of me. That's how little respect they had.

'Business been good, Grace? Do you take it up the brown or stopped that? Can't be too careful with AIDS around. Had yourself checked? You're a bit of a menace aren't you to respectable folk who do it nice?' The cop was very troubled. He circled her like a lover, then choosing his moment punched her in the kidneys. I could smell his acrid sweat.

'Excuse us, Glory.' Grace bent over double. Her long strong body folded in, swaying on her plastic high-heel shoes with the pain. Her face, when she brought it up again, was comically resigned.

'They usually pay for me to beat them,' she said and went down beautifully with the second blow. The other cop said to me, 'A bit unfortunate.' I recognised this as a phrase he used a lot.

I said to his friend quietly, 'I wouldn't if I were you.' The cop looked up from his play, his eyes shining.

'Oh you wouldn't, eh?' He came quite close to me and I could see his pitted skin. His breath was disturbing, it was metallic with some kind of festering emotion. A secret man. The other cop motioned with his head. He wanted him out.

Grace was gasping with the pain her eyes bloodshot with tears, her long beautiful body dropping. She leaned on the cop as he took her out, he put a friendly arm around her as he escorted her to another room. She was obviously in for a beating.

'Tends to be a bit over-zealous, Glory. Needs his leave. A very good officer. Friend of yours? The transvestite?'

'Yes,' I said.

'Ever seen her before?' He showed me a photo. It was the girl junkie, in more prosperous days. She was sitting at a restaurant table, her mournful eyes fixed on the camera. She was wearing a lowcut dress, and the bones of her face were stretched into a kind of stricken vulnerability. I felt a rush of grief to see her alive. Like all photos of dead people, it had faded, it already looked ancient.

'That's the kid I met at Mainstreet last night,' I said.

'Never seen her before?'

'No.'

'Know who her father is? Bet you don't know him either. A well-known businessman in Auckland. You and I don't move in those circles. Very religious, moral majority type. Doesn't like sin in any form, Glory. He's wondering who administered the fatal shot. Some friend of hers must have done it.'

I said nothing. No wonder there was all this hassle about a drug overdose.

And that was the first time you and your friend saw Marianne Lucas? OK. Why did you take her to hospital then? Out of the kindness of your heart, or second thoughts maybe, clever cover-up, genuine remorse?' He had a very quick mind, full of surfaces.

I said, 'Are you arresting me?'

'Not yet, Glory. But we're very interested. You're not new to this, are you. I've heard it runs in the family. The Days are pretty well known to the New Zealand Police Department. You're no exception.' He read from some notes. 'Idle and disorderly. Consorting with known criminals. Both your hubbies by way of being pretty devious characters.' He said the word 'pretty' so slowly he almost dislocated his jaw. He must have been doing some research. He was still obviously feeling his way, being delicate with me, which was a surprise. I got the impression he had great hopes of me, that he had other sources of information.

'OK,' I said. 'I've got nothing else to say.' I just wanted to stick to my story, unconvincing as it was, stay laconic and hope Grace wasn't losing her head.

He said, 'Fair enough.' I could tell he was itching to keep me in there for safety's sake.

'I'm waiting for my friend as well,' I said, as I got up to go.

The cop went out of the room briefly and came back with a businesslike air.

'She's been booked. No point in waiting.'

'I'd like to see her,' I said. They were overdoing it.

'Sorry. Not now.'

'OK, I'll ring a lawyer. You've got no right to keep her there anyway.'

'Just a minute.' He went away again and I waited in the little grey room for what seemed like a fair while.

And then, like a glorious bird of paradise wafting perfume, slightly subdued, Grace came in with the other cop. He was quite twitchy. He pointed the way and left us to it.

'OK. If there's a hint of bullshit we can pull you in on any number of charges. We'll be back, so don't trying anything. We'd like you to stick around.'

'Notice how nothing was official,' I said as we went out. 'That interrogation? They didn't write anything. That's influential parents for you.'

'I'm buggered if I know. Let's go for God's sake before they change their little minds.'

'Do you want a drink?' I felt bad about the trouble this was causing her.

We went to one of those smart plushy old-fashioned type of midday bars with red upholstery and fake English sideboards, all boring Victoriana and dim lights. Full of well-dressed old office people bland as butter. The sort of place I wouldn't go near normally but I was longing for a drink. There was a slight hush when we came in, but I didn't feel in the mood for playing up to it. I bought her two whiskies.

'There is definitely some kind of set-up,' I said. I drank the whisky moodily. I felt dirtied by that whole scene back at the police station and responsible for Grace. She was powdering her face and fixing her rich hair back into the punky backbrush she had before the cops started giving her a hiding.

'They pulled us in with no evidence. It was like they were in a real rush. All over an OD. They were acting real nasty.'

The people in the bar were staring at Grace in that superior bemused way straight people always had when confronted with vulnerable oddity. She sat there all fluff and gentleness, trying to patch herself up, the tiny glass clawed inside her long red nails.

'There's nothing they can pin on me.' She was philosophical about it all. You could see she'd been through it so many times it hardly signified any more.

'I can't get that kid out of my mind,' I said. 'There was something so pathetic about her. I was hoping she'd pull through.'

'Well we did our little bit to help. Not that we got any thanks. It's true. A mate of mine's always telling me off about it. She says a whore with a heart of gold is just too much of a cliché.

It comes of being a country girl from Te Kuiti.' Grace flicked a professional eye around the pub as she was talking.

'Well, dear, I don't know about you, but I'm getting out of this place. Some lovely little boys of course, but they all look like rugby players. Kick shit out of you before they look at you. If you know what I mean.' She grimaced. 'I've had quite enough of closets to last me all week thank you very much.' She was out of her usual stamping ground and I could see she was getting twitchy. There were too many dangers for her in a place like that.

'I'll take you home in a taxi. Do you want to stay with us a couple of days?'

Grace looked at me with her humorous face. She was amused.

'I took you for the strong silent type. With that wonderfully bushman face. No, dear. I will accept a lift though. There are so many straights around today.' She shuddered without affectation.

A red-faced young executive with hard eyes leaned over us as we stood up to go. He was right on cue, rigid with suppressed excitement and contempt. The buzz from the bar died down as people waited for what was coming to her.

'Don't I know you from somewhere, dear?' he asked to shouts of appreciative laughter from the group behind. He was obviously the dag of the gang.

'Hardly, dear,' said Grace. 'I don't associate with wankers.'

I thought the situation looked quite nasty. I've always found the men with suits and nice open drinking faces can turn quite vicious if any cracks appear on the surface of things. This was all about manhood, a fraught subject.

'Watch it, you fucking fag,' he said, showing his teeth. But his advantage was lost, and he knew it.

'Not today, dear,' said Grace raising her voice and, I thought, completely losing her head. 'I'd have to charge you twice the price for dirt money.'

Even she knew that was too much for a great lump like that. He made a rush for her, leaning his body heavily against the table and smashing all the glasses off the top. I tripped him as he stumbled, and gave him a little secret chop to the stomach. It was so fumbly and slack that people didn't even realise it was happening. He fell heavily against the chair I had just got out of.

'Come on,' I said to Grace and we both made our exit to the door, still retaining a certain amount of dignity before racing for the taxi stand outside. For once we were in luck.

'I must learn karate,' Grace said, leaning against the car door, her eyes closed, panting and dishevelled from the run. 'It's so hard to fit it all in.'

When I dropped her off home, svelte once more, she posed briefly, Hollywood on her high heels in front of the boarding-house, and waved to me before she made the long descent.

3

When the phone rang in the middle of the night I woke up cold, and sat up straight away. I got to it before the end of the second ring. It was an unfamiliar voice, very curt.

'Glory? It's Trish. Nettie's very ill. She sent for you.'

It was my first husband's sister. A courtesy call in the middle of the night. She must have been ringing a fair few people, there were ten brothers and sisters in that family. Not to mention ex-wives.

'Oh yes?'

'She won't make it. Can you come down?' When she said that I felt a catch at my heart.

'Is she at home?'

'Yes. You know where Mitch is?'

It felt like the pay-off for loving me all those years. It was Nettie's innocent way of making sure she saw her Mitch. I was the only connection she'd been able to keep with her son.

'Who?' I asked, to gain a bit of time.

'Mitch. Your ex-husband.' She sounded impatient as if she didn't want to do this — ringing strangers in the middle of the night, talking about her vermin of a brother.

'I haven't seen him for years. I wouldn't know where he was.'

'Ah the poor thing. She wants to see him bad.' Unexpectedly the voice cracked and broke off, overcome.

I knew it was probably Mitch Nettie was thinking about now as she lay near death. I could see her clearly, lying very still, thinking about him and her failure, her narrow old forehead and painful eyes shadowy against the white pillow. Her coming death pierced me. I knew she'd want to see him and that she was relying on me.

I said, 'I'll do my best to find him. I'll be down right away.

Getting in touch with Mitch was letting another man-eating lizard out of the mud, and after the last day or so it was the last thing I wanted, but I felt obligated. The least I could do for Nettie was to find her rotten son. I tried to stay calm as I dressed in the dark, but I got the shakes and couldn't stop. In the end I rang Cash.

The phone rang about ten times before he answered, his voice clotted and rough with sleep.

'That you?' I asked.

'Christ, Glory. What now?'

'Just a favour, Cash.'

'Oh shit. This time of night?'

'Nettie's dying. Mitch's mother. She wants to see him. I have to get hold of him.'

'Oh. Why didn't you tell me?' His voice cleared, became respectful. 'You know I'll always help out. That's a terrible thing. She's a wonderful woman.'

'Thanks, Cash.'

He always sounded as if his deepest sentiments, most holy thoughts came from Christmas card messages, care of Stamfords. He could well have meant it for all I knew, but it never rang true.

'I'm going down. Can I rely on you?'

'Yes of course you can, Glory. No worries.' He was exulted by the nobility of the moment, I could tell by his voice.

I took my wallet and my bag and let myself out of the house. It was really cold, the wind howled round the roof, flapping and banging it. I got into the car and started it up. The engine whined and whined. I tried again and again till it was completely flooded. The fucking battery had finally gone. I might as well get it towed off for junk — it wasn't even worth a hundred bucks. I leant my head on the steering wheel despairing.

After a while, sitting in the dark, stiff with self-pity, it gradually dawned on me that I had just walked out of the house, leaving Rina, the paintings I was doing, not even telling Al where I was, to go off in a car that would never have got further than the Bombay Hills. It made me realise how desperate I was to get down to her, get her blessing, tell her I loved her. I had never told her anything like that, and it stuck in my throat, even here in the middle of the night in my clapped-out car. I had to think. As I sat there, a small white figure wandered out through the long grass, peering for me through the darkness.

'Mum. Mum. Glory,' Rina called.

'I'm here.' I opened the car door and gathered her into my lap. She was still half asleep, her body bed-warm, red sleep crinkles on her cheeks.

'Why did you get up?'

'I heard the phone ring and I heard your car. You kept rrrring it.' She gave a huge yawn. 'What are you in the car for?' Snuggling up.

'Johnny's nan is sick. Nettie. We have to go down and see her.'

'Before she dies? John's mum?'

'Yes. Down in Glen Afton.'

'We could go in the train,' said Rina sleepily. 'In the morning.'

'You're a bloody genius, Rine,' I said. 'That's right. We'll go on the train tomorrow morning.'

'What's a genius,' said Rina and fell asleep.

I sat there listening to the wind crashing around the car and the dogs' paws skittering on the wooden boards of the verandah next door as they made their rounds. Occasionally a car zoomed past on the highway in the darkness. The sound of each lonely journey died faraway in the distance.

I tried to take an overview of things, it seemed important to make an inventory before I even moved out of the car. It was as if the kid dying at Mainstreet had triggered off something that had been fuelling me for years. I had to take notice of the strength of it all before I went any further. It was as if I had to repeat the catechism — I am still a young woman with my life before me — just to keep my head above water. For years now if I ever thought about my childhood or about Mitch and Weasel, it was just as a passing shadow, a mild curiosity, nothing more. My two marriages were just chance, a foggy mating in the dark at a time in my life when I was damaged and nutty from the decay around me. My husbands and their mean worlds were just an extension of my family — they formed a link I still hadn't got around to cutting. And once they went out of my life, there was a gloss to things I'd never had before, everything took a turn for the better. When I was living with them, it was me and them and the kids and drama off and on TV. There were so many fights and little secret aggravations. We ate out each other's hearts just like my parents before me.

I started my married life in a little North Island town near Scrubsville, Taumarunui. Anyone could imagine what that was like. I nearly lost my mind there, with my jerk of a husband going over the accounts in the cold kitchen at night, the calendar always on the same month. Mitch was the first man I had sex with, at the tender age of fourteen, and I got pregnant, I was so desperate to get away from home. Childbride that I was, pregnant already, at fifteen I entered into the trap. There was a photo that survived, of the group outside the Registry Office, with me looking like an Appalachian mountain girl — a face already old and deprived, thin little whippet body, lots of mean power in the eyes. I had all the growing awareness of the misfortunes of life to tighten my mouth. I was playing it all by ear essentially and knew nothing about health.

Of course Mitch had come a long way from Taumarunui. I didn't know the exact details, only that he lived out in Albany somewhere, a Mr Big in the crim world. Ex-bankrupt dairy owner, ex-shark car dealer, it was only a few years ago I was reading in the *Star* that he was given time for some scam to do with stolen car parts and softball batting recalcitrant payers. Not to mention the big time in drugs.

Nettie was forever telling anyone who would listen that her father was a well-known chief round Wellington way, she probably mentioned it in court as well, bless her. Her scummy son would have loved that. He was never embarrassed by his mother's snobberies, but then I don't suppose he should have been. It was about her only fault. Nettie always had a soft spot for him, her only bad egg out of a family of ten. She still called him her baby. There was never any question that she'd take my

John, Maori style, once I'd proved my incompetence — and I had the grace never to question it. Even then I trusted her absolutely.

See, my Nettie was a healer, a magician. She carried power around with her nonchalantly as a queen. Her specialty was binding lost souls to life — she could heal them, love them in a way which was spellbinding. I grew up with them, the ones she helped. They were strewn throughout my life, so more than anyone else I could appreciate the miracle of her connection with them. She could do the equivalent of making someone like Weasel sleek and happy, pull him from the grave. These were people who were so damaged that they had no inner core left, their lives had no meaning to them other than bottling a man in the pub or smashing a woman senseless.

Even the most minimal comforts were denied people like that — the small human pleasures of loving a child and looking after it, watching TV with a friend in a cosy room, being praised or wanted by someone. Child molesters, druggies, violent crims, killers, their veins were brimming over with the poisons accumulated in a lifetime of neglect, losers enmeshed in a life of cheapo violence — a quick fix in a public toilet, a crack over the head with a broken bottle.

These were my childhood companions, flesh of my flesh, so I knew them like the back of my hand, I knew the hopelessness of them. And Nettie could speak to them in her own language. All except Mitch, her one failure. She had never been able to heal the wounds he tore out of his life and hers and their family's, and it was her lifetime's regret.

She had done all she could in her clear sure way to clean up the mess her son left wherever he went. She had loved me, her daughter-in-law when I was a difficult, grotesquely lonely child, and I had never got over the surprise of the cool gift of her love. I had always stayed grateful. And then she brought up our John with a delicacy and sureness of touch marvellous for someone so old, so bowed down with the troubles of the world. She had no separations in her life, the current of her being flowed through everything and everyone, and there was my smiling serene John to prove it. She'd given him his fine life and now she was dying.

None of these good acts had even registered in Mitch's garish life. He let her love him, and was passive and unyielding on the surface — he knew he owed her respect, but his death-dealing instincts were too deeply rooted for her to soften. Mitch's power almost matched hers. He was a blank, cold strong man, a gangster, and he had no need of healing.

It was here in the car I had to make the decision about all this. There was never any doubt about me going down. That was nothing. It was seeing Mitch, handling all the old malice, and trying to keep things clean for my Nettie that preoccupied me. I hated having old memories reopened.

I dozed off with Rina heavy on my lap, and woke cold and bad tempered with a crick in my neck. I piggybacked her into the house and put her to bed. She must have been dead tired. I packed a few things, wrote a note to Al about recharging the battery and sat in the kitchen, drinking a cup of tea and watching the dawn come up.

It wasn't till we were going to the station when the taxi driver said shockingly, pointing at my sleeping Rina, 'She handicapped?' that I realised how stirred up I was by all this. He was a huge beefy man who filled up half the front seat, he had his well-thumbed *Best Bets* laid like a sacred vessel between his thighs. I raged at him in my foulest voice.

'What do you mean handicapped? You keep your fucking observations to yourself. She's probably brighter than you, creep.'

He said nothing, but I could tell his silence was not happy. We rode quietly through the cold streets.

'You're lucky I didn't throw you out. A fat hag like you. Cheek,' he said as we drew into the railway station. 'Fifteen bucks, and any more crap from you and I'll radio the cops.'

Rina stumbled out glaring at him blearily. She was still asleep on her feet.

'You fuck up and die,' she said, lugging off with the suitcase. We walked through the cavernous, tiled lobby alive with echoes of footsteps, children racing up and down, the hum of travel. The smell of mustiness, of trains, the magazine rack were all old as the hills, and even in my morning daze I registered the comfort of their timelessness.

'Where'd you learn that?' I asked her as we waited at the little ticket hole.

'What?'

'Fuck up and die,' I said.

'Johnny,' she said. She was watching a little girl, very seriously. The kid was wearing a snazzy red wool skirt and matching socks and shoes. She looked so clean and immaculate next to my Rina.

'What's your name?' asked Rina, drawing close to her.

The little girl didn't answer.

'What's your name?' she repeated, her voice testy. The little girl started to wail and skidded away from her, running down the hall.

'One and a half return to Huntly.' The man in the ticket office was very old. That was one of the things I liked about the Railways. He was like an ancient gnome in a cave, with all the tickets hanging like promises above his thin old head.

He filled out the forms so slowly that I could see the minute hand leaping the spaces. It had already been a hard morning. We raced down the echoing stairs onto Platform Four. The Silver Fern was just easing out with a magnificent slowness; the guard's whistle, the people standing back, the long, slow stir of the train, was like a running on the spot dream.

'Jump in, Rina!' I screamed. I wasn't going to miss it.

We just made it, and I leant against the toilet door in the swaying midsection, looking down at the floor parting and creaking. I was panting and exhausted. Dragging my bulk so fast down the platform had just about done me in, I'd never done so much exercise for years as I had in the last few days. It wasn't doing me any good.

My face was hot and wet with the strain.

'Not bad, Rina Loo,' I said. It was little victories like that which kept us both going.

We made the long swaying journey up the train, grasping the backs of seats, tripping over luggage, feeling like sore thumbs as all the other passengers looked blankly at us from their own little comforts. The musty smell of the train, the rustlings of peoples' food wrappings and the authoritative motion were instantly familiar even though I hadn't been on a train for years.

When we finally got to our seats, Rina stumbled into the window one and settled down to sleep. It was still so early I felt soiled and jumpy from the rush. And not only that, but as I sat there looking out the window trying to relax, it all hit me, like the re-run of an old movie. There, hurtling past in all their glory, were the images I thought had disappeared for ever. Framed by the dark peeling wood of the train windows, they were visions that could only ever belong to this train journey, and me as a deranged ten-year-old all those years ago. They were like a series of images I could measure myself against, a loop into time. I was back there, a kid staring out the window on one of the family's innumerable vagabond migrations up and down the North Island.

We had always been on the move, our ratty family, but for years I'd never thought of those dumb journeys we used to make. They overwhelmed me as I sat in the train. Always having to make a run for it in the dark, us kids shivering and whingeing. There were usually people after us, rent-men, creditors, cops, ex-partners my old man had done the dirty on. I knew all the warning signs of imminent departure by heart, my father coming home dead-drunk, oozing with the resentments of a lifetime, punchy with the latest defeat, my mother screeching out of control when she knew we had to move again. Us kids crowding together in the kitchen ready to hide when the shit hit the fan, listening fearfully for the sinister scuffling in the bedroom.

Our family life together was like living in an airless dingy cave littered with the bones of small animals, and wherever we moved, we took the sourness with us. It was my old man who blocked out most of the light, it was either us or him the way he saw it, and when it came to the crunch he decided to leave us to it. If you look at it one way, there was even some credit in his pathetic attempt to drag us with him. There he was, a small-time crim, trying to stay inconspicuous, with five scabby children and a half-mad wife the size of a house trailing behind. He used his great fists to keep us together — in exchange for the gift of his presence he required total submission and he would have broken us without a qualm to get it. The sound of his blatting frog-voice in the dark would set my heart beating as if it would break. The fear of him kept us all like hunted animals, and made our journeys together a nightmare.

For years now I hadn't even wanted to think about all that. I just assumed, wrongly as it turned out, that I'd finally got the past off my back. So the last twenty-four hours had been real razor-blade stuff to me. It was like riding on a ghost train, with all those old terrifying shadows coming at me in the dark, and now on the train, just when I thought it was OK, a whole brick wall cracking soundlessly over my head.

Nothing had changed out there, I was journeying through the bleak vistas of my childhood. There might have been a few more trees around the rest-rooms, but the same toy houses offered up their shy gifts — minuscule backyards where the business of people's lives was carried out beside the lemon trees and clotheslines, the selfsame houses I used to stare at as a kid and wonder what sort of kingdom reigned behind the curtains. I used to think about the little arrangements of each life, as we thundered past into the future, and I never doubted even then that irredeemable cruelties festered away in those family strongholds. I remembered a house, painted an innocent ming blue, with wrecked cars out the back, just outside Pokeno, and there it was still, older, but there, just waiting for me to flick it back into life with my attention.

This trip was absorbed into my skin and I hadn't even realised — the waking up, surprised, to find we were climbing the Raurimu Spiral, place of dreams and middle of the night groggy wonder as the train clacked on, burrowing through the darkness, the landscape outside unknowable through the dark night windows. Huntly, Te Kuiti, Taumarunui, Ohakune, Waiouru,

Taihape, Mangaweka — the names became more potent the further into the night and dreams I went — the coldness, the snow, the wild horses, as the guard walked through, repeating the name of each station like an incantation, an implacable person with a torch. The litany of those names was as familiar to me as the back of my hand. It was all there for the taking, the sad, dead towns, raggedy macrocarpas struggling against the wind, farm houses boxy beside the idiot green, my starvelling heritage, and I sat there transfixed by the memory.

'That your little girl?' asked a smiling middle-aged woman. She was sitting opposite with her bag in her hand, her smiling scrutiny. I hadn't even noticed her coming in. Certainly I wasn't in the mood for any conversation, let alone with this dopey-looking woman.

'Yes,' I said, looking back out the window, glancing at my sleeping Rina for confirmation.

She took out a bag of paper-wrapped toffees and started eating them like a child, stuffing them into her mouth, chomp chomp, papers falling everywhere, her wrinkled jaw masticating loudly. She didn't give me one, she ate her way all through the bag, her eyes unblinking on me, the smile fixed.

'Why don't you tip the back of your seat over? Then you can see where you're going.' I said in a soft voice. I was getting irritated by her smiling ridiculous gaze and the steady ugly sound of the soft caramel between her teeth. She didn't answer, but after a while she got up, banged the back of the seat over with a thump, and sat herself down on the other side, with a meaningful sigh. I could hear her starting on another bag of toffees. Then her voice started in a low monotone, full of unmistakable spite. I could hear snatches, 'Bitches, think they're smart, some fatso,' floating over me.

I looked around at the other passengers and twigged. It was like a walking Diane Arbus photograph. A train expedition for retarded adults, all looking at me unsmiling, chewing. You could tell they were pissed off.

'What's wrong, Elaine?' I recognised the guttural tones of my Rina deepened by adulthood. It was the thick mongol tongue that got in the way and made her talking so dense and heavy sometimes.

'That bloody bitch,' sobbed Elaine, and I couldn't catch the rest.

There was a real stirring and murmur from the people all around and I felt hemmed in, half amused. They gave off a kind of dull powerless anger, a seething resentment. There didn't appear to be anyone with them. It was strange to see grown-up Rinas everywhere. I could see the two of us, me even fatter and more awkward with age, huge and sepuchral, Rina with her wrinkled monkey face and the tawdry clothes she liked to wear, going to places together, shuffling along, a couple from the funny farm. It seemed a good proposition to spend my old age with her, but I was surprised how depressed they seemed. Usually they were relentlessly cheerful in a group. I hoped Rina wouldn't get so sombre when she grew into adolescence.

A fussy little woman with a working mouth came down the aisle at full speed, her throat was going with the tension of it all.

'Elaine! Hush! What are you talking like that for?' She bent her head over and there was a hastily whispered consultation. Now and again she glanced over at me fearfully. Finally she gave me a collapsed sort of smile as if to say, don't mind us, and escorted the weeping Elaine further up the train. Rina woke, and was instantly hungry. She stared around her, and I could see she recognised her mates, but she didn't say anything to me except to ask me about breakfast. She was always careful about things like that. She hadn't forgotten the taxi driver. In the end, once we got off the train, we had to wait for an hour for the bloody bus in a draughty waiting-room with a concrete floor, and dusty rubbish under the seats. We ate chippies and blocks of caramello for breakfast and mucked around — and the air smelt fresh even by the railway.

Nettie lived right out in the backblocks of the Waikato, a long way from the emerald farms of the wealthy cockies. Here the land was sour and bad, no sun, the trees looked mean and exhausted. I was never sure why Nettie came up here to live, away from her own roots, except that one of her sons went to work at the mine and she wanted to live near him. Her house was a wooden unpainted one on the main road just up from the mine. The settlement snaked up the hill — all the houses were poor and small, with old American Pontiacs and Fairlanes parked outside and great branching TV aerials poking out of the tattered old corrugated iron roofs. The settlement looked real though, as if there was some past to it, and some other investment besides money. The miners were all big men with country faces — they walked down the road to the mine, talking to each other, relaxed in the early morning. Some of them had worked there all their lives. It wasn't a closed-in little claustrophobic rural community, there was a sliver of past at least and some shared hardship, tradition.

Big hills, sombre and dark, towered above the little sprinkling of houses. I felt a great dollop of grief rise up in my throat when me and Rina finally arrived at the house and the first person we saw was Johnny. He had changed suddenly in the short time since we'd seen him. He came down the dark little hallway to me like a little brown wraith, but he was dignified in his new position. His eyes were red-rimmed and I felt awkward in the face of his adolescent grief.

'Do you want to see her?' he asked. He seemed resentful of something, maybe that I was still alive and his Nettie was dying. 'She's pretty crook,' swallowing back his tears.

We went into the bedroom. There were people everywhere, her sons and daughters, friends, but somehow they kept in the background. They were all concentrating on Nettie, who was half sitting on her bed, propped up with cushions, like a doll, her chest bubbling. Years of fags and hardship had broken her old body and her chest was heaving with the efforts of a lifetime.

'Glory, is that you?' Her voice was harsh with the breathing.

'Yes, Nettie.'

'And Rina.' Rina had already gone up to the bed and was staring at her.

'Are you going to die?' she asked holding her hand. But Nettie had other fish to fry.

'Is he coming? Is Mitch coming?' she asked. She was very

plaintive, her shrewd eyes troubled as she strained to hear me.

I sat beside her and held her other hand. She had the sick sour smell of death on her. The family had dressed her in a fresh nightgown and put clean sheets on the bed, but you could smell all her old juices leaking away. I could hear her labouring horrible breath right in my ear.

'I rang a mate of his, Aunty. You remember Cash? I rang him because I don't know where Mitch is. He's promised to find him.'

She jerked her hand away in a disappointed gesture, and flopped it down on the bed, her breath coming in stinking gusts. She was irritated with me. She couldn't even be bothered to hide it. I tried again.

'Cash just has to get hold of him. He'll come,' I said. 'He won't ignore that.'

The people in the room were quite silent, it was bizarre to hear them listening, feel their disapproval, in this most intimate death conversation.

'I tell you what,' she said clearly, 'he's always been a shit.' And then in case we didn't understand, 'Mitchell.'

Everyone in the room shifted, there was a clearing to the air, even some soft laughter. She had never spoken like that about Mitch ever. It was so unexpected it was comical.

'There's my Johnny,' she said sentimentally, taking his hand. She was really sparking for a minute. He stood there awkwardly, looking so young and handsome it made my heart lurch for him. 'Don't you turn out like your old man. Or your old woman,' she said. 'I've been lucky with my family. You've been a good family.'

She got very tired then and slumped on the pillow. 'I need a sleep,' she muttered, more to herself.

The eldest sister, the one who had rung me, said sharply, 'Let's give her a rest.'

There was a silence in the room. Outside the rain started, clattering on the iron roof. The room was very shadowy, with the venetians pulled against the grey day, all the bodies of her family there amongst her dark furniture, trying to breathe for the labouring old woman in their midst. She roused herself and mumbled.

'Is my Glory there?'

I said, 'Yes, Aunty.' No one showed surprise. This had obviously been going on for hours — she'd been checking all her family, wanting them within earshot. I held Rina in my lap and sat leaning peacefully against the bed. It creaked and juddered with her dying breathing. Everyone sat there caught in her net, the loving net she had spread around the room. She had blessed each of us with her dying already.

I drifted off, the peace of her dying reminded me of my own mother's life and death, something I didn't usually want to think about. But the air in the room was so alive with grieving, family love, old memories that you could almost touch it, and in my heightened state my own past, my mother, came to me easier than it had for years. Beaten into the ground by her punishing life, wrecked with booze long before she died, she was a person I never knew well. She was a frightening figure when I was a kid, full of unpredictabilities and sodden angers, but I recognised soon enough from my own experiences how easy it was to be made vindictive by circumstances. We had all discovered very early on that we could get nothing in the way of emotional and physical nourishment from either of them anyway, so we made our own adjustments as kids do.

When we did eat, for instance, it was greasy fry-ups, of leftovers, nameless masses, things like sausages cooked in fat she kept in the fridge in a broken cup. I would sit down to the table famished, but feeling sick to the bones before I even started eating. The warm grease used to congeal on the plate like yellow wax and our houses were always full of the sweaty smell. When I grew up to my own devices, I always ate with passionate delicacy — the chickens, grapes, puff pastries were all to set my stomach right. I had become huge on the past, it was compensation for the deprivation.

My mother would drag herself round the house, never sitting to eat, her huge shapeless nether regions ripe as mutton fat, a source of satisfaction to my old man right up to the time he left, him being a man of ripe sadistic urges. Dull-faced, puffy with the booze, she used to talk to herself, long abusive strings of nonsense, like one of those derros in city parks who catch the eyes of innocent bystanders and berate them. It never even occurred to me to blame her for her neglect of us, she had her own problems and even as a small kid I knew what to expect.

By the time Roach and I had come along, any love she had was gone. She got religion about then as well, Pentecostal or some other frantic hoax, and even that gave her no rest, with her brain half eaten out by the booze, it was just another irritant.

When she died, me and my sister were the only ones who went to the funeral, and unwillingly at that. All the rest of the family were scattered in Aussie and in gaols and borstals up and down the country. My old man was still alive, but I'd heard he was inside too — he'd long gone down the road by then. Roach could have asked for compassionate leave, being only a hop step and a jump away in Parry and a free day out, but he still had a lot of grievances. As the youngest he had the hardest time of all of us. Mum used to give him fierce hidings and lock him in the washhouse for hours. It was the booze and the religion mix which gave her no mercy. I would sneak down to him being only the next up in the terrible pecking order, full of pity for his little sobs, trying to comfort him, not being equipped with any of the natural ways of expressing love. She was three-quarters off the wall by then and a small boy's weary whimpering was the least of her worries.

She died of pneumonia after she was caught wandering in the rain during one of her mad spells. She'd been out all night, and in the end we even called the cops. Pally, my sister, finally found her crouched in a bus shelter up the road, her hair hanging down her face, singing to herself. I'd never heard her sing, but that was what Pally said. As sweet as a bird too she reckoned, and she was rocking to herself in the darkness.

I'd never been close to her, never knew her, spent all my time hiding from her rages, but once or twice since her death I'd thought of her singing in the bus shelter. At the time I had such a strong image of it in my mind I'd wanted to paint her, but I always thought better of it. I knew I'd just be a stranger intruding on the only moment she ever had.

So, sitting there in the half-dark with Rina crashed on top of me, waiting patiently for Nettie to die, even the ghost of my mother acquired its own dimensions for once. Whether I liked it or not I had her build and probably her liking for the booze, so I was still her daughter. But the vital difference for me was that the same uglinesses which had crushed her were my saving. I had my little prides and conceits, and that was one of them — the way I'd used the disease around me to flourish instead of dying of it. It had been touch and go, a precarious balance between selling out and going under but I rode all the way. Painting was survival to me, I found a freedom and a power through it for the first time in my life. My mother took to the booze, I painted my life up, and produced form out of the bad blood I was born to. And Nettie went further, she healed others as well as herself, she gave me love I never would have known, and it was her I always stayed grateful to.

A long time afterwards Rina woke and started whimpering. I took her outside to play in the backyard with Nettie's old cattle dog. I felt like a drink, and as I made a cup of tea instead in the kitchen, I heard the first sounds of mourning. The chilling sound wound round my ears, clinging to my nerves. I could even see Nettie in the room for a minute, sitting at the table drinking tea, her poor old eyes looking lovingly at me.

Other women came into the kitchen after a while as I stood there working in silence. They had already begun the work of preparing food for the people who were starting to fill the house, but none of us spoke. We peeled potatoes and kumaras, buttered the thin white bread, boiled eggs, washed the puha. I'd seen those preparations before — always done with style and casualness, the women moving stately in the bare kitchens, the plenty coming from them without effort. Plain plates, plastic cups and white paper spread over long tables. The food thick and filling and stodgy, bread-of-life food, but I didn't have the stomach for it without Nettie there.

4

Of course later on that day Mitch finally made it. I didn't even see him for hours after he arrived because I just stayed and worked in the kitchen. It was the only thing I felt like doing, a way of grieving for Nettie, standing there in her kitchen peeling potatoes like a zombie, my legs planted solidly to stop myself falling. It got through a certain amount of time, numbed my brain, it was even a way of making up to her for not getting her son to see her in time.

When he walked into the kitchen he was radiating tension, he looked pissed off, preoccupied, he barely even said hello. He had turned into a big man, fleshy with an overcharged electric skin on him — he looked sick, with his yellowish eyes and bloated face. He was still handsome in a spivvy middle-aged way, dressed in an expensive suit, his nails buffed and pearly like a businessman's. He still had sleepy eyes, black lashed.

'Jeez,' he said to me as soon as he saw me. 'You've packed it on.'

I recognised the tone. He had always been irritable with me.

'Look at you! You've let yourself go.' He was frankly disgusted, but the sight of me gave him some obscure satisfaction as well.

I said, 'At least I don't look like a fucking third-rate gangster.

He gave me a long look, nasty. Then we both collected ourselves. It was over ten years later after all, and the women working in the kitchen were all openly listening. We went out onto the verandah by tacit consent.

'Were you here when she passed away?' he asked. He wasn't upset about it, but there was a slight disturbance going on somewhere in his glacial depths. There was that coldness in him even about his mother's death. He'd never known how to deal with her, her open love was an anathema to his secretive nature.

'Yes,' I said. I certainly didn't want to talk about it with him. He was edgy too, you could tell he hated being there at the mercy of the family. He considered them yahoos, suckers, envious of his dough. He used to call them hicks even when he himself was a shit dairy owner in the wop-wops.

'It was a shame I didn't make it. Cash reckoned the old lady really wanted to see me.' He paused. 'He said you rang him.'

'Yeah. Your sister rang me.'

'You staying here long?' he asked.

'I should be going back. I wanted to pay my respects. Couple more days.'

'Trouble?' he said so quick and smooth I should have taken notice of it then.

'No,' I said. I still had healthy instincts about not telling him anything.

'I can run you back. I wanted to go sooner, but I've got a couple of things to talk to you about. I was going to come up and see you anyway.'

I didn't say anything. It seemed really strange that after all these years he could have something to tell me. I was feeling unreal anyway, to say the least.

'So what are you doing with yourself? Make anything out of that stuff you do? As a matter of fact I saw something about you in *Metro*.'

His forté had always been taking the ground from under my feet, and it was interesting to face him now and not start doubting myself. It was the same with my old man — after years of domination I discovered they were just jerks, not even worth thinking about. Years of my life down the drain trying to please violent fools. And now here he was with names like *Metro* tripping off his tongue. He must be on the up and up. When I knew him all he read was *Best Bets* and *Truth*.

'*Metro*? Shit, eh,' I said, deliberately offensive.

'There was a story about car salesmen in the same issue,' he said smoothly. 'I don't usually read the wanky arts pages. You always were a bit of a snob, Glory. You never thought I had anywhere near your brains. I don't know what you're doing with that shit band. They've got no class.'

It was strange sitting on the rickety verandah looking out onto Nettie's scrubby garden with this well-dressed stranger, father to my son. I had honestly thought I would never see him again. The circumstances of our parting had been ugly to say the least, even at the best of times there was never much in common between us.

The last time I saw Mitch as my husband was when I drove him to hospital with a broken arm. What had happened was, when he went off with another woman I was so pissed off I smashed all the windows in his car, let down the tyres and then tipped red paint all over the seats. I rang his work — he was a car salesman by then — and told them all about his under-the-counter deals as well. I've never pimped like that before or since, but my pride was hurt. For some reason nothing happened and he didn't lose his job, he never said anything to me about it. With all the shit flying round about the car, he didn't have time. When he finally came round to heavy me, I got this dyke friend of mine to scare him. In those days he was a bit of a wimp for all his country blubber, that's why I wasn't surprised later to read in the paper about the softball bats.

Anyway, this friend of mine broke his arm with a chair, quite by accident in fact. He cried like a baby with the pain so I took pity and drove him to hospital.

I never actually saw him to speak to after that, just occasionally at pubs or on the street. That was years ago anyway. He tried to have my friend up but she was leaving for Australia to escape another charge, and after a lot of letters he just let it lapse. I sometimes wondered if he'd bring a group of heavies round one day and knock my teeth out for it, but it was so long ago I couldn't see it. Probably out of respect, me being the mother of his only son, some sentimental crimmo idea like that. I wasn't physically worried, I learnt karate almost straight away after that incident and now with my weight I'd probably knock him flat just by leaning on him.

I was eighteen by then, involved with a real hood who used to talk all the time about wasting people, and his continual talk of violence and death had influenced me. After that incident with Mitch, I went with Darcy down to Christchurch to do some big deal. We even had a posh rental car. It was probably smack — I was unclear about the details because I was always out of my head in those days. We ended up borrowing a clapped-out Holden off some drunken friend of his and I drove it all the way up the South Island — he wouldn't drive because he said it interfered with his concentration.

Someone was after him, I wasn't sure who it was. The deal had obviously fallen through because we only stayed one night in Christchurch in a crummy little house in Sydenham and then shot through first thing. It was a nightmare trip which ended when the engine block fell out on that winding road to Picton. I just left him and hitched back because I wanted to see John.

By that time anyway, none of Mitch's family would have anything to do with him either after he did something slippery with the family finances, and they wouldn't let Nettie near him. She used to go and visit him later when he was inside the first time. Once I even caught her getting into the bus in her best black dress, a bit dusty, her great shopping bag bulging with stuff for him. I made her come in my car at least that time, an old woman of seventy bumping all the way out to Parry in one of those bonejerkers. She, as usual, retained her coolness the whole way, her handsome lined face staring gravely ahead as we drove in silence to the jail. I suspected he had bled her dry as well. He used to borrow money off anyone without compunction, not that I would have dreamed of mentioning it to her. Nettie had her pride.

In those days she wouldn't admit a thing about Mitch. I thought of her old voice as she lay dying, her swearing at him, the faint hint of laughter as if she had finally at long last given up all pretence. I felt a wave of loss like a physical blow, but I knew I had to control it. Mitch was the last person on earth I'd ever cry in front of. He was sitting there, restive, looking moodily off into the garden. He probably thought I was trying to bluff him by my silence. It was the sort of thing he did. I said, just to break the ice, 'So what line of business are you in?'

'You were always the same,' he said, twisting his bull neck around to glare at me. 'Too smart for your own good. Even when you were a kid.'

'Me?' At age fourteen?' I wasn't even aware of having brains or talent till I'd had two kids, and two broken marriages at twenty.

'You were always up yourself,' he said. He sounded as if he still resented it.

'How did that woman — Sheree — go?' I asked. I couldn't help myself.

'Oh great. A couple of years. I don't know what's happened to her. She's got a kid too.' It was strange, but he was definitely boasting. I had always thought Mitch was as indifferent to me as I had become to him, but there was obviously still some seething stuff going on in that massive meaty head. He wanted to pay me back, for all sorts of things, but for some reason he had to stay nice. He was controlling himself with an effort.

'So John's got another half-brother or sister somewhere?' It was the first time I'd mentioned John and Mitch's reaction was physical shock. He jumped and twitched as if I'd pricked him.

'Look I know I've been slack. You had Weasel to support you and then all my capital was tied up in the business. I'm doing alright now, and I've been thinking for a while of fixing him up. Couple of grand?' It was the same old Mitch and all I could do was just look at him.

In the end I said, 'OK,' and held out my hand to him, just for my own secret satisfaction.

'Come on, Glory. I don't carry round cash. I'll arrange it through the bank. What's his bank? You know?'

'Fucked if I know.' I was irritated by this charade. He should have known it meant nothing to me.

'Well you're no bloody help. I'd like to help the boy.'

Mitch had always whined a lot. Like a lot of professional crims he was sentimental, basically stupid, his emotional apparatus smeared with lies and crooked dealings, the ever

present tension of missing out on the big one always preoc-
cupying him.

'Oh cut the bullshit,' was all I said. It wasn't that I didn't want
the money. I didn't have any hang-ups about pride or anything
— I just knew from bitter experience that I would go through
some complex rigmarole and then still not get it at the end. It
annoyed him, my flat refusal, because he liked playing sadistic
games like that. I wondered why he was being so dangerously
patient with me as we sat so genteel on the verandah.

In our early marriage he used to give me hidings every time
he got drunk and then try to drag me to bed, all sexually charged
by my bruises and tears and childish body. It was razor-edge
stuff for both of us. Some of the women I knew got beaten up
every weekend regular as clockwork, but I was strong even
then. After months of these beatings and dangerous sex I got out
the carving knife and stuck it right into his side. He bled like a
pig and, pissed as he was, realised cold that I meant it. He never
touched me again, it was like a connection burnt into his brain.
It reminded me of the nights when Dad came home drunk, threw
Mum against the wall punching her and then dragged her off. I'd
hear the old bed squeaking under the gross weight and it was like
two monsters coupling and groaning right in my ear. I knew my
mum hated it all — the only thing she ever told me about sex
was that it was better to move a bit and they'd finish it quicker.

I watched Mitch play out the same game with me, just as
tethered to the past. I never knew for sure, but it was likely his
father beat up Nettie. The virus of violence passed down the
line. Mitch was still a violent man, I could see by the way he sat
in the chair — alive with irritation, staying smooth with an
effort. Being in jail had certainly taught him patience.

'You're still the same bigmouth,' was all he said. 'You never
did learn to leave well alone.' There was a silence. It was a real
free-ranging conversation.

'Are you ever going to do anything for Johnny?' It was just to
make conversation, I'd never relied on him and neither had
Nettie. He pretended to give the matter thought, shifting his big
hypocritical body around.

'Well I could get him a job. I'm back at the yard up there. Good worker is he?'

The day lengthened, broadened on to us, sun streaming onto the paddocks and scrubby hills surrounding the house. Inside we could hear the sounds of grief, people with hard healthy faces filed past us continually, averting their eyes up into the front door, to pay their respects.

The gangster and the prostitute. The family renegade and his ex. With Nettie gone I could feel the weight of their displeasure with me and Mitch. Some of them tried to be civil, but we were an embarrassment to them. Mitch had done them all down probably — and I as an ex-wife was part of the whole mess, there were probably some weird tales circulated about me anyway. It was for John and Nettie's sake that they were not rude to me and put up with Mitch's presence in the house. He was unconscious of this, social intricacies had never interested him.

A woman brought us each out a plate of food and he accepted it as his due without thanks. As an elegant piece of social handling, intricate in its intention, it was beautifully and courteously done. The message was: Mitch you are a bastard and a thief but because you are the son of our mother, and the father of our son we will tolerate you today and perhaps tomorrow. The mark of courtesy was not for him as a person. It was all wasted on Mitch of course. He thought only about himself and how to wangle the next buck, and that was a continual process with him. His shark brain mashed and meshed out complicated deals, schemes, muddy practices and, since he'd been inside, it had hardened in him.

As we sat in silence, John came out on the verandah. He didn't even look at Mitch. Thinking about it later it must have been a moment of shame for him. There for all the world to see, his great bizarre mother with dyed hair and tattoos on her arms, and his father, a shifty-looking gangster just out from the boob. I could see he was worn out, the poor little bugger, with grief and his responsibilities. He was being the man of the house, tending to all the kuia with his old world courtesy, jollying all the aunts and uncles, arranging food and accommodation. His eyes were ringed with purple shadows. He looked remarkably fine and dignified there in the doorway. His hair was almost blue it shone so dark in the sun.

He said, 'Are you OK, Aunty Glory?' I heaved myself up off the chair and went and hugged him. It was special occasion.

'I'll come and give you a hand again,' I said. 'I've just been having a breather. This is your dad.' It was so bald, but I didn't know how else to say it. They didn't seem to be any more related than a shark to a sheepdog. He looked at me with such a mixture of fear and rage and exhaustion on his face. For a moment he looked like my own father.

'Oh.' He swung round on Mitch. 'I've heard all about you,' he said, not even trying to conceal the sneer in his voice. I could see he was absolutely overwrought.

'Have you now? And what have you heard?' It was not a promising beginning, and I stood there alert, balancing on the balls of my toes, apologising in my heart for giving him such a father.

'You treated my nana like shit. That's one thing. And my mother.' There was an electric silence. 'And you never saw me, you never cared about me.'

I couldn't believe it. John had a horrible tight smile on his face, it was like a rehearsed speech that he'd wanted to make for years. Mitch made a movement, I almost expected to hear applause from hidden watchers inside the house. The sun was suddenly quite warm. We were certainly both sweating.

Suddenly, to my horror, John burst out in sobs. They were great harsh wrenching ones, right from the heart. He wiped his face with the back of his hand, like a kid, and just stood there crying. I said, 'Johnny, I'm sorry.' I was overcome with grief for my son. I never even knew his private sorrows, the thoughts he had at night in bed, staring up into the darkness.

'They've turned you into a fucking poofter,' Mitch said. 'The two of them. You're like an old woman.' The boy's beauty meant nothing to him.

Johnny stepped up very close to his father, the tears glistening on his cheeks. He whispered to him, virulent with baffled love,

'At least I'm not a wanker.' He chose his words for the maximum offence. It made me realise he wasn't my son for nothing.

Mitch went into overdrive, his eyes narrowing, the adrenalin packing out his cheeks as he leapt to his feet in a gesture surprisingly agile for such a heavy man. All the aggro he'd been suffering at my hand burst out. He was frightening.

He said, 'What did you say, you little milk-fed cunt? What are you calling me?'

Johnny was blind to his cruelty and strength, he was still crying and murderous with rage. There was a confused scuffling as the two moved into a grappling seething fight, silent with concentration. It was such an old score between the two of them, and I had nothing to do with it.

I said, 'Pick on someone your own age, you jerk.' I couldn't resist it. He flicked such a bloodshot look of sheer hatred at me, it put him off his stride for a second. For such a professional that was a surprising mistake. He was just raising his big meaty arm to hammer his son to the ground and Johnny, quick to cash in on the second's inattention, got in with a punch. It was such a crack, it even made me wince — and there before our startled eyes was Mitch crashed to the floor, half unconscious, with a bleeding cut over his eye.

It was so unexpected that Johnny stepped back, startled by the suddenness of it. We both stood staring, at a loss. It was such an abrupt end to what could have been very serious. It was an embarrassment to both of us, Mitch's huge, bleeding comical body, but Johnny quickly recovered himself.

He said, averting his eyes from the sight, 'Tell that cunt I never want him near me again.' It was the sort of absolute decision you had to make in our family.

'That was for Nettie,' he said to his sleeping father, a shade too dramatically. His sincerity was never open to question though and it made my heart ache for him. 'You never even turned up for her. She wanted you.'

I'll give it to Mitch that caution won out over machoism — even he knew not to say anything. He was probably feigning unconsciousness. Johnny turned around with full honours, and went out into the hallway and I followed him. He had turned adult so suddenly it was disconcerting. I was floundering a bit, trying to find a different tone with him.

He said, not looking at me, 'It wasn't right to do that with Nettie in there.'

'Oh shit, Johnny. The family's a better place for it. The bastard's had it coming for years.' It was on the tip of my tongue to say I was proud of him, but the words couldn't come out, I could never say things like that.

'Yeah, well, I don't want him here again.' He gave me a small austere smile — we both secretly saw the funny side of it, but that was as far as he'd go, out of respect for Nettie. It was hard for me to tell whether he was pleased or disappointed with my answer anyway. He kept walking up the hall.

I said, 'I want to talk to you for a minute. What are you going to do now? Stay here or what? There's always a bed for you at our place.'

'I know.' He stopped and looked back at me. 'Aunty Rita says I can stay with them. I can get a job at the works with Charlie he reckons.'

I didn't know he'd left school already. He hadn't told me that. It was like losing him twice when he said that. It made me realise what a small space I took up in his life.

'You happy with that? Are they OK?' I knew for sure I had to withdraw quickly. I was taking too many liberties.

'Yeah.' He wasn't that interested in the conversation any more, but he always stayed polite. I turned back.

'I'll see you later, son.' It was the most intimate thing I'd ever said to him, but he gave no sign.

'See you,' he said, his shoulders hunching over with the cares of the world.

Mitch was sitting up moaning when I got back to the veran-dah. While I was sure everyone in the house was well aware of what was going on, no one came out to help him. Mitch carried his city plague around with him, and these people didn't want to catch it. They genuinely wouldn't have cared if he'd died out there.

'You alright?' I asked without much interest. He was stone angry, as if he had been brawling with some upstart stranger who got him with a lucky punch. He knew there was nothing he could do for the moment, a defeat was a defeat and he had a very precise idea of the balance of things, but there was no generosity in the man. I knew his capacity for grudges from old.

'The shit,' he said. His lack of emotion about either his son or his mother was startling.

'You shouldn't have called him a poofter. Kids that age are very sensitive about their sexual preferences,' I said to remind him he was dealing with a kid, even if he wasn't making any other allowances. Mitch seemed to be taking the humiliation to heart, son or no son.

'Oh, fuck up, will you?' he snarled at me, straightening himself up and dabbing at the cut. 'They're all like him. You've brought up another fucking inbred country cousin. That's all.' He imitated Johnny's country Maori accent, 'Eh, boy.'

'You've hurt him,' I said. 'You're his bloody father.'

There was a silence and I thought it was possible I had been underestimating him, but he was just shifting into another gear.

'I'm getting out of here. I've got work to do. It's alright for some. You want a lift?'

'No thanks.' I'd forgotten his idea of running me up. Whatever he wanted to talk about was bound to be a mass of lies and double-dealings and I couldn't stomach being with him so long. Even thinking about the whole mess up home was enough to put me off — I felt like staying down here just to keep away from it. The phone rang at the far reaches of the house and there was a long silence after it was picked up. It was just like the movies. I knew it was for me. Finally as we sat there a little girl with a snotty face came racing in importantly.

'Aunty Glory. It's from Auckland.'

It was Al. He was always hopeless on the phone. I'd seen him talking on it — handling it as if it was a grenade. Basically any method of communication made him uneasy.

'Glory, you've got to come back now. The cops were really pissed off.' There was a long silence, then, 'He reckons, the smartarse one, that you promised to stay around. I said you'd be back today. Can you make it?' He sounded very harassed.

'OK.'

'They've arrested Grace.'

'What for?'

'Fucked if I know.'

'I'm coming. Tell them I'm coming.' I put the phone down and went back through the throng of people to Mitch still sitting out on the verandah. I'd been trying not to think of it all and the phone call from Al was like an electric jolt.

'Yeah, I'll come.'

'A little trouble at home?' he sneered. He never could resist kicking people when they were down. It was one of his trademarks.

'I'll get Rina. And say goodbye to John. Give me quarter of an hour.'

It was a shock. I wondered why they'd arrested Grace, when it was transparent she had nothing to do with it. Something to show they were in earnest — a gesture to me? I didn't like the intensity of it, just for one death by overdose. They were usually a dime a dozen in Auckland, heroin deaths. Acts of God everyone felt sanctimonious about, nothing more. There was no doubt I had to go, even if only for Grace.

It seemed ridiculous to turn down Mitch's offer in the light of this latest news. I'd be up there in a few hours. I went into the house to find Johnny and Rina.

The little house was bursting at the seams, it was sighing and creaking with mourning people, the murmur of voices, the sound of the keening in Nettie's closed bedroom. I finally found Johnny in the corner of Nettie's shadowy lounge, sitting with a kuia. He was leaning towards her for comfort. They were not speaking. When I finally pushed myself awkwardly through to him he looked up at me tearfully.

'What do you want?' he asked.

'To talk to you.'

'This is my mother, Aunty.' Her hand felt like a leaf, soft and dry in my hand. She looked up at me, her old eyes flashing welcome. She had no teeth, she looked sly and vivacious with her sunken old soft face.

'I'm Nettie's sister, Aunty Marie. Pleased to see you here,' she said. She was being very helpful and friendly to me. I could see tears trembling on her old cheeks, she didn't even seem to be aware of them.

'Hello Aunty Marie,' I said. 'I'm sorry about Nettie. She was the best.' I was desperate to get away by now. 'Do you mind if I have a word with Johnny?'

She waved her assent, her face creased in a smile. She didn't judge me for my lack of courtesy.

I said to Johnny out in the hall, 'I've fucked up again, Johnny,' genuinely regretting it. 'I have to go.' It was a big admission for me, but he wasn't having it.

'They'll be insulted,' he said, coldly.

'I'm in trouble.'

Johnny was not going to be shaken. He looked fierce.

'OK,' was all he said.

I said nothing. I didn't want to quarrel with him. Out in the kitchen Rina was sitting on an old woman's lap being fed sweets and having her hair combed. There weren't many kids around and they were making a lot of her. The women were talking in Maori and chuckling over her. When she saw me she said, quickly, knowing the expressions on my face by heart, 'I'm not going.'

'We have to. Al wants us.' I had to use the magic name because I could see she was readying herself for a major tantrum. Johnny had come behind me and was speaking to the group in Maori, and they all looked at me nodding and clucking their tongues, disbelieving. They'd put nothing past me, you could see that.

I said to Rina, 'Come on,' and smiled at them with as much sincerity as I could. I was feeling the strain, and Johnny's disapproval was electric.

'Let's go, kid.' We went out into the hall and I heard a car horn outside. I said goodbye to Johnny and he muttered some sulky answer. If we'd been more intimate I would have given him a clip over the ear just to break the tension, but I had a lot on my mind and I couldn't do a thing like that easily with him. It was another black mark with Nettie's family and with Johnny, but there was nothing I could do. Then to make matters worse, when I took Rina outside to Mitch he looked at her with undisguised distaste. If he'd been religious he would have made a sign of the cross. As it was he sat at the wheel of the car ignoring her.

He said to me with contempt as we got into the car, as if she couldn't understand, 'I didn't know you had one of those.' Rina was really chuffed about his snazzy car and didn't even notice. It was a Mustang with shiny upholstery and spotless inside. It smelt plasticky. She settled down in the back. I could see she was still reeling from the whole trip.

Sometimes her brain would buckle under pressure and she'd go blank. Then she really did look retarded, remote — her brain hardly seemed to move behind those raisin eyes. It was probably the strain of processing too much information. She could sleep all day and night if it got too much or her. She lolled in the back, looking white-faced.

'Is that Johnny's favver?' was all she asked.

'Only in the biological sense,' I said. It was a cheap shot, and totally wasted on both of them anyway. But I was irritated at the thought of this car journey and all the crap at the end of it, worried about Grace and aching about Nettie and the loss of my son. Mitch started the car with a roar and we shot off down the road. I looked back and Johnny was standing on the verandah. I waved, but he stayed motionless.

Rina was already asleep, curled up in the back. I leant over and tucked a car rug over her. I needed to perform some little attention like that just to establish my territory with someone.

'Jeez, what a relief to get out of that,' he said, genuine for once. 'Well, how's things?' he asked, as if he really wanted to know.

'Alright,' I said.

'Still singing at Mainstreet?' I could see it wasn't going to be easy. Whatever he wanted wasn't going to come out straight.

'Yes. Every now and again.'

'I heard you had a hassle the other night,' he said, carefully.

So that's what it was. He knew about Marianne. He was somehow involved in that sordid business. I realised that was what it was, it was probably why he'd come down and everything.

'Oh it was alright. No real hassle.' I caught his eye and we both smiled. The air was dangerous.

He said, clutching the wheel grimly, his big hands white, 'Was she unconscious? When you took her up?'

'How did you know about that?' I was careful to keep aggression out of my voice. I kept things light.

'Oh, around. Mates. They knew you were my ex.' He was lying wonderfully, his fleshy nose twitching casually as if his mind was on something else.

'Semi,' I said.

'Dirty business. I'm surprised you were involved. I thought you'd left all us dirt behind. In your new career. In the Arts.' He couldn't keep the venom out of his voice. He had me all to himself and there were years of resentment to spray all over me, captive in the car.

I just stayed silent, looking out the window. The car swerved and bucked over the loose gravel, sending up showers of dust and stones, like rain. I'd give him a few miles. There was a long silence.

'How were you involved? One of the distributors?' I asked. There was another silence, Mitch stayed very smooth, a dangerous twitch going on the corner of his mouth, the only sign.

'Is that a nice way to talk, Glory?' he asked. 'Come on now. There's no connection. I wouldn't be involved with all those fucking no-hopers. They couldn't organise themselves out of a paper bag.'

'Who? Who couldn't organise themselves?'

'Junkies, small-time drug dealers. They're all cuckoo. Greedy.'

I smiled at him. The day was getting quite warm and I felt my thighs sticking to my dress and the shiny plastic seat. My stomach felt queasy from the rough ride.

'Who's your witness besides the queen?' he asked.

'Friend of mine,' I said. 'The queen saw nothing anyway. The cops aren't interested in her.'

We drove for miles in silence. I put the car radio on. We were on the main drag now, past miles of bright paddocks, and brick houses. 'I'm going to Graceland, Graceland,' I sang. I looked in the glove box for cigarettes and there was a flask of whisky in there.

'Want some?' I asked. He shook his head. We didn't have a lot to say to each other. It felt like a soft light in my stomach, glowing, calming the sickness I was feeling.

'You're a mate of Roxy's, aren't you?' he asked.

'She's my model.'

'Roxy's a mate of mine.'

'Is she?' He was pleased. He could tell by my voice he'd got a rise out of me at last.

'Yeah. Off and on for years. As a matter of fact she and I — had it off for a while. Lovely bird.'

'Jesus. Roxy knows everyone,' I said. I didn't particularly mean it to sound insulting but it staggered me. She'd never so much as mentioned it to me, though I suppose I never talked about Mitch either.

'Ah. Jealous, eh? She's a good-looking chick alright. You with Al I heard.'

The whisky was rolling round my stomach. I said to him, 'Let's stop and get something to eat.' We were coming up to a little township, a petrol station, pub and general store and takeaway bar. Tattooed kids were sitting on a bench outside the public toilets, watching the cars go past.

He stopped obediently. 'Whaddya want?' he asked. He seemed to be pleased about something.

I got out just to stretch my legs and let the air circulate.

'Hey fatso, pull in your puku!' yelled one of the kids. They all sniggered.

'Hamburger,' I called after him. 'Two!' I yelled. 'No onion!' Waiting at the takeaways, he looked like Mafia in his blue business suit. The tan of his skin looked more Calabrese than Maori and he had that air of beefy malice, the brutish ignorance I saw once on the face of a Mafia informer being interviewed in a TV documentary.

'Where are we?' asked Rina, and then vomited all over the back seat. I got her out and cleaned her up in the petrol station toilet. I got yards of toilet paper to try and mop it up on the back seat and the floor. It put me off hamburger. Rina looked white and exhausted.

'Shit, what's that pong?' Mitch asked. He had the greasy-looking bundles in his hand.

'Rina's been sick.' I went and sat in the back with Rina lolling languidly on my knee.

'You won't want these I suppose. Fucking waste of ten bucks.' He was in a real temper over it.

'Just leave them and we'll have them later,' I said.

'No, she's no fool that chick,' he said sitting back comfortably. 'She's in on a fair few things, that kid. I've always said you can still keep your femininity even if you are brainy.'

I could smell the vomit still in Rina's hair. She lay soft as a jelly baby, her head lolling on my shoulder. I had the sudden feeling that if I stayed quiet he might tell me something else about Roxy. He never could resist boasting, in the past. I was impressed in spite of myself when he didn't rise to the bait. He was becoming a very smooth operator now that he could control his vanity like that. It made me very interested in what his connection with Marianne was.

It was almost cosy driving along with the faint smell of vomit in the air, Rina tossing and snoring in her sleep, flashing past the farmlands of middle New Zealand. We were like a comical travesty of the little family back from the holidays. Any minute now we would start playing car games — first person to see a white horse, a red car and yellow roof would get a Mintie. Or we would stop at one of those rest places by the highway with the little wooden tables and rubbish bins. I'd seen them there, famished, eating salad fresh out of red Tupperware containers, drinks for the kids, the man in the towelling hat gazing off into the middle distance with a longing stare.

It reminded me of my first exhibition at Outreach. It was

called 'Families' of course. Parodies of family portraits, all of them gazing out without a smile. There were the dwarves, the child rapists, the violence kings of my dreams holding tortured children, their mad mothers like ghosts in the backgrounds. It was crude and evil looking, but even now I had a soft spot for that series.

Certainly there was a love/hate tie-up with my childhood in my pictures, but I didn't paint it all bad. It wasn't as if I didn't appreciate my grotesque heritage. Without it my paintings would have been different, and if most of the other painters I knew were anything to go by, much weaker, more adaptable to changing fads, apologetic. Even as a kid I knew instinctively that in all our squalor I'd found a bastard vigour in my life which would stand me in good stead.

I was a very fast learner. The few flavours hard-won from the ugly lives we led were mine forever, no one else could really taste them. As a result I wasn't so swayed by the trappings of life as other painters I saw. My upbringing gave me the hard edges to my life, my easy acceptance of certain kinds of ugliness.

Here I was, getting on, and I still liked things open, people around me who had no other connection besides easy familiarity, a house where people came and went on their own business and didn't feel they had to admire the furniture. All that was a gift from my childhood. In contrast, some painters I knew swept their lives clean of all extra baggage. They sat in an empty room with an easel in front of them, and some poor sucker of a wife drained her life out in their service. Daily morning tea and letters from dealers on a resentful tray. All the time life was humming away outside, just out of their reach. I wanted to keep my feet firmly placed in the mud and slime of it all.

Not that I'd deny it took me a fair while to sort my priorities out — my upbringing did not exactly equip me for health. Not only did I have the white-trash heritage on my back, there was also a whole sister culture of agorophobics, no-sayers, Calvinists and sodden respectable alcoholics to deal with from my mother's side as well. I was probably listening to all their voices when I chose my two death-dealing husbands. The fact was, vigorous or not, it was a bastard class that I came from, ignorant, diseased and spiritless, a thinned-out version of the English working class without any connection with the land we perched on. Even the ceremonies of our daily living, births, deaths, marriages, were without dimension, fouled up by the worst gifts from the mainstream which had rejected us.

Mitch, Rina and I driving along on the highway was a burlesque of what I had always known about families, in the full juicy mix. Thrown together by bad genes, chances, a death — kept together by fear and resentment. Mitch, bless him, head of the house, twitching as he drove, preoccupied by his violent crimes; Rina, like a little white soft slug, dead asleep, her slow brain almost at a full stop; and me weighing down the car with my huge bulk, thinking about my paintings, trying to avoid the police. Extreme, but a pretty accurate exaggeration. I even ate one of the hamburgers at the thought — it was cold and greasy, but delicious, and I settled back to enjoy it. After all there wasn't a lot else I could do anyway.

5

When Mitch finally dropped me off at home, he showed no interest in coming in. He just sat there without turning the engine off. He was genuinely incredulous but delighted.

'Is this your dump? Christ, I wouldn't be seen dead in a place like this.'

I lifted Rina out of the back seat, but she woke and wriggled out of my arms. 'Al!' she screamed and raced off into the house.

I said, 'Thanks for the lift.'

'Don't mention it,' he said. He kept revving the engine like an adolescent. He still looked very pleased about something. He even said, 'Bye, Glory. Nice seeing you. You want to watch your weight though.' It sounded like a threat but I couldn't be bothered even answering. I had a lot to do at home.

The car ripped off down the lawn so triumphantly I could feel bits of mud and grass on my back. When I walked up the path Al was sitting on the verandah with Rina on his lap.

'How's things?' I asked dropping beside him.

'What?' He was in a filthy mood. He looked sick and hungover. 'Who's that arsehole?' he asked.

'That's Johnny's favver,' said Rina, pushing her nose into his cheek lovingly.

I made a cup of tea. The milk looked off, but I was thirsty after the hamburger and all the little games with my ex. There was no beer left. Al came stumping back.

'And I'm not your shitty secretary either.' I'd never seen him in such a rage. 'I haven't been able to do anything to my bike — the frigging phone hasn't stopped. I've had transvestites and cops and arseholes swarming over the joint. I'm just about jack of this fucking place.'

'Do you want a cup of tea? The milk's a bit strong.'

We sat at the kitchen table, the three of us, and drank our tea. Rina still looked pale but the smug look was coming back. It was school tomorrow and she was back with me and Al.

I said, 'What's the story about Grace?'

'Well in the end I rang your mate.' He had always admired Sarah. He told me once she was real class.

'What did she say?'

'Oh, she'll do something. You know her.'

'Al, you're a beauty,' I said. I was so pleased with him for that. It took a load off me leaving Grace in Sarah's hands. I got up and moved towards the phone.

'Yeah, well it was a bloody shambles,' he said, slightly molli- fied. 'You ringing the cops?'

'Fuck that. They know where I am. I don't owe them a thing. Sarah, is that you?'

'Glory, what is going on? Can you come and see me? I've been trying to ring you since yesterday.'

I felt a real glow of pleasure when she spoke to me so crisply on the phone. Whenever I was with her I always felt that the world was basically a decent place. I could see the cavalry thun- dering up the hill to save the goodies just in the nick of time. She was such a precise baby-faced English woman, she looked as if butter wouldn't melt in her mouth. Sarah acted for unfashion- able people — small-time crimmos, street people, derros, and it wasn't just token. She really slogged it out for them. Nothing was ever tokenism for Sarah.

Our connection in the beginning was paintings, she was the first person to buy one of mine way back in the early days. She became my lawyer after I got to know her, and I always paid my fees in pictures, she still owed me for about a quarter of a painting of Rina. She was a real live patron of the arts, with no strings attached.

'I've got to work on those paintings. I just rang to see if Grace's alright.'

'I think she's coming to see you. Where have you been?'

Rina disappeared into her room and a sudden blast of Brucey

nearly knocked me over.

'What the hell is that?' asked Sarah, startled into swearing.

'It's Rina.'

'Rina?'

'Her Bruce Springsteen tape.'

'I'm going down,' he sang. The whole place was vibrating.

I said, 'Did you find out why they arrested her?'

'I don't know what's going on,' Sarah said. 'That arrest of your friend was ridiculous. I mean they knew it too — they rescinded it as soon as I went to see them. Not that I knew anything about it either. I just had to bluff my way through. They as much as admitted it was premature. Some young cop being overzealous. Of course your friend now wants to sue for wrongful arrest, and I'm afraid she's not very happy with you either. She said you disappeared.

There was only the very faintest hint of reproach in her voice. Sarah hated to impose any moral strictures on me. She had very fixed ideas on the role of artists.

'It was a promise. A dying woman's wish, my real mother. Her last wish, Sarah. What do you want me to do? Tie myself to a tree? I haven't done anything, and the cops are just bullshitting when they think they can ask me to stay where I am.'

'I'd like to see you.' She gave a very small polite sigh. It was touching to hear her do that. 'It doesn't look good to me. I don't understand what's going on.'

'I'll be in touch, Sarah. As soon as I can. Thanks for helping me.'

'Glory, look after yourself.' She sounded resigned, but she knew I wanted to do it on my own. I was too weary to put my mind to explaining. I said, 'Bye, Sarah,' and heaved myself back into the chair.

'Everyone's mad wiv you,' announced Rina, bustling about full of self-importance. She'd put her pink tutu on and was dancing about in the hall. It was good to see her back to normal again.

'That tutu's getting too small,' I said absently, giving her hair a ruffle. 'You being a good girl?'

'Nah,' she said, looking up. 'Yes,' really quickly in case I didn't get it.

You never knew with Rina, sometimes she thought like a little old woman, other times she was like a three-year-old. I didn't know whether that was just normal with kids or part of her condition. Rina was my only experience with kids, you couldn't really count Johnny, so I was never quite sure what was expected in the general run of children.

She said, 'Can I have a dollar for some chippies?' She'd already seen I was in a good mood with her. Sometimes it was hard to believe her brain was slower than other kids, she was so quick off the mark. I've never seen her waste an opportunity. I gave her the dollar.

Al said, 'Roxy came round about three times.'

'What for?'

'How do I know?'

'Is the car OK?' I asked Al.

'Yeah. It was just a flat battery.'

I smiled at him and we just sat in silence in the warmth of the kitchen. The music stopped. Rina had obviously gone off to get her chippies.

'Go to bed,' Al said. 'You look rooted.'

I can't even remember how I walked to the studio, but I fell like a log onto the bed and into a deep sleep. It could have been hours or days later, in fact it was next morning, that I woke with a great sweating start to Al bending over me, shaking me wildly. In my groggy state he looked like a demon, his nostrils were distorted with panic.

'They've got Rina!' he shouted right into my face, as I sat up, my heart thumping.

'What do you mean? What the fuck are you talking about?' I caught his hand, wrung it beseechingly. It felt like a lightning flash on my heart.

'Someone rang! They said Weasel's got Rina. It was like a threat, Glory. It sounded like a threat.'

'Weasel? Weasel? Who? What do you mean Weasel?' I wailed. I could see fear in Al's eyes. He hardly ever saw me lose control.

'Her father. Weasel. Your fucking ex.'

'Come with me, Al. Come on. We've got to go now.' I jumped out of bed stark awake and pulled on my overalls.

'Rina was playing next door. I was home all the time and then I went up the shop on the bike for milk. It was five minutes. Ten. That was all, I swear. They must have been watching her.'

'But why? Did they talk about money or what?' I raced out of the room, Al close behind. 'Weasel's never even seen her. What does he want her for?' Out on the front lawn I wrenched open the car door and crawled in.

My insides felt icy and light, I was stern with panic. I graunched the car into gear and started off with a stench of burn from the clutch.

'Who was it rang? Did you recognise the voice? What did they want?'

'No. They said nothing. Whoever it was said tell Glory Weasel's got Rina. That's all they said. The voice sounded funny like she had no fucking roof to her mouth.'

'She?' I asked.

'Or he. I dunno, Glory.'

We drove wildly in silence for a while.

'I bet she's not scared,' I said as we went into a sideways skid just before the motorway on-ramp.

'Glory, stop the car will you, you mad bitch?' He was shouting, I realised, but it sounded a long way away. I could hardly hear him in fact.

'Stop it, and I'll drive. You're still half asleep.'

'No. I'll be a lot quicker,' I said in my light mad new voice.

'Don't panic, Glor. You're panicking. For God's sake, he's her father. He won't hurt her. You're panicking.' He cowered as I veered into the fast lane — with cars screeching sideways to avoid us.

'His brain is completely smashed out. He's dead. He doesn't even know what he's doing. He's mixed up with some real dead-heads, bloody zombies. You know what I mean?' I turned to look at him seriously.

'For Christ's sake, Glory, watch that fucking car!'

I swung off the motorway. The engine was really clunking now and it was so hot the needle was nearly off the dial. There was an ominous smell of burning rubber.

'You'll fuck the car,' Al said calmly.

I wheelied into Levenes' car-park, hitting the judder bars.

'It's tow away if you're not a customer,' he said.

I left it straddled across three spaces and ran up the hill, Al labouring behind me, burst through the scabby little back entrance and upstairs. There were about ten doors in the passage. I knocked at each of them like a madwoman, the sound of the banging echoing and swelling around my head.

An old woman opened one door, letting out a great stale blast of heat and piss and cat.

'You after those druggies, dear? Next door. There's always people coming and going. I haven't seen him for a while.. Heard the door bang a while ago now I come to think of it. Could have been yesterday or the day before. That kid came up again most probably. He's old enough to be her father. Of course I'm only here for a while. My daughter, she's taking me to Kawau Island.' Her mad old rheumy eyes sparkled and snapped coyly, her sunken mouth mumbling and mouthing. All the stiff white hairs on her chin were thick with snot and food.

'Yes, Kawau Island. It's in the Hauraki Gulf you know.'

I knocked and knocked but there was no other sound. Al said, 'No one's here. It's probably crap. She's probably home. Some creep having a joke.'

I put my shoulder against the door and smashed it open with all my strength. We stood there, the three of us.

The scene in the room was too much for the old woman, who started screeching like a bird, little inarticulate cries close to my face. When my eyes got used to semi-darkness — the one grimy window gave little or no light — and the first impact of the stench had slightly receded, I saw the most horrific creature stretched out on the floor. A bloated, stinking, stiff corpse with a green smiling face. Rigor mortis was just starting to flop into jelly, I saw little movements around the mouth, which were flies or maggots. The remains of an Irvines pie were on the floor quite close to it and some of the maggots from it had found better, more juicy food.

My ex-husband lay there quietly, flies buzzing around his dead rotting head, and I felt my stomach turning. The room seemed full of a malignant buzz, like dark waters lapping at the brain; the smell was the unnameable sweet bone-crunching stench of a mean death, and a living death before that. I had noticed a slight rustling movement at my side, and realised Al had disappeared. I said to the old woman, 'Is there a phone up here?'

'Downstairs in the shop,' she said. She kept fumbling at me with her dry old hands. I looked into the room.

Piles of curdled dark rubbish lay all over the floor and dripped off the walls, there were strings of cobwebs and darker, wetter substances hanging off the ceiling and from the lightshade. The window was matted with filth. It was the room of a person no longer bound to life, an old derro, impersonal and final.

Traffic raced and roared like a beast below, people passed on the footpaths, shopping, sauntering along as the dead man lay above them — his corruption gradually leaking out the door and all over the territory he laid claim to. I thought of our brief miserable marriage.

There was actually a great hole in my life somewhere around Weasel, there were only a few vital things I remembered about him. His appearance, for instance, because it was so odd — little and dark with a foxy face and flicked-back hair — he had a great egg-head domed forehead, throbbing with babyish blue veins. He was always ghost-pale.

Weasel was a con-man, a thief, and he had no heart. His eyes were washed out, crooked from years of lying and cowardice. I never saw him smile or laugh, he was like a somnambulist. He found grown women repulsive, his grinding parents, Jehovah's Witnesses, had terrorised him all his childhood. I only had sex with him a few times and often wondered how I actually conceived Rina (my half-moon eggchild barely caught by the lick of his washed-out sperm). Sex with him was like being with an insect, his limbs used to grate against my skin. His dry body had no warmth in it, it was bloodless with the slightly gritty dead texture of fake veneer stone. He'd flick his little cock out and race off to the bathroom, his pimply buttocks sucked in with the strain and spend hours in there washing himself down, scrubbing me off his sad little body. He was already an old man then. Poor Weasel. I must have sent him completely off the edge. I was already starting to put on weight then and I probably became a nightmare figure to him. I had just started to draw seriously, and I still had one early drawing of him sitting watching TV, his starveling face immobile, frozen, held to the flickering screen like a man from outer space. Trapped unhappily in a parody of domesticity. His parents made him marry me because I was pregnant and they knew it was their last chance for grandchildren. Weasel disappeared like a little wraith long before Rina was born, and I don't think he'd ever seen her.

It was hard to match those few memories I had of him with the body in front of me. I hadn't even seen him to speak to since then, and Rina was ten. His works were lying by the body with the blood still caked on the tip. But there was no Rina and that was all I could really concentrate on. I just wanted to get out of it, I was only interested in her. His corpse forced me to pause and pay my respects for Rina's sake, if only for a minute, but even dead, Weasel was an irrelevance. The horror of the room was hitting me physically and I felt as if I was going to keel over. I said to the woman, 'Where'd that guy go? With the shaved head? That guy who was with me?'

'You'll have to call the police,' she said. Saliva was bubbling out of her mouth, she was half excited, half horrified. The scene had completely set her off, poor old thing. She could have been anyone's loving grandmother in better circumstances.

'You go and ring them, dear,' I said. 'Just go and tell them about it. I've got to go.'

'But my daughter is coming. She's coming to take me to Kawau.' She suddenly became terribly busy and preoccupied, pursing up her slack old mouth like a drunken judge. The change happened in front of my eyes — uncanny, as if another person had suddenly materialised. It was a horrible sight.

'I've got to go and get ready. Get a few things packed. Say goodbye to my old life. It's a new start, dear,' She leaned so close I could feel her warm spit pricking on my skin and the stink of her breath.

I said loudly, 'Will you ring the cops?'

She said, 'I haven't time, dear. A big young woman like you. There's a lot to be done. There's the cold meat in the fridge and you need warm woollies for night. There's a lot of water at Kawau. You can't get it into your bones at my time of life. My daughter's told me time and time again, bring your woollies, mother.'

She gathered herself up, trying for a ghastly semblance of gentility — lowering her wrinkled lizard eyelids like a coquettish girl, mincing and drawing herself up.

Behind her the corpse waited on the floor, polite, unassuming. I could hear that line from Mick Jagger's song in my head clear as day — 'Flies buzzing around your hide.' She started to laugh, came closer and grabbed me, her hands scratching and scrabbling at me.

'It's such an opportunity for me.' I broke free and raced down the landing, my heart thudding.

'Ring the cops!' I yelled and kept going.

Down in the car-park, Al was vomiting against the car, his poor face white. I hustled him in.

'For God's sake, Al, get into the bloody car.'

I felt sorry for him. He'd always hated blood and guts. That's why he never got his patch though the boys always had a soft spot for him.

'Did you ring the cops?'

'No. I asked the old woman to.' I backed the car out so fast Al jerked in his seat and fell back, knocking his head. He was proving to be a bit of a handicap, but I didn't have the heart to dump him. He meant well, Al did.

'Where the fuck are you going now? We have to go to the station, Glory, or you'll be had up for accessory.'

'I've got to go and get Rina from him. He's capable of anything.'

'Who?'

'Mitch, you dumbo.'

I had such a strong image of Rina's little tear-streaked monkey face, when she was miserable she could become so passive and animal-like. Crouching in a corner in that pink tutu, her hand up to ward off the blow. She didn't like Mitch anyway. I couldn't stand the thought of it, it was burning out my heart. I felt frantic, a huge instinct was rising up in me and I felt it fuelling me, propelling me down the highway. It was almost a magic push. I hardly saw anything, I drove so fast that, glancing sideways for a second, I could see that Al was literally crouched down in the seat. He was still sick, I could see that. I never even realised the car could go that fast, but it hummed like a bird. I almost felt like singing. I must have had a mad look on my face because I could feel the freezing of muscles around my cheeks and mouth, a kind of grin of desperation.

'You're a fucking death mother!' Al screamed, at the end of his tether with me. 'You'll kill us both!'

I said, 'I've got to go and get her,' but I slowed down obediently. The whiskies, Weasel's corpse and no Rina had all welled up inside me like a big clotted ball of misery. The drive became dreamlike, it seemed to go on and on interminably through the streets. the ordinary world out there, people passing through the air with their soft bodies and flesh were hallucinations. They strode and danced uncaring past the car, luminescent, past the wooden houses of Kingsland which crowded into my mind like old memories. The streets glowed and shone outside and I felt huge, disembodied, watching it all like a stranger. It was an old re-run nightmare, everything in slow motion and nothing I could do.

'What would he do that for?' I asked Al. 'Why would he do something like that?'

'Where are you going?' Al asked.

'I'm going home first,' I said. 'I have to trace him from there.'

'Why don't you go to the station? I'll go witness,' Al said. I looked sideways at him as we stopped at a red light. His sinister mirror glasses were askew on his shiny skull, he sat there white as a sheet with vomit still clinging to the corners of his mouth. I felt a surge of affection for him.

'I can't stuff around with them. He's got Rina,' I said as if I was explaining to a child. 'They won't fucking believe anything I say anyway.'

'You'll be had up,' he said. 'They'll want to know why you went there.'

'That'll make two of us,' I said. I was concentrating on driving, trying not to think of Rina.

After I parked the car outside home I had to force myself to walk up the path. In the hall, a loud infant voice suddenly rose to a shrieking wall of sound, so loud and sinister in the deserted house I leant against the door trembling. It was with relief that I realised it was only the radio left on, playing to itself in the lounge. The venetian blinds were still closed against last night, empty bottles were piled behind the sofa, there were dishes and glasses in nearly every room.

It was that computer-voice song, 'Girls just want to have fun', and Cyndy Lauper's shrill innocent voice rose in silvery bubbles all over the room. It was so loud I thought my head would crack. I went to the fridge for a beer and her voice followed me in. Rina's kitten tottered into the kitchen gazing into my face and mewing piteously — he wound around my legs and I could feel his skinny little body under the soft fur. He was hungry. I heard a movement behind me and, overwrought, whirled round with a knife in my hand.

There was Cash, watching me, holding Rina in his arms. I picked her up, holding her sweet little bones and softness against me and sat on the sofa in the dark.

'I missed you, Glory,' Rina said in her nasal little inhuman voice. I cried and cried as if my chest would explode. The hot sweet tears flowed over me and Rina, bathed us, rocked us, her nubby hands burrowed into my flesh as if she wanted to hook into me. Her little snotty animal face pressed all its sweet juices into mine and bathed me with her tears and snot and sweat.

'Girls just want to have fun,' she sang and the whole house shook.

6

'OK, Cash. What the hell is all this about?'

We were sitting in the kitchen drinking beer, still shell-shocked. Rina was on my lap very subdued, stroking her cuddly, her face tear-streaked. She didn't want to tell me anything and I was reluctant to push her. Knowing her, she might get it wrong and give me a false lead anyway. She was still in a state of shock.

'I can't tell you, Glory, God's honour. I swear on my father's grave. Just trust me will you? I swear it'll come out right. Look I can tell you this much. I'm in this half-cocked deal and I can't get out of it. There could be something good for you at the end of this, Glory. Just take it easy. For a couple of days. A day even.'

Even at a time like this he couldn't resist looking knowing, but it didn't last long. He was nearly as shaken as I was, I could tell by the way he was talking. Sometimes Cash just talked to cover up the terrible void in his head, but this time I was losing patience with him. I had to clear things up quickly and I didn't have the time to pander to his panic reactions.

'Look, I've just seen Weasel's body and it's made me feel as sick as a dog. I want to find out what's going on. Whoever you're working for did it, mate.'

'I don't know what you're talking about.' Cash was so jumpy he kept lighting cigarettes and putting them out, walking round the kitchen as if he was going to break into a run any minute.

'Alright. Just tell me and stop fucking about, Cash.' I realised I should have used that tone at the start. He was so easy to intimidate, and it was quicker than trying to appeal to his sensitivities.

103

'I can't tell you. They'd eat me alive.'

'Who was it?'

'I swear to God I don't know. I'm so down in the whole thing they keep us couriers right out of it. I swear. They just asked me to come to an address in Parnell and pick up a kid. I nearly fell over when I saw who it was. That was all I knew about it. Honest. I wouldn't lie to you, would I? I couldn't believe it was Rina. I'd just seen her a while ago.'

'What did they tell you to do with her, for Christ's sake?'

'He said take her home. It was some weird kid. He said just ask her where she lives and take her home.'

Obviously even Mitch drew the line at hurting Rina but it was still so close to the bone I couldn't stand it.

'Give me the address,' I said.

He was being stretched far enough as it was. He was probably lying through his teeth. But at least he'd brought Rina back and for that I could forgive him anything.

He said fearfully, 'What are you going to do?'

'I've got to go and find out what the fuck's going on. No one takes Rina. Don't worry, I won't mention you.'

Looking back on it, I was in a manic state bordering on hysteria. I hadn't even understood the events of the last few days, let alone processed them, and I was starting to act on adrenalin, react from sheer nerves. Even Cash with his startling lack of nous could see it was risky to go there, and though he tried to talk me out of it mostly to save his own skin, there was an element of concern for me as well. But at least I had a few things up my sleeve.

One thing I knew, hanging round at home waiting for the next blow to fall was definitely not to my taste, especially if they had the gall to involve Rina. It wasn't even as if I was deathly frightened of someone like Mitch either, I knew him like the back of my hand, he was like a lot of men I'd grown up with. I had his measure as a passionless, small-time jerk who'd do anything for dollars — there weren't any extra dimensions to the man to catch me off guard. I knew where I was with him, I knew that whatever happened he'd always play dirty, and that he was riddled to the eyeballs with grudges against me in spite of his smiling old exterior. That was a comfort in itself, but all the same I didn't know enough about the actual details of what was going on to be really safe. I only knew that this malice beaming down on me for whatever reason had to be stopped by an act of will on my part.

As soon as Cash gave me the address he cheered up, as long as he was safe that was OK. He even started talking about percentages and deals for a minute before I told him to go. The lifetime of any emotion of his was usually ten minutes, so he'd done alright. He went out whistling between his teeth, his fear gone, obviously in the grip of one of his latest fantasies.

My next problem was Rina, because I wanted her looked after day and night, and even in my present state I wasn't mad enough to take her with me. I couldn't very well ask Al, he was probably locked in his room. Now that his most paranoid suspicions about the world were confirmed, I wouldn't see him for hours. In the end I lugged Rina next door. Only Kingi was home watching TV.

It was really smashed up after the weekend party, there were beer cans, butts, Kentucky Fried cartons, newspapers sodden from old chips, and cigarette packets all over the floor. It was like an ogre's cave, with the blackened pots in the kitchen, flies crawling over the diseased surfaces, the TV on all the time, but it was a friendly place. I liked their cheerful acceptance of the basics of life. Rina always liked staying there, but this time I found it hard to leave her even in their tender care.

I said to Kingi, 'I'm in real trouble. I've got to go somewhere urgent. Look after Rina, will you? Don't let her out of the house till I'm back.' I even gave him the address, at least I had the presence of mind for that. Kingi took what I was saying seriously. He hardly ever talked but I could tell he was respectful of what I told him.

Our houses had gradually evolved into a common patch for both of us, it was no haphazard arrangement either. Like most gangs, they had certain rituals which made their world safe, cast-iron agreements which were taken for granted. There was respect there, and I liked the order of it myself. Rina, Moe's dealings and Al's eccentricities were kept sacred and not talked about lightly. Moe and his mates were always living on the edge, there was danger wherever they went, so they had to evolve these intricate structures for sheer survival. I nearly always knew where I was with Moe and most of the guys.

I said goodbye to Rina, but she was already absorbed in the telly, and went outside, feeling light-headed with the stress. The car started like a beauty thanks to Al's work on the battery and I sped off again, concentrating on the road, not thinking too much about anything else.

It was a house in Parnell. I was sure I'd been there before, an old house with willows and an ancient garden damp underneath the hedges. The front door was ajar, and there was a long dark passage stretching the length of the house. There was the unmistakable smell of junkies in the air. I went down the passage, annoyed to feel how hard my heart was beating. I felt a powerful urge to get out of there fast. It was very sleepy and sluggish and evil in there, like a murky pool, the air was stagnant with secrets.

All the doors were closed except one halfway down the passage and I was drawn to that half-open door in spite of myself. I looked around to see if anyone was there, then I slipped in, the thick dark air was like smoke in my mouth. The room was so dark I couldn't see anything at first. The curtains were all drawn and there was a dead smell, something was stinking in there. Gradually I became aware of a very faint rustling — the room seemed full of eyes, small creatures, bats. But even before I turned the light on I knew by the smell it was Roxy's room.

I saw my bright and star-like princess, my Roxy standing there, her cheekbones beautiful in the half-light, mouth fixed in a forgiving smile. Her blue blank eyes stared cold at me. I had made her come with the sheer force of my will — it was such a strong hallucination I could almost reach over and touch her soft arm skin and feel her wicked breath on my cheek. Roxy! It was unbelievable. I turned the light on and blinked with the shock of it. The fluttering was paper, tacked onto the walls, the ceilings, over the window. The slight movement of my body turned the whole room into a great living breathing cell seeded with strange growths — spotty, mangled, blind, each piece of paper rose and fell with a sigh as I stood there aghast. Above the bed, around me dangling from the ceiling, tacked over a mirror were crudely torn-out newspaper cuttings, paper growing from the wall like ferns in a cave, stuck on sellotape, blue tack, safety pins, and drawings pins. All of them were torn out carelessly, with ragged holes and tears and rips; they were dotted with crude underlinings, scribbles, comments in patchy felt. To me it looked like the work of great speed and stress, a compulsive labour of love, and a propitiating gesture set up as a shield against some impending punishment, a shrine.

I could see just from where I was standing, four copies of one article tacked together, dotted with exclamation marks, question marks, scrawled comments in Roxy's tight little handwriting. When I looked closely I saw that every review, every article, every interview, every photograph about my career sat up there — and it had been xeroxed three or four times. The whole grotesque room was all about me.

My first thought was that the crazy bitch was trying to do some kind of copy-cat exhibition of her own. There were photocopies and separate copies where she'd obviously just gone out and bought a dozen copies of a newspaper or magazine with a story about me in it. Glory Day, the sinister face of Glory Day, my career and life stared down at me mockingly. Looking at it, shocked out of my wits, I could see what she'd been doing. She lay down on her bed there, among the soiled mangy sheets, took a shot and grooved on me, her mother, her mentor, her deadliest enemy. It made me sick to think that Rina could have been there.

The decay was so advanced it was awesome, a pyramid of madness so intricate and deeply layered that there was no way to begin digging into the base. I stood there paralysed, my mind racing with the implications of it. It was like turning up a stone to uncover a nest of rats gnawing at each other.

Roxy, the junkie model. It was so completely out of the blue that I just stood there paralysed. Weasel's room, his corpse and the young girl's death, the nightmare of the past few days started off somehow in this room. Roxy was trying to frame me. She was as mad as a meat-axe. She'd stolen my kid. She was not just picturesque, junkie mad, but murderous mad — and I could be next. I had to shift everything into another gear, rapidly, even just to understand what had happened in the last few minutes. Everything had changed so completely, I was like a sheep standing there, mentally bleating.

The door creaked open, sending the paper off into a mad dance, and a tall thin guy stood there looking at me. His face was very pale.

'Gidday,' he said. He was quite blank.

'I'm looking for Glory,' I said.

'You mean Roxy, doncha?' he prompted.

'Yes,' I said, flustered.

'Oh, Roxy.' He stood there at the door. He was so tall he nearly hit the lintel. 'She's a bit of a collector is Roxy,' he said, conversationally, surveying the room with approval. 'Good chick.'

'Where is she?' I asked after a silence.

'You a friend?' the strange kid asked in the same tone. He had a faint North Country accent. I noticed he was carrying a knife, it was just sticking nonchalantly out of his pocket.

'Where is she?' I asked again. I was getting a bit jack of him staring at me. He was just a young punk.

'How do I know?' For a minute he sounded like Al, and just that memory jolted me into registering the danger I was in, not so much from the boy but if Roxy came back. This new Roxy was too sinister to even contemplate, much less cope with now.

I moved over to the door and said, very cool, 'Tell her I called, will you?'

He didn't move. 'What name shall I give?'

'Rina. Tell her Rina,' I said. It was a stupid thing to say, and I instantly regretted it. There was a little flicker of recognition in his blank eyes which I didn't like. He obviously knew her from this morning.

'Oh, yes,' was all he said. he would have liked to keep me there, but I pushed past.

'Remember to tell her,' I said, using all my power on him. But all the way down the passage I kept feeling as if my back was a huge vulnerable space ripe for the picking. As I went down the stairs I glanced back to see him standing at the doorway like a stick-insect looking after me, his face impassive. I could see the knife glittering in his hand. If it wasn't so creepy it would have been comical.

Walking down Parnell Road in the bright sun to my car, the dinky colonial boutiques and wealthy women shoppers with their starved iron faces took on a nightmare tinge. The white soft clothes they wore, their utter cleanliness did not hide their harpy bodies stringy tough, their parched ski tans, their fear of me. Roxy's room had spilled over into the sunny streets, it was like Weasel's corpse leaking corruption back into the place that spawned it.

I walked down the street in a daze. I couldn't think straight. All the little comforts I'd built up so painstakingly in a lifetime of autonomy seemed about to crumble and I felt my shoulder blades twitching with a new feeling of exposure as I walked. Images kept jostling in my head every time I tried to fix onto some face to ease the shock.

A film I'd once seen of a beautiful cold girl with a rotting animal in her handbag, Roxy's face when she was giving me the last chance, the defencelessness of Weasel's corpse, the whispering of paper on Roxy's walls. It went against my grain to accept the humiliating fact that it had been Roxy all the time. The beautiful Roxy with her cloying love and dependence, scrabbling at my life like a demented child. Coming straight to me red-handed from her crimes.

I had never taken her into serious account. For instance, I had just dismissed all the intensities of the last few days as her usual affectations. It was her beauty I had valued and wanted and that was it. There had been no willingness in me to recognise signs of her dangerous mental processes — they were only important to me for the tinge of depravity they gave my paintings. Apart from all the other considerations, my pride was hurt. I had always prided myself on my street instincts, I saw them as the key to my survival, and here I was completely taken in by a creepy-crawly kid with a suicidal bent. She was up to her neck in it, that was clear, but the implications of all that were too much for me at the time. My brain had seized up with the enormities of it.

As I stumbled off into the side road where I'd parked the car, a bike suddenly roared up beside out of nowhere, so close I could feel the heat of the engine. It almost singed me and in my jittery state I screamed. I turned to curse the driver and there was Moe, full of spunk and *joie de vivre*, smiling at me. I was so pleased to see him I couldn't let myself show it.

'I've been looking for you,' he said.

'You nearly run me over, you bastard,' I said. My lips were so stiff it was hard to shape the words.

He said, 'You want to come to the pub?'

'Yeah.' I was heady with relief, just to see his friendly face.

He parked the bike and walked down the road to the pub. I was so used to his general mode that the violence of public reaction always surprised me, and even in my present preoccupation it was hard to ignore.

To be fair, looking at him through the eyes of passersby, there was no doubt he was a huge machine of a man. His grime-stiffened red curls and jeans were hardened by the sheer duress of his life into something inanimate, even his pores oozed oil like black blood. Moe was charged with symbols of power so electric it was like being in a forcefield walking next to him. All the signs of his calling, his tattoos, the crust of filth on him, the blackened bandage wrapped carelessly around his wrist sent ripples of fear and delight through the crowd. Moe never gave a sign, his face turned impassive against all the secret attentions. He was like a knight, weighed down, made clumsy by his own power. We didn't even talk till we actually sat down, a jug of beer between us on the table.

He said, 'I thought I'd find you somewhere around here.'

'How did you know?' I asked, suddenly paranoid.

'You want a beer?' he said imitating a Chinese accent. 'Plenny beer for you. You like?' He waggled his fingers obscenely, I could smell the bike grease on his skin. It was like the pelt of an exotic animal.

'Yeah, why not.' As I sat down I noticed I was shaking. It had easily been one of the worst days of my life, and I hadn't even caught up with Rina disappearing, let alone this latest discovery. I rolled a cigarette and sat there trying to calm myself down. Moe was talking about some deal.

'See, that's where the bucks are. They reckon it's the biggest business in the States. You're fucking printing money. All you do is go into it for a couple of years, buy off a few people, put it into some legit business and then sit back and let it roll in.'

'Oh yes,' I said. There was silence as we sat and drank.

'Kingi told me where you were going. He was worried about you.'

'Oh,' I said.

'So what did she say to you? Roxy?'

'She wasn't there. You ever been to her room?'

'What for?' Moe said, giving me a funny look.

'She's got magazine and newspaper stuff kind of pinned every-where. It's all about me. She's made about ten copies of every review. It's the most disgusting thing I've ever seen.' An image of Weasel's body flashed into the space as I said it and I actually shuddered. I was in a bad way.

Moe said again, 'What for?' He was obviously disbelieving, but tried to hide it.

'She's nuts. She's off the air. She's trying to steal my soul. She's out to get me,' I said, and stopped. I was starting to sound like one of those people who think they've had radios planted in their brains. It just didn't sound like a very sane remark.

Moe said, 'Are you OK, Glory? You've got the shakes. You're shaking.' He went up to the barman again and I heard him ordering a double whisky. When he came back with it I could see he had been coming to a decision.

'Look, I heard about Rina, and all the other shit that's been happening. I'm prepared to tell you a few things if you keep your mouth shut.' His hand holding the glass out to me was so engrained with grime you could see the whorls of his skin, a thin black tracery.

He said, 'It's about time you knew. See Roxy'll hang onto you till you crack. That's her speciality. She's been talking to the cops for years. That's why they believe her, not you. She's been on a thin line for a long time now. She's a real street-corner princess.'

'Roxy? An informer?' It was so staggering I couldn't believe it. Moe was not happy about telling me either, so I could tell it was true.

'It's gone to her head. She thinks she can control the weather now that chick.'

'But how does she do that? She's out of it half the time.'

'One thing she does. She screws your ex. That's one thing. And she's got it up here,' he said tapping his temple. 'You can slag her all you like but she's got what it takes. She's good-looking, she's got the gift of the gab and she's four jumps ahead of everyone.'

'Mitch? But he told me it was in the past.'

'He would. That fucker don't like saying anything honest. It might affect his image,' he said bitterly. He'd obviously had dealings with him.

'I knew he was in it up his balls,' I said more to myself. 'Does he know? She's an informer?'

'What do you think? You breathe a fucking word to anyone and she'll knife you. She knows Mitch could blow her away in a minute, no worries. He's cunt-struck, that's all, he can't see what's staring him in the face. Roxy plays him for a sucker. She told her cousin she don't even like him, she says he can't get it up unless it's real rough. But she knows if she's got him the world's at her feet. He keeps her in with all the big importers see. You have to be nice to Roxy. She's a hard bitch — she'd cut someone's balls off it it meant money.'

'How do you know all this?'

'Her cousin. She was my old lady before she went religious.'

'Sharon?'

'Yeah. Sharon.'

'Roxy never told me about Mitch. Shit,' I said. I didn't really want to let on to Moe how much she'd conned me. In a way I had to admire her, she had it off so well. The poor little junkie and the great painter. She really played it, the flattery so subtle I didn't even pick it up. I thought of the long hours she spent lying in the chair as I painted her, the stories of her life she poured out so relentlessly. It was all too much to grasp, the energy she'd put into trapping me. And yet it wasn't insincere unless her whole room was another bizarre lie. It was confusing to say the least, like stumbling around a great mouldering castle with labyrinths leading nowhere, and secret passages. We both fell silent. I drank my beer moodily. There was no reason to disbelieve Moe but what he told me made it worse. I was dealing with people who had no remorse, no conscience, steely freaks with junk in their veins instead of blood.

'I don't know why you fucking didn't tell me before,' I said irritably. 'She's been coming round to my house for a year nearly. You could have warned me.'

'You reckoned to me once she was the best model you ever had. That's what you said. Her other dealings never came up.'

'That sounds like bullshit,' I said. 'I would of told you. I told you Weasel was an informer. Your friends should know things like that. You don't know when it might come in handy.'

'You've got such a bloody big mouth when you're drunk. That's one of the reasons,' he said looking at me long-sufferingly. 'You ask anyone. They'll tell you. Glory bloody Big Mouth. And I tell you if you blabbed about that you'd know. Those mates of hers are rank. There's going to be trouble with those drug deaths and they're all running scared. It was a fuck-up. They'd slit anyone's throat if they had to. They'd eat you alive. When the shit hits the fan I don't want to be around, and I tell you one thing, I wouldn't want to be known as the leak.'

It seemed reasonable when he put it like that. It made me wonder what exactly I had told Mitch. He had made a round trip of hundreds of kilometres to get that information so it must have been worth it. I was a ding-bat, off-beam, naive as a fucking bunny to let him do that to me.

'Well, it's just like the old days,' I said. 'I can't get over it. An informer, a killer and mad as a bat. That's my model. And you not telling me.' I was getting drunk, on an empty stomach and the stresses of the day. I could see Moe's great buffalo face across the table from me.

'I'd only do it for you, Glor. I can't let you be fucked over by a chick as gross as that. You've been a good mate to us.'

'Do what? Tell me about it too late? Thanks for nothing,' I said.

'Don't blame me,' he said, shrugging.

'I'm not,' I said. 'Blame isn't an appropriate word in the circumstances. It would be like finding fault with the weather.'

'Anyway,' he said, 'when did you see Mitch? I thought you hadn't seen him for years.'

'We came up together from the tangi. It was his old lady who died. Nettie. He must have just come to get it out of me. Whether Marianne said anything.'

'Who's Marianne?'

'The junkie who died. The one they overdosed.'

He said, 'See? Shit I told you didn't I? Those bastards have really got it in for you. You better lay low, Glory.'

I said, 'I'm going to. I've only just found out it was Roxy.'

It was a typical late afternoon at this kind of crummy pub, the lassitude of smoke and stale beer and saturated carpets — the red-faced barman drinking on the sly. It was one of those working-class pubs I could never find now — most of them have been done up in salmon pink with pot plants, and filled with hordes of tidy, obediently civilised drinkers. I felt at home in a pub like this, it reminded me of the old days, dust motes in the air and 1ZB whining out the races, the smell of beer and fags in the air, and faded old beer-soaked carpets. Hardened drinkers with red bottle noses, caricatures of themselves, lighting up their smokes with trembling Korsakov fingers, already awash with their morning's booze. Their dim old brains slithering around for some suitable social nicety.

'A beer please, Bob. Nice afternoon. Give us a packet of

Winfields, will you?' It was the only power they had left, the leisurely purchase of their poisons on pension day. I felt an affection for them, the derros like my old man and Weasel. At least what you saw was what you got.

'The real Roxy,' I said. 'Dah dit dah. Here she comes folks, riding into the ring.'

'You see,' Moe said, sententious. He was on to his second or third jug of beer. 'You see she thinks the world of you. That girl said to me you were the greatest.'

'Me? Roxy? That's what she's been trying to make me think. Is that why she pinched my kid?' It was comical, I didn't know whether to laugh or cry when he said that. The beer combined with the whisky was blurring my responses.

'That's why she's so fucking tinny,' he said. 'She means what she says at the time. She don't know what's truth and what's not. So she sucks people in. I've heard of her conning real hard bastards.'

'Like you?' I said. I was in a real shitty mood.

'Look I wouldn't touch that chick with a fucking barge pole. The first time I met her I knew she was poison. She'd eat you alive.'

We sat in the crapulent old bar, both preoccupied. I felt the beer seep and soak into me, my tissues sogging under the steady trickle of it. This new picture of Roxy as the clued-up together crimmo leader, with Mitch in the palm of her hand, and the psychotic addict with an obsession about me was still too startling to take in. I'd always associated that kind of eerie possession with cheapo American lives I'd read a lot about. Son of Sam, the creep who killed John Lennon — restless zombies reacting to indifference, men with blank eyes fucked up by the American dream, too disturbed by it even to be successful crims. False tinsel motel ceilings, those big raucous American cars chewing up gas for nothing, hamburgers gulped into acid stomachs, a gun in the drawer of some crummy hotel room, along with maps of other people's journeys. I knew all about it, it was the sort of nutty violence I was interested in.

But Roxy didn't have the background somehow to produce

115

such single-minded zombie madness. She had style, she wasn't cut off at the knees like those other deadheads. It was their ordinariness which drove them to kill the person they loved, while Roxy had power, startling beauty, people were never indifferent to her. The suicidal course she was pursuing was magnificent in its selfishness and courage, so I'd never even sus- pected the dead core which had to be there for her to be designer of that death room, the killer of children. And why she was picking on me as the object of her ambivalences was equally dis- turbing, to say the least. Here I was minding my own business, full of the confidence of years of hard work under my belt, trying to forget the grievances of the past, and bang, this she- devil was doing her best to blow up all my most careful con- structions.

I was getting pretty close to the edge with the anxieties of it — my past coming up all the time, the almost continuous bom- bardment of grotesque facts, and now this last shock, were definitely taking their toll. I couldn't confide in Moe, he was so steeped in gang-land rituals of style and power that he would only see emotion like that as a weakness. Moe didn't possess anything else except the power of his presence, so the way he used it was vital for his own survival as a leader. He couldn't afford to let the mask slip. I understood the necessity for this in his kind of life, because to a certain extent it was the way I oper- ated as well. He'd gone as far as he could, with all the tender- nesses of finding me and getting me drunk in this scummy bar, not to mention giving me information which could kill us both. Listening to me voice my fears was not on for either of us.

I said, 'OK, let's go. I've got work to do.' I had to think about Roxy on my own.

On the way out, one of the grizzled old derros raised his glass to me. 'Good on you, lassie. Good on you, lassie. I've always liked them well stacked. Plenty to get hold of, heh, heh, heh.' I bent down on an impulse and kissed him as I went past. His little wrinkled mouth and toothless gums felt like something putrid on my mouth, the stench of beer and rotting breath was truly rancid. It was like my father kissing me when he was drunk. The old man's cackle followed us out into the street.

'Heh, heh, heh. See that, boys? See what she done?'

'What did you do that for?' Moe asked. 'You'll pick up some disease.' I could tell he was pissed off, but the booze often took me like that and I sometimes felt I had no other means of protection.

7

We were all sitting out the back in the winter sun. Rina, Al, Sue, Cash and me with some bottles of beer, the trannie playing 1ZM middle-America pop songs. There was even John Denver. Rina was waiting impatiently for Bruce Springsteen. Al had bought her *Born in the USA* and *River* and she'd played them so many times I could hear his voice in my head when I was trying to paint. When 'Glory Days' finally came on she made us all jump by screaming at the top of her voice, and turning the trannie up till it vibrated. She danced her little shambling two-step in the sun. There was even a cheer from next-doors.

'Me mum!' she shouted. 'That's me mum! Glory Days!'

'I'm Glory Day, Rina. Not Days,' I said, rolling a cigarette. I had taken up smoking again over the weekend and it was peaceful to sit in the sun with my rollies and Rina and Al. I had been up nearly all night working on the painting, I had kept Rina there in my studio so I could hear her peaceful breathing as she slept in my bed. Neither of us much wanted to leave the other.

All night I had been trying to work out the best thing to do for Rina and me. I knew I needed all the painful cunning I'd scraped together over the years just to get through this. It was a test of the usefulness of my life's directions, and failure meant the whole rickety structure that I'd built up by my own hands could collapse around my head. Roxy meant business, that was clear, and with Mitch hovering around in the background the cops against me and my own weaknesses, I was on very shaky ground. Half the trouble was that I still couldn't jerk myself out of the feeling of unreality, of being utterly lost. It was like one of those dreams when you are trying to run away from danger, and a nameless force holds you back.

As Rina danced in front of us, I said to Al, 'It was just like exposing her to a virus. She can't protect herself, she can't always throw them off. I mean what kind of effect would that room of Roxy's have on her?'

'Oh crap, Glory, Rina's a bloody champion. She's seen plenty. She knows how to look after herself better than you.' He was offended for Rina.

He and I were both feeling very fragile, floaty, after yesterday. We were being unusually considerate with each other. It was like recovering from an illness. He and Sue had only had one minor spat.

'So it was bloody Roxy,' he said. He didn't seem that surprised. 'Jesus, they must be pricks. Fancy doing that to a little girl like her.'

We both watched her spinning and weaving clumsily in the sun, her thin hair glinting as she twirled her little swollen hands in unconscious parody of a ballerina. She expected nothing but praise and love from people around her — she tripped and curtseyed on her red fat legs, deep in her princess, Bruce Springsteen fantasy, one eye cocked out for more applause. She was like a wonderfully grotesque little fairy.

We all watched her silently, drinking, content just to be quiet. Brucey's nasal voice wound off and someone stood at the gate blocking the sun. It was Roxy. She was slightly soiled, dishevelled, but still beautiful. Her brilliant red hair glowed. We watched her approach, stunned into immobility. Rina saw her last and reacted instantly. She came running for me, burrowing under my skirt. She was muttering 'bastard, bastard' under her breath, her cold little nose pressed onto my thigh.

'Gidday,' said Roxy. 'How are youse all? Enjoying the sun?'

We were all struck dumb. I just stared at her in disbelief. Out of the corner of my eye I could see Cash slithering off into the house. Rina saved the day.

'Gidday, bastard,' she said, muffled under my skirt.

'Manners!' said Roxy. There was a slight twitch at the corner of her mouth. 'That kid's getting fucking cheeky. You spoil her, Glory. Just because she's a bit sub it doesn't mean she should be allowed to get away with it.' She squatted down in front of us. 'What's wrong with youse buggers? What's wrong, Glory? You OK?'

I looked at her and her eyes were quite blank. She wasn't putting anything on. For one wild moment I thought the last few days had been just one long hallucination, that nothing had happened and once again she was my flighty model, come to annoy me with her demands and unreasoning love. She squatted there in front of us, quite still, one soft white hand covered in junk rings, balancing her body on the grass, her purblind blue stare, tremulous mouth.

'You got a cup of coffee for a thirsty friend?' she asked. There was anxiety in her voice for the first time.

'Nah,' said Al finally.

'Oh.' She looked uncertainly at me, 'Glory,' she said, touching me with her soft hand, 'I've been thinking, I'd like to model for you for free. I decided last night. I know how fucking broke you are and I want to help you? I know with looks like mine I could name the price, but we should stick together. That's what friends are for. I've always said, eh Al, she could do with a minder? Our Glory?' Her voice cracked with the strain of it.

'Were you just minding Rina? Eh Roxy?' Al asked.

'Oh that,' she said flatly. 'You talking about Rina?' She got up and started to back away keeping her great blank eyes on Al. 'You've always been a smart little shit haven't you? Always trying to get Glory on your side. Little shit bubba. Hiding behind mama's skirts. You believe him, Glory? You really believe that little cunt, that I'd do a thing like that?'

I realised that she must have genuinely thought we knew nothing. Looking at her killer eyes, I saw she had moved in and out of so many games and deals and characters for so long that she was gone, lost in them permanently. She'd gone into overdrive with the panic of it and all the different roles were flashing past like speeded up tape, blurring in a gabble of sound and light.

I said, 'It's true isn't it? Weasel, Rina, you name it. Marianne.' After that there was a silence. We all sat there poised for flight. I could feel the adrenalin hammering away in my temples. Even Rina stayed silent, her body damp against my legs. Roxy froze, her face going blank in that scary way of hers.

'I can see I'm gonna have to come back when you're in a better mood,' she finally said. 'There's certainly some pretty fucking weird vibes round here. I was trying to save your precious Weasel, stinking little informer that he was. I tried to save him for your sake — I knew how much he meant to you. That's what I was trying to tell you the other night but you wouldn't fucking listen. Too wrapped up in your own ego. But I'll come back when Al's not here. We'll have a smoke, we can sort it out on our own. My offer's still open, Glory. I'm not a petty person.'

From under my dress Rina said tensely, 'Anyway, you're not the boss of the world.' There was a silence.

I said to Roxy, 'Over my dead body, honey,' which I realised straight away was a pretty dumb thing to say to a homicidal maniac. It just slipped out before I even thought. I was so shaken by seeing her. I couldn't work anything out. She laughed at me, genuinely amused.

'You always were a funny one, Glory Day,' she said.

She turned to go, the sinister bitch, and nearly crashed into Nigel, who was rushing up the path, a grim look on his face. It was a heaven-sent chance, a perfect way of getting her own back, and quick thinker that she was, she leapt to it.

'Hello,' she said, enchanted, all her bracelets jingling. 'Nigel. Where've you been hiding?' She couldn't wait to pounce. 'Heard about Glory?'

'What now?' Nigel's face was a picture. He looked disapprovingly at me. He was never at his best in the morning. For some reason Roxy always flirted with him and it made him touchy as a cat.

'Oh, police, murder, kidnap — you name it! I wouldn't be her agent, dear.' She was so light there on the path, her beautiful body inclining towards him full of grace and warmth and animation. It was the kidnap that did it. I pushed Rina out of the way, walked up to Roxy and smacked her one on the mouth. I did it coldly and deliberately, but my heart was thumping with rage.

She reeled back, and I had a glimpse of the surprise in her eyes, and then she backed off watching me blankly.

'Piss off,' I said. 'I don't want you here.'

She said at the gate, 'Catch you later, Glory,' and I could see her mouth was already swollen. It was a really heavy whack.

'I seen you, Mum,' said Rina cuddling up to me. 'I seen you give her arseholes.'

Al said, 'You shouldn't of done that, Glory. She's going to do you. She is right off the air, man. I've never seen anything like it.'

Nigel said, 'Wonderful, Glory. Terrific. Now you're becoming a real thug. You should have seen your face!' He was titillated by the punch for some reason. Whether he was pleased for me or just liked to see women fighting was beyond me — unless it was to do with my business, I had long since ceased to fathom the working of his processes.

'Private business,' I said.

'Well,' he said, still staring after Roxy's retreating figure, fascinated. 'Never a dull moment on the Highway.' It was his coy name for our house.

I sat down again on the step, offered him a drink of the beer. It was just an automatic provocation, he always reacted with the same distaste. Anyway I was tired of all the games with him, I needed some time to myself.

'I can see you've been up late. Look at those bags! Not a healthy colour! But almost marvellous that violet,' he said in his nagging way.

'What do you want, Nigel?'

'Just passing,' he said fooling no one. 'Done any more?'

'Yes. I worked all night.' I slipped that in to shut him up.

'Fitted it in with the drug dealing, did we? Well, I suppose I'm the last to know. It's only right.' His bitterness slipped sideways from the false jocularity. 'I mean I only stand to lose thousands. Fuck the money, dear.'

'It's got nothing to do with me,' I said very carefully and softly.

'I've been hearing a few things. Extraordinary things, really.

I'm not as insulated as you think. You haven't got the monopoly on being one with the people, having your ear to the wind, you know. But I'll give you one thing, you're the looniest painter I've ever heard of. Certainly female anyway. We all know about creative people rampaging around society, outsiders with their savage eye on us poor straights but you go too far. Why did you take it into your head to paint for God's sake? Why not poetry? Why pick on me? Why did I have to be your agent?'

'I'm getting jack of you, Nigel.' I chose my words with care. 'You're talking to me as if I was a halfwit. I've got enough on my mind without you hassling me.'

'I thought you were trying for that image.' He looked at me. 'Alright. Sorry. Just a bit of razzing. If you can't take it, I'll try not to. Really. It's just hard for a Parnell boy like me to cope with all this real life out on the Highway. I've never seen a grown woman punch another one. Except on TV.' Whenever he was at a loss Nigel went into overdrive.

'Do you want to look at the paintings?' I asked finally. I wasn't interested in helping him out. I had other things to think of.

'No, no, no. I'm in a bit of a hurry. We'll have to hang them some time of course. When you're ready. I'll ring you anyway. If you're not in chokey.' He couldn't help himself, his malice was so close to the surface he had to fight to keep it under. It bubbled up when he least wanted it.

I said, 'Goodbye, Nigel,' in case he thought he was staying.

'Alright, Glory,' he said. 'You can stop staring at me with that great monolith of a face. I've got my own troubles too, you know.' He went off reasonably satisfied. Right on cue Cash came out and stood at the door. He'd been filling his face while he was inside, dodging Roxy, and his mouth was shining with grease. He winked at me.

'Remember we've got a band practice tomorrow. Don't worry about that other thing, OK? I'll see you right,' and sloped off quickly before I could say anything.

Rina and me sat on the step, but the day was clouding over and it was getting chilly. More rain clouds on the horizon, a wintry day gone sour.

'What do you want for lunch, chicken?' I asked.

'Chippies,' said Rina. She was quite happy again. She was the spitting image of Cash like that, it was all water off a duck's back within minutes.

'Let's go,' I said. Rina took my hand, danced and skipped and sang all the way to the dairy. She was in a terrific mood. When we got back there was a letter for me, jammed under the door. As soon as I picked it up I knew it was Roxy's.

I realise you take me as a joke. You've never really considered me in any deeper light. Not like I think of you. You, Glory, have always been a mother to me — I thought of you as a person who could always solve my problems. I used to try and think what you would have said before I said anything, and to be like you. I tried painting, not that I told you. I wanted to become one with you.

You're so old and sexless, you're like an ancient monument. Once, on acid, I had a hallucination of you as a giant spider, hairy and bloated with your victims, your men, your kids, your mysterious past life and now me. You've got freaks all round you, Glory, or haven't you even noticed. I dream of you a lot, think of your painting sessions when you watch me with so much intensity, it's almost sex, you paint and paint me as if you'd like to strip my body down to the bone and then suck the marrow out with your great brown teeth. You were perfect till little things started to creep in.

I wanted even then to give you one more chance but everything went numb and I can't help thinking of you with hatred and viciousness. (*Something crossed out deeply.*) You know? I need help, Glory, but I know you're not the one to give it to me any more and you are now my life-denying enemy, try as I did to reverse it. I'm not going to write anything about all that to you, about that kid, and Weasel and your snivelling Rina or anything — I have too much respect — but I'm watching you, and I'm frightened of your size, your grossness, that pudding grey face of yours, and I will defend myself if necessary. Never forget that I loved you dearly but I can only take so much. I am a forgiving person but you have thrown my love in my teeth,

— Roxy

I never knew she was that poetic, she had a real flair for dream language, intensities which you could never pick from the way she talked. Her handwriting was so tight and small and malignant it was hard to read. I once read a greeting of Son of Sam's to the world — it was, 'Hello from the cracks in the sidewalks of NY city and from the ants that dwell in these cracks. Hello from the gutters of New York city which are filled with dog manure, vomit, stale wine, urine and blood.' That was the sort of language which really disturbed me, and this letter of Roxy's had the same kind of passionate skew-whiff logic, the lyrical intensities of threat, entreaty and a death vision — the feeling of being trapped inside the fierce words, her world, where there were no horizons, air or light, only a blind iron process triggered off by random signs.

In black and white, on a sheet of creased paper, a flat statement like that was chilling. It had the ring of authenticity about it; a bulletin direct from her subconscious. The creepy creepy merging of identities that I saw in her room, the incandescence of the enmity and love, the whole rich mixture of my paintings, my strength, her life.

At least I knew more, that was something. I knew more of what was actually going on in her head. The sheer intensity of her convictions was a shocker — I hadn't realised the full extent of it. To her I was to blame, there was no doubt about it. Roxy had a talent for making people feel responsible for her own fuck-ups and against all odds, the letter, with its eerie insights, put me on the defensive. In my shaky state she had homed in on my doubts. Why me? The old question had a pungency to it which gave me pause.

The fact was that just about the only common factor in the whole business was me. Ex-husbands, acquaintances, friends, you name it. It was uncanny. They were my own people and it was a point of pride with me that I'd never betrayed my origins, but all the coincidences were starting to disturb me. It was Roxy I had chosen for my model, and it was me she had chosen for her soulmate before things went sour, those were inescapable facts. And whether I liked it or not it was me who interfered, however briefly and well meaning, in the disorderly process of the life and death of Marianne. And there was no doubt either that I was painting pathological human states, however careful my motives. I might have known the lovingly arranged deaths, murder on shiny surfaces, plus all the money, excitement and pain tied up in the paintings would have been dynamite for such a suggestible kid, her brain curdled as it was by smack and speed. She took them at face value, being a born troublemaker.

The proof of that was her behaviour that night when she came to see me, fresh from Weasel's room, and saw a picture which mirrored her wildest fears and guilts. I could appreciate all that, now that I'd seen her own room. But I still didn't know what these facts added up to, if anything — whether it was just a bizarre series of coincidences complicated by Roxy or whether it was just my old sins catching up with me.

I knew I had to stay very careful there, though, and not lose my head. The last thing I wanted to do was read some mysterious meaning into it. Deliberate mystifications would just be dangerously misleading. I'd seen where it got Roxy, her inability to look at the simple truth of something and to face the discomfort and ultimate release than came from it. In her junkie way she chose to dress the truth up, distort, complicate things endlessly in her wormy brain, so that she was always protected from that sort of clean pain. Signs, portents, mysterious congruences, dreams, stars, all the paraphernalia of the junkie world had finally sent her spiralling off forever.

I went inside with the letter burning a hole in my hand. I said to Al, 'Look at this will you?' I gave him the letter to read.

He sat at the kitchen table, propping his head up on his bare elegant arms as if it was almost too heavy to support, and read it slowly, frowning with concentration.

'She's got a way with words. "Spider", for Chrissake. "Bloated with her victims". What a lot of muck.'

'It's like the room,' I said. 'She's totally obsessed. "I want to be one with you." In the bloody grave probably. Yuck.'

'You're a hard case,' Al said. 'I've always thought she was a nutter. She's right off the fucking edge. You wanted a model for "Senseless Violets" and that's what you got, baby. A model alright.'

'It was her face,' I said, feeling a fool. 'I've never seen a face like that. How did I know she was a fucking psychopath?'

'I never knew what you saw in her myself,' he said.

I said for something to say, 'Thanks for yesterday, Al. You were a real mate.'

We sat there in companionable silence. Upstairs I could hear Rina playing with Sue:

'Say say you play me,
Come out and play with me
and bring your darling sweet.
Climb up my apple tree
slide down your rainbow
into my candy store.
Forever more more
shut the door!'

Her voice sounded innocent and far away. We sat listening, entranced, till it died away as unexpectedly as it had started.

'That's that clapping game she learnt at school,' Al said absently. After a silence he said, 'Do you realise she must have written this in half an hour? Less even.'

'Come on. The whole thing?' It made me feel sick to hear him say that.

'She came round, you belted her one, Nigel came, you went up the road with Rina. Half an hour. Maybe more.'

I said, 'She probably had it all written out before she came this morning. She wanted any excuse, the bitch.' We both shivered like kids playing a scary game, daring each other in the dark. Al put on his mirror glasses again.

'Hard to say,' he said austerely, obviously as thrown as me at the thought. 'Me and Sue are going round to Griff's place to jack

127

up that bike part. See you.'

I couldn't see his eyes behind the glasses, but he seemed to be taking it OK. It was always hard to know which way he was going to go. I said, 'See you,' and went back inside.

I felt like doing something physical before I went back into the studio. I needed to clean up a bit, really get stuck in, shift things around me. The house had become patchy, full of secrets — I suddenly wanted order around me, fresh air, scented cleanliness. I went into the kitchen and filled the sink with hot soapy water. I scrubbed the stove, wiped all the stains off the walls, got down on my knees and scrubbed the floor with a stiff-bristled brush. I sang at the top of my voice, and tried not to think of anything at all, flopping round the brown soapy water.

At times like these I enjoyed all the clean smells of a kitchen, of Ajax, soapy water, my sweat, the floor cleaner fluid which smelt like synthetic daffodils. The room gradually assumed shape, solidity, all its old surfaces had new clean lines. Each object became more distinct as I worked like a madwoman, rinsing off the accumulated dirt. I even did the fridge. Inside were three bottles of beer, half a squashy tomato, a little hard heel of cheese and red jammy meat stains all over the bottom and sides. I threw everything out and sloshed at it till my back ached. Kettle on the stove all shining, I yelled out for Rina.

She came down sniffing like a little boxer dog. 'Neat,' she said appreciatively. We had some biscuits, so it was a bit like a commercial, the cup of tea in the clean kitchen, mother and daughter. I sang 'Ajax the foaming cleanser da, dad, da, da' to Rina, which she'd always liked since she was a baby, and she sang 'Wash your hair, too clean for dandruff, too clean for dandruff with new cleaning shampoo', which was a real oldy. The lino shone, the fridge motor snorted and chug-a-lugged as if it was on its last legs, and we ate three biscuits each.

'Did Sue read you a story?'

'Yes. I saw her and Al kissing on the lips.' She pursed her own mouth up, deeply excited by the thought. I was suddenly sorry, thinking, what's going to become of her? I hoped someone would want to kiss her mouth too, besides me and Al. She sat close to me, dunking her biscuits snuffling and content.

I said, very nonchalant, 'Roxy didn't hurt you did she? When she took you yesterday?' Rina looked at me, her grey eyes unfathomable.

'Yes. She pinched me and pinched me.' Looked at me sideways to see if I was getting the joke.

'You were OK? She was kind to you?'

'She give me a Crunchie. She said, "Don't tell Glory." She said you mightn't ever see your mum again.' A slight shadow passed over her earnest face. 'That's not true, is it?' It was only really a perfunctory question. It hadn't even entered her head that it was likely.

'No,' I said. 'Hell, no.'

That night I dreamt very intensely, very methodically, fire-works shooting out of my skull as I tossed and turned. It was an underground muddy, exhausting dream and I used all my physical strength to stay there. Whenever Roxy appeared in it, there was such power in her that I was blindly driven to explain things, to bow myself out from her presence. I went onto my knees, almost sobbing with the force of my emotion. I groaned with it, even begging her, but I couldn't make a connection. She was a smiling angel with a heart of stone and blind stone eyes come to root me out and destroy me for reasons that I couldn't begin to understand. I felt the full force of my powerlessness in my dream, I protested my innocence, I groaned, I knew it was only me who stood between Rina and her smiling menace.

It was my own involvement in this which really obsessed me, whether I really was innocent, or whether it was some just punishment from my past which Rina had to pay for. I dreamt of Weasel's rotting body and his death room, the smiling cops, the newspapers growing on Roxy's walls. In the dream I knew that Roxy had killed us all — the little junkie my namesake, floated, her green face congested in the nightmare twilight of Mainstreet. I had to wake myself in the end with a huge jump as if devils were leaving my poor old body. I was completely wet through and I felt huge, lumbering and old as I heaved myself out of bed. As I went up the dark passage there was a bar of warm light from under the kitchen door and I could hear the radio on softly. I was so relieved I almost wept. Al was there morosely sitting over a cup of beer. Opening the door was like entering into another dream, the room was so sparkly it took me by surprise. I had forgotten all about that cleaning work. My dreams had been so muddy and blood tinged in contrast to this innocent room.

'You done the kitchen really nice, Glory,' he said without even looking up.

'Yes. You want a cup of tea?' I went over and made one. The beer looked so flat I wondered how long he'd been sitting there.

He said, 'Sue wants us to move out. She reckons there's too much going on in the house and we'll get into trouble just living here. She was really shocked about you smacking up Roxy. She says Roxy'll get you for that. I haven't told her about Weasel yet.'

'Oh, she's got a fair idea,' I said. 'She's no fool.'

'You don't like her do you?' Al said.

'Oh, she's alright.'

There was a silence as we thought it over, both of us embarrassed. I said, trying to encourage him, 'I don't blame her. It's not easy living with two emotional retards like us and with all this shit from Roxy on our heads as well.'

'She's young,' Al said. 'In her mind, I mean. I think this is the first time she's ever got involved with a man. A lot of sex, different guys, but I don't think she's ever moved in before. She's only young.'

'Are you going to?' I asked, settling down in the chair with the warm cup in front of me. I'd never seen him so unhappy.

'Dunno,' he said not looking at me.

'Well, I'm easy. I'm not in a hurry for another tenant if you're still not sure.'

'What's an emotional retard anyway?'

'Someone who's had their emotions stunted as a kid.'

'Oh,' he said. 'Thanks a lot.'

'What did you say to Sue?'

'Nothing.' We stayed silent. We've never had to say much to

each other anyway. Al and I had been living in the same house for a long time and we knew each other's moods.

'Oh well, that's alright. You can come back if you change your mind. Unless you decide it's permanent.'

When I said it and the words were out there hanging in the air between us I felt a sudden bad ache. My dreams about Roxy had made me painfully aware of the dangers around me. I felt if he went it would be a bad sign.

'We had another fight anyway,' Al said, 'so I don't know what she's thinking.'

'So what's new?' I said, I couldn't resist it.

'What about the money?' he said. He didn't sound relieved, just resigned. It made me sad for him. He even accepted a cup of tea.

'Oh, Nigel reckons the opening'll really go. That'll tide me over.'

I settled down, suddenly feeling more comfortable. This late-at-night feeling, the strange night brightness of the kitchen, my dressing-gown, reminded me of staying with Nettie one time when I was pregnant. The smell of toast and lino in her little house, the same deep feeling of peace in a war zone. Intimacy between two people cocooned comfortably in the night, the slight chill, the bar heater burning my legs. As if in our slow sleepy conversation, we had left our bodies still warmly asleep in bed and were communicating in sign language from innermost least-guarded secret places. The words became shorthand for something much deeper — the inarticulate, unformed sounds of love and despair and understanding could at last come out freely without the inhibitions of daylight.

'I'm worried, too. About Roxy. I kept dreaming of her. And Weasel's body. And Marianne.'

'I know,' said Al raising his startling head to look at me. 'I'm shit scared of Roxy. That bitch could kill us.'

I said, 'I can't tell the cops anything because they won't believe me. And Roxy is so off her head she could kill me and still think she was the Virgin Mary.'

'I reckon Roxy did them both. She's got a lot to lose, that's

---

why she's trying to get you in the shit.'

'Her and Mitch,' I said. It was a huge relief for us both to say it. 'I'm worried for Rina more than me,' I said. 'And the opening.' We both moved positions on the creaky old kitchen chairs.

'I'm not going yet,' Al said. 'I'll tell Sue I'm moving later. You can't do this on your own. Just because she's jealous. She's feeding on my entrails as it is.'

I looked at him really taken aback. 'What an image! Entrails!'

He looked at me with his opaque eyes. 'That painting of yours. You know the nuclear family one? It reminds me of her.'

'Sometimes I think I'm a bad influence on you,' was all I said.

He turned the cup round in his big delicate hands and looked up at me again. 'How about it tonight, Glory?' he asked, his eyes on my face. I might have known that was coming. On the face of it the whole thing was strange, me in my grossness and his clean beauty but whenever we were in bed it was always right. Nice clean sex it was — he revered and loved and was surprisingly tender. I lay in his arms like an old queen pleasured from head to foot. It was slightly awesome to have such beauty at close quarters all for me — and he always looked so flushed and young and enthusiastic. But now that Sue was around it wasn't worth the hassle if she found out; now that I was older I'd learnt that keeping the peace with other women was more important than the odd stray fuck. Doing other women down was my forté when I was a kid, but I didn't have the taste for it anymore. Al was the man I missed out on when I was young and spunky and ready for real love. Now it was too late — I didn't take it all that seriously any more. I was much too involved in my work, my singing, my daily life, to feel passionate about a man, especially a friend like Al.

Something had been burnt out of me with all the years of my father, and the lovers and husbands I'd had. I wanted to get on with other things, I'd believed for years now that life was easier without men and their demands, the little smiles on their faces when they wanted something. I never knew exactly why Al was so keen on it, but there it was, and we never really discussed it.

It just happened sometimes. He used to make me a cup of tea and sit on the edge of the bed talking about different things while I drank it. We'd just go on with life, which was comforting to me — it never seemed to affect us either way. It was easy I suppose, and there was a good feeling behind it.

That night it was the perfect suggestion, Sue or no Sue. I wouldn't even have thought of it, full of worries as I was, but I realised straight away that sex with him would be magic for nightmares.

'I'll just finish this,' I said. I felt an unusual tenderness for him. He stood at the door waiting.

'You've changed, Glory,' he told me. 'I've never seen you so out of it these last few days.'

I didn't like him saying that because now of all times I had to keep my wits about me, stay strong, watch out for my back. That dream I'd had about Roxy reminded me painfully of me as a kid begging one or other drunk parent not to give me a hiding. Powerlessness was a condition I thought I'd left behind forever, but the dream made me realise it could hit me between the eyes the minute I let my guard down. It was a necessity for me, keeping control.

'Not with you and Rina,' I said, and let it pass. I didn't want even to voice a fear like that out loud, it was such dynamite. Besides, I could feel my body getting ready for sex, warming, softening, and I didn't want to talk any more or think any more or worry. I was numb with it all.

We got into bed so delicately, like an old married couple. It was nice to feel his strong loving body all round me and inside me. I could smell his clean sweat as he laboured. I was surprised by his urgency — he even whispered, 'It's been a while, Glory,' his young skin was like silk against me. When he finally went to sleep, his whole long strong body curled against my back, his even child-breath in my ear warmed and calmed me and I slept dreamless.

8

I woke early to the sound of magpies out the window. A pair used to live in the wasteland up the road. Their harsh musical voices always made me think of cow paddocks, the innocence of country mornings.

I lay there looking at the paintings stacked around the walls, checking my children. The death one — the woman on the lino — was still my favourite. There was a quality of immediacy I liked about it, it made death look somehow humdrum, almost friendly. No wonder Roxy had reacted to it so violently. It reminded me of Weasel's corpse. All the paintings looked menacing, diseased, silently stacked there in the grey morning light. Around them like offerings were strewn ashtrays, glasses, rags, paints, empty cups, the tobacco packet, Rina's dolls, knickers and lolly papers. The sharp clean smell of turps and paints and canvas hung over the room.

I stayed still for a while, thinking about the painting and Roxy and watching Al curled up like a dog on the other side of the bed, dead to the world. Sometimes you could forget that great shining skull, but this morning it looked almost painful on my red pillows.

When I leapt up out of bed, he stirred, puckering his lips like a baby. I pulled on my painting overalls, a great garment which crackled like the sails of a yacht, and shouted at him. 'Al, come on, wake up!' I wanted to start work.

He always woke gracefully, it took a couple of minutes before the day's paranoia settled onto his face like a cloud and his shifty expression took over.

'I was dreaming about you, Glory,' he said, stretching like a god. 'Shit!' and leapt out of bed. 'She's coming early this morning.'

'She being the cat's mother,' I said absent-mindedly, my mind already on the day's work. My mother had said that to me so many times, it was a knee-jerk reflex. The long sleep had made me refreshed and full of energy, and now the plan that gave me most comfort was just to keep on painting.

'You and I were in a boat. One of them little dinghies?' He dressed nervous and fast. I always liked seeing men doing up their pants. They looked serious and somehow sad about putting their armour back on. He said, 'Do you want a cuppa?'

'You'd better hurry. She'll give you arseholes if she finds out you've been here.'

It was time to wake Rina as well. She always took a long time to get herself dressed. It was her first day back to school after the holidays and I wanted to walk her there.

Al said, 'See you later, Glor,' and ducked out. He had things to do as well.

When we finally hit the pavement, Rina and me, it was still early in the morning. She was wearing one of the dresses her grandmother had made for her, it had frills on the sleeves and sat strangely on her hips.

We passed groups of big Samoan men in overalls and work-boots waiting for the pick-up van to the freezing works. They stood swaying slightly, half asleep, their big bodies relaxed inside the loose work clothes. Their sleepy faces looked exotic in the grey Anglo-Saxon street. That kind of wintry early morning light was the purest I knew — it touched people's hair intimately, softened the hard angles of streets and buildings and the glittering cars. People seemed more friendly, their bodies bigger and softer in the glow of it.

We took our time, Rina and me, enjoying the freshness, even going to the dairy to buy a Crunchie each. The wooden shelves in the shop were quite bare, it was like being in a country shop somewhere on a Pacific Island. There were three big women sitting on a bench there, talking Samoan in their soft lilting voices, and they smiled lovingly at my Rina when we came in. On the counter, that innocent mixture of goods you find in country general stores, dishwashing liquid, Samoan newspapers, yams, some lemons.

We walked on down the street, biting recklessly into the Crunchies. Rina had insisted on wearing a Madonna bow in her ratty hair and it perched like a mad butterfly above her cheerful morning face.

She said, 'Miss Benson is really mad with me.' She had the rolling eyes and twangy voice of the American kids' programmes off to a tee. 'She says, "Rina, stop your talking,"' Rina said, trudging along with her bow.

'She probably gets pissed off with all those kids yattering away,' I said.

'Oh no,' said Rina, shocked. 'I'm her pet and so is Tracey and Moana. We're her pets. We're allowed to do *anything*,' rolling her eyes again.

'Teacher's pet, I wanna be teacher's pet,' I sang. We both sang it for a while. I held her dry little hard hand. 'Don't go anywhere without me, Rina, will you. I'll come and pick you up, or Al.'

'OK,' said Rina very seriously. She knew I was serious. When I hugged her at the school gates she asked, 'Are they coming to take me away, ha ha?' looking at me slyly. She was always quick for a laugh our Rina. She liked that song. 'They're coming to take me away, ha ha, they're coming to take me away.' My mother used to clamp her hands over her ears whenever she heard it.

I suddenly had the idea of going in and talking to Rina's teacher. Rina would never remember a warning — the only thing she remembered was words of songs. It was a measure of my uneasiness, me even going near the place. It was a recognition that I had to take a few precautions.

We walked to the classroom, all the smells of the school turning my stomach. That musty dead institution whiff of chalk and rubber and clothes. The nearest thing to it was the Sally Army shop up at the shopping centre.

The teacher was so neat and sweet and bright. She was like a little well-groomed bird. She kept her face very professional and I remembered too late my overalls and general appearance. I didn't want to shame Rina, but she led me proudly up to her Miss Benson.

'This is my mum,' she said, with terrible pride.

I said, 'Hello, Miss Benson. Rina enjoys school.' I felt very awkward. It was like being a kid again. The paintings on the wall, all the busyness and care by this Miss Benson was somehow a terrible lesson to me. Rina drifted off to her desk. I heard her singing 'Teacher's Pet' to herself in a meditative kind of way.

'I've come to ask you something about Rina,' I began.

'Yes?' she said. She was longing to get away from me and tell her colleagues all about it. She was a kindly young woman, but I could see my huge, paint-daubed overalls and general demeanour were not to her taste. I hadn't brushed my hair and my skin was still crushed and scented from Al.

'Could you make sure that Rina doesn't get picked up by anyone apart from me. Or a young guy called Al? He's bald,' I added helpfully.

'Sure, sure. Yes,' said Miss Benson, buttoning her lips in with the effort not to show any emotion. She fiddled with her neat set of felts. They all had lids on I noticed. 'I wouldn't mention it — but it's pretty important,' I said clumsily.

'Right. Thanks, Mrs Day.'

I kissed Rina goodbye and walked out thankfully. It was a most ancient reaction, that working-class cringe at the power and self-satisfaction of schools, the awesome magic of teachers striding around busy rooms, the cars parked in the car park, the playground all nice out on the grass. They had things so much under control, the world was theirs in their charts and maps, while I, threadbare and somehow inferior, had nothing. Once, when I was a kid, I looked out the window of my classroom and saw my parents walking past quickly, shamefacedly, looking neither left or right. Shabby, despicable, they were going up to see the headmaster.

Roache, my brother, had broken every window in the music room and was, I knew, held captive there. They had come to agree with the headmaster about Roache's wickedness, kowtowing and bowing before him. I saw them, my huge and fear-some parents, stripped of their power and mystique and realised we had no hope. They had sacrificed Roache without a qualm, and they'd do the same to any of us if they had the choice. It's always put me off schools, seeing my parents lose their power like that.

I walked home preoccupied, thinking of the painting I'd work on today. It seemed like a concrete step, warning Rina's teacher, and it made me feel better. The beautiful morning had turned into one of those grey skittish Auckland days, tossing from blue sky to grey, to cold wind, to sun. I thought greedily of staying in the studio all day, sweating out the images of these last few days, painting myself back into control.

When I arrived home, the kitchen was full of the smell of food cooking. Al was at the stove frying up some eggs in a dense cloud of fat, Sue was at the table reading *Truth*, with Cash hanging avidly over her shoulder.

'Hello, Glory,' he said looking up. 'Well, I tell you old Bob won't be amused. Not to mention the management of Main-street.'

I sat down. 'Give us some eggs and bacon, Al?'

They showed me the paper with relish. There was a big story with a banner headline — 'Mystery Death of Young Junkie.' There it all was in that juicy empty journalese — well-known nightspot, father a prominent Christian businessman. Police making enquiries and have questioned well-known painter and singer Glory Day. It is alleged she knew the girl and is connected to another suspicious death in an inner-city flat, a well-known heroin dealer. There was even a fuzzy picture of me — it was an old promo shot for a blues concert about three years ago. I looked big and tawdry and dangerous. Perfect for the story.

'What are you going to do?' Cash was definitely excited. He'd obviously already formed his own conclusions and felt exhilaratingly safe.

'What can I do?' I said, throwing the paper down.

Al said, 'Get a lawyer, Glor. Ring Sarah. It's really connecting you with it, that story. They're saying you done it, kid.'

He was sorry for me, but he didn't want to show it in front of Sue.

'I mean if it was me, I'd do anything to clear my name,' Sue said in her ratty little voice. She looked dried out, full of secret, spilling resentments this morning. Her tee shirt had big ragged holes cut in it. You could see her soft skin inside. She never seemed to feel the cold, she sat there like a little dried-out lizard, watching Al, her face puckered with the angers of the morning. Cash was eyeing her automatically, even in the midst of his excitement. The smell of female flesh alone was enough to set him off, you could almost see him sniffing it in twitchy gasps. He was waiting greedily for breakfast. No one had invited him either, for sure.

'What can you do?' he said, feeding me.

I was thinking murderously. It was really disturbing this cold little story. I felt dangerously exposed, crucified by the relentlessness of it. It seemed a crazy thing for *Truth* to do, sailing as close to the wind as the story did. Whoever gave it to them must have sounded very confident, shown excellent credentials. The cops wouldn't have gone that far unless it was some kind of half-arsed idea about a lure, and if it was Roxy she must have been on her best behaviour when she spoke to the reporter.

I thought of her beautiful face and the power of her, there was no doubt that she was quite capable of charming the pants off some guy. She'd probably said she was an undercover cop or something, in terrible danger. I could just see her beseeching eyes, brave smile. Glory Day, the spider in the centre, searching for her victims, dealing in the snowy death powder.

I didn't realise the extent of my rage till the phone rang. It was Nigel, he'd seen the story, and he wanted to know the truth, he was only my agent and he thought we were friends. It looked like the opening was down the drain. His whining set me off.

'I've got nothing to do with this!' I shouted into the phone. 'Thanks for being a mate, old dear.' I mimicked him dangerously, 'It's really terrific to know you *believe* in me, Nigel. All this time it hasn't just been dollars. I appreciate your faith in me.'

He never knew how to let things go. He still went on whingeing about the opening.

I said very softly, 'Nigel, you can stuff your opening up your arse!' and put the phone down. It was a cheap shot but I was trembling with rage. It must have been awesome because everyone in the kitchen had gone quiet. Al put a plate in front of me as if he was feeding a wild animal. I ate in silence, my stomach churning acid, rage and fear distorting my face as I chewed into the hot grease. It was like old times. The phone rang again.

'Tell him to get stuffed,' I growled, my mouth full of runny warm egg.

'It's Sarah,' said Al. He sounded relieved. He knew I was getting out of my depth when I was like that.

'Can you come up and see me, Glory? Have you seen —'

'I was going to ring you. Yes, I've just seen it. When?'

'It might be a good thing if you came pretty shortly,' she told me. 'If you can. You should have got in touch with me again before it came to this.' She said it very gently not to hurt my feelings.

I went back into the kitchen feeling lighter. Cash was saying, 'But you know what she's like. I told her, but she wouldn't listen,' to a contemptuous Sue. He stopped in confusion when I went in.

'Can you pick up Rina after school? I'll probably be back, but if I'm not?' I asked Al.

Al said, 'I'll be here all day, mate.'

Sue stood up, noisily dragging the chair back on the lino.

'Well fuck you, Al. I'm not hanging round here then. You said you was coming up to the furniture place with me.' She looked at me guiltily. Even Sue was scared of me sometimes. She wasn't to know Al had already told me about moving out.

Cash said, 'What are you looking for, Sue? I've got a mate — he's got his bloody basement full. He's giving it away. Dirt cheap. What say we go over? We can have a look around, bound to be something you want. It's good stuff. I've seen it myself. Mattresses, lounge suite, kitchenware. The lot.'

Al said, 'Why don't you, Sue? It's most probably hot stuff

but, eh Cash? We know all about your mates, don't we?' he leered. 'Did you do it yourself? Eh?' Al was sometimes danger-ously mad. He just said things like that from the top of his head. We all knew being a third-rate muso didn't pay that well and Cash did a bit of receiving on the side, not to mention the courier work I'd just found out about, but no one would have dreamt of saying it. It was a real breach of etiquette. Al was just lucky it was only Cash. One day Al was going to get flattened. He never realised he was pushing it. He seemed to have none of the normal social graces.

'Come on. What are you talking about. Come on, Al, who do you think you're talking to?' Cash wasn't sure how far to go. He kept darting little glances at Sue and gulping down his breakfast as if we'd take it away from him, like a bloody dog. He was blinking rapidly, staring at Sue and Al in turn with his goggly eyes. He was genuinely outraged.

'Well, are you?' asked Al to Sue. They were locked into some kind of muddy little manoeuvre. Cash didn't come into it.

'Yeah, I might,' she said, very deliberately. It was like playing with razor blades. Al told me once that Sue had stabbed a friend of hers by accident. Looking at her bone-thin little face I could see that it would come easy for her. Cutting someone's flesh with a knife takes a lot more physical strength and cruelty than anyone gives credit for. I got up.

'Don't overdo it, youse two,' I said. 'Don't leave the blood on the floor.' They hardly even heard.

'Can you gimme a lift?' Cash asked. He had abandoned his hurt pride stance. He knew a good game when he saw it and he realised it was useless even trying to get them to take notice. He was really pissed off, though. I got him to push the car while I crash-started it, it was really slow this morning, and he kept pushing it stupidly before I could even get the engine going. We nearly ended up in the next-doors' verandah. It was the action of a hostile man. The neighbours' alsatians started barking and growling. They were half-wild beasts kept chained up round the house and they had hard savage eyes. The next-doors didn't feed them much on purpose. Cash was petrified. The stupid little bastard leapt into the car just as I managed to jerk it into life.

'Did you see those bloody brutes? They were after me. Did you hear the buggers howling? They were like bloody wolves.'

We drove soberly over the kerb onto the road. Out of the corner of my eye I could see Kingi strolling nonchalantly out onto the verandah to have a look at the tyre marks, studiously not looking after us out of politeness.

'I don't know how you can live next door to those people. They're killers. You only have to look at them.' Cash was really wired up this morning.

'Where do you want to go?' I asked.

'Symonds Street'll do. Coming in for the rehearsal tonight?'

I didn't answer. I was savagely tired of him and everyone. I hadn't even thought of the bloody band since last Friday. All I wanted to do was finish my painting, and the idea of another trip into the city was burning me up. The car was playing up again as well and every time I changed gear there was a graunch in the engine. I'd probably burnt out the clutch with that wild driving yesterday.

We drove in silence for a long time, but he was always hopeful.

'Are you?' He was holding onto the car door handle when I was cornering too fast, but staying stoical.

'Here. Get out here will you? I've just forgotten something I had to pick up,' I said and stopped the car unceremoniously at the lights by Hobson Street.

'Oh, this is good,' he said, collecting himself. 'I've got to get something here anyway.' Cash never took offence for long. Insults bounced off his tough little hide. 'Don't let it get to you, mate.'

'I'm not, Cash,' I lied. He gave a comical wave and darted off into the traffic, looking back now and then to see if I was watching him.

It was a relief to get to Sarah's office. She was sitting there among all her files and books, looking like a kind little girl in a fairy story. There was the familiar framed slogan on her wall that I always read admiringly: 'A large group of people must struggle to survive in order to sustain the few wealthy, who will always disdain them for their gift', and her immaculate pot plants. I could have cried on her shoulder.

We went straight down to the coffee bar on the first floor of her office building. It was called The Cellar or something like that and was a complete freeze frame of sixties hip, right down to the hessian on the wall and posters of the Lovin' Spoonful. The people who ran it were all middle-aged hippies with kind sloppy faces and the smell of patchouli in their clothes. We always went there.

'It's nice and comfortable here,' Sarah said, sitting down looking around her with a wonderful twinkling complacency. She'd bought me wholemeal muffins which I can't stand. She's one of the few people whose feelings I've never been able to hurt, so I tried to stuff the whole heavy, healthy mess into the back of my throat without tasting it.

'Glory, you don't look very well.'

'I'm not too good,' I said.

'Now, what's going on? Al's told me something, but you know what he's like on the phone. It was all basically in grunts and long meaningful silences, with heavy breathing. And then that woman Grace, I talked to her briefly at the police station. She was saying such fantastic things, it was hard to make any sense of it.'

I certainly didn't want to be reminded about Grace. I had a conscience about her. God knows what she'd think after the *Truth* article.

'It's a fantastic story,' I said gloomily. I don't know what's happening either, except some madwoman's trying to scare me, fuck up my life and kill me.'

There was a silence. I could see Sarah was anxious, not to mention incredulous, but trying to hide it for my sake. She had always seen herself as my protector, the good fairy who waved her wand and cancelled the harsh realities of the world which got in the way of my painting. She was like a Renaissance patron, she believed fiercely in my work. I had never had anyone like her in my life before, and sometimes it was a real

143

temptation just to slide into the comfort of it, especially now when things were closing in so fast. But I'd never had the stomach for any kind of dependency, however legitimate — it made me uneasy. I knew instinctively that I had to keep my reflexes sharp or I'd go under, and Sarah, pure as her motives were, could quite easily lull me at the wrong moment, out of sheer good nature. All the same I was grateful, and couldn't help playing up to her wicked sympathy. Her naivety always made me feel like being childishly gross and rough.

'I think we should start off with a proper statement. Just get it all down in writing. You want to come back up to the office and take a statement on the dictaphone?' She was unconsciously dropping into the tone she used for Rina. I recognised it instantly.

I said, 'Yes, if that'll help. I want to start legal action too.'

'Legal action?'

'Yes. I want to get *Truth* for this,' I said, savagely.

'Yes. I think that's important.' She paused. 'I wonder who gave them that story. It had the appearance of a real put-together job.'

'Roxy, that's who,' I said, choking on the last dry gollop of glutinous wholemeal, 'and probably Mitch. The cops. It could have been any number.'

'Do you want another one?' she asked, so formal we could have been at tea in an English garden.

'No thanks, Sarah,' I said. I felt sick again from forcing it down.

'She was a friend of yours, this Roxy?' asked Sarah delicately, not looking at me. She had acted for several of my friends in the past, including Cash, but she wanted to stay tactful.

'Yes. She wants to be at one with me in the grave.'

'I wish you wouldn't joke,' she said. Her face was genuinely quite pale. 'It sounds horrific.'

'It is. We're quite freaked out.'

'We?'

'Al and me. She's got this thing about me, she modelled for me for this series, and somehow she's flipped into thinking she's me. I've got inside her head. The whole thing, the pictures, all of it has just tipped her over.'

'Inside her head?'

'Look. All I know is she's completely nuts. I'm not a shrink. The smack's rotted out her brain, maybe she thinks I'm responsible for her crummy life, who knows? Since this has all happened, she acts like I've failed her in a big way. She's a fuckwit.'

'Did you quarrel or anything?'

'It's malice out of a clear blue sky. I've got a few enemies but never her. Bitchy yes, but my mate, my admiring fan. Never an enemy. Until a couple of days ago.'

'Christ,' said Sarah, awed. 'It's hard to believe.'

'I should take you to see her room.'

'But I don't understand. Why did you go anywhere near her?'

'I didn't know it was her at the time. I was trying to track down who kidnapped Rina.'

'Rina? What? When was this?' Her clear face was very solemn. 'My God, Glory, you're a fool not to get in touch with me straight away. Why in the world didn't you?' She'd never been so sharp with me.

'It seemed OK. I thought it was all under control until this business with Rina. And then the *Truth* article.' I hadn't thought of phoning Sarah since that last call. I couldn't even remember what day Rina was taken away.

'I'm getting in touch with the police,' she said. 'This all sounds like a set-up.'

I sat there, the coffee warming me. At least I was doing something official, but looking at Sarah's vulnerable face, I had my doubts about how successful it would be. Just talking about it with someone made me realise again what a bizarre tangle it was.

'Let me finish my tea,' she said, 'and then we'll go up and do the statement. I'll draft a letter to *Truth* as well. We're wasting time stuffing round here.'

I loved it when she tried to sound ordinary. Her street language always had inverted commas around it. I could tell by the stillness of her body in the chair that her brain was going like a computer.

'What about witnesses? Did anyone else see you? I tell you what. Grace's got a list of convictions as long as your arm. She's not a reliable witness as far as the cops are concerned.'

'Grace's alright,' I said.

'Isn't there anyone else?'

'Yeah. Patrick.' I realised that I hadn't got round to talking to Patrick yet. He had been avoiding me I noticed. Even the *Truth* article hadn't brought him out. 'Patrick,' I repeated. 'That zippy little Remuera kid? Art student? Fast lane Patrick? He didn't let on to the cops — I think Roxy scared him off.' I felt more cheerful for some strange reason. Talking to Sarah had in some mysterious way tipped the balance slightly — her class-nurtured certainties had affected me, even if it was only fleeting.

'I really don't know how you're coping with all this, Glory, and trying to get your paintings ready. I take my hat off to you,' she said emotionally, finishing off the last of her tea in her finicky little way.

'It's been very hard,' I said, drinking my coffee in big childish gulps. There was no doubt about it, the sympathy was finally going to my head. I was almost getting carried away. I said formally, to stem the tide, 'We'd better go. I've got to get back.'

Afterwards, driving down the motorway towards the Mt Wellington turnoff, the taste of the muffin was still clinging like a cobweb to my mouth and teeth. I felt lighter, easier in my mind about Roxy. It was probably Sarah's calming influence. I just didn't want to worry about it for a while, however misguided that was. Instead, I thought about the colour of the curtains in my painting — I wanted them to look like bandages at the window. I worked out all the different greys and sang all the way home, for my own private rehearsal.

9

The warmth had brought them all out, they lay on the grass out the back drinking quietly. The bulk of them, the sheer weight of equipment hanging off them, made them look like a herd of buffaloes basking in the sun, huge and shaggy and dangerous. One of the younger kids was perched up in the branches of the grapefruit tree, staring up into the leaves. His bare feet were wrinkled as a baby's. I could tell it was dole day by the pile of empty cans around them and the smell of dope in the air. Rina was there too, a little dot of colour in the middle, leaning trustfully against Al, her face solemn.

'Jeez, Glory, your clutch sounds stuffed. You probably done it when you and that joker did those wheelies on the lawn,' Kingi said, expansive with the beer. They all smiled secretly.

'Yes, I know,' I said. 'It was Cash as usual.'

Al said, 'You've had that many phone calls I come out here to get away from them.'

'Who?' I asked, sitting down in the long grass and taking a swig of his beer. It was a blue day, almost hot. There was a city smell of onion flowers and petrol in the air.

'Nigel. Three bloody times. Some jerk who reckoned you'd done in his daughter. Sarah. Grace. And a chick from the paper.'

'Take the phone off the hook,' I said. I had another drink. It was that *Truth* article of course. I felt really hunted, nervous. 'Can you? I'm going down to the studio and work. I don't want to see anyone.' I picked up Rina and hugged her. It was like a tidal wave ready to drown me. 'Gidday,' I said. She had a great smear of jam across her cheek and her ribbon was hanging on by a thread, like a floppy dead insect. I pulled it off.

She said, 'Where was you?'

'Up at Sarah's. How was school?' I desperately didn't want to know.

Rina wriggled in my arms, her body soft and smelling of grass and jam. 'Al picked me up,' she announced. 'He said, "Don't you go with no Roxy. Don't you go with no Roxy."' She imitated him solemnly. There was a silence. 'That Jason, he hit me and punched me and hit me.'

'You didn't let him, did you?' Moe asked concerned.

'Nah. I kicked him in the stomach.' They both fell silent. I had obviously interrupted a conversation.

'Sue reckons she saw Roxy hanging round this morning. By the workshop,' Al said, looking at me.

'What was she doing?' I could just see her face, looking over at the house.

'Nothing.'

'She'll probably fucking firebomb us next.' I started drinking in earnest. The idea of her being anywhere near us made me feel queasy. I didn't feel like working any more once I'd found that out. It was safer here with the boys in the warm sun than in my studio. 'Who reckoned I'd done in his daughter?'

'I called the cops,' Al said.

'You what?'

'I'm not having no fucking madwoman hanging round here. They go, "Are you laying a complaint?" I said not yet. This is for your information.'

'I seen her. For sure,' Moe said. 'She was up by them old bombs. In the grass.'

I didn't say anything. Al could see I was pissed off. I knew the cops were probably waiting for me to make a false move. I was reduced to staying quiet, keeping out of their orbit, and hoping that Roxy would hang herself. It was a feeble strategy, but I was too shell-shocked to attempt anything more ambitious. Now they probably thought I'd put Al up to it, and to them it was just more evidence of guilt. It was all going Roxy's way, facts or no facts. She had their confidence, she could tell them what she liked. If Moe was even half right they would know from long experience that she usually had good information for them. Here I was right in the sights, ex-wife of the deceased, last seen with the girl, crawling with crimmo associates, and with a kind loving friend into the bargain, a friend who found it painful to pass on these facts about me. Roxy was a show-woman, you'd have to be a jerk, an insensitive creep, not to believe her. Al ringing the cops was another liberty taken with my safety, another act which undermined my control of the whole thing. It was like driving a car with no gears, as I raced crazily down the road — all I could do was just miss certain death and try not to listen to the voices in my head.

'What did Sarah say?' Al asked. He wasn't taking any shit from me in front of his mates.

'She's taken a statement,' I said shortly. 'She's suing *Truth* for me. Plus she's talking to the cops again.' I realised now I was away from her seductive aura, that even Sarah with all her competence was simply known to the cops as another do-gooder young lawyer who would eventually settle down into some serious profit-making. In the meantime they probably didn't take her very seriously. She'd backed too many losers.

I lay back full length on the damp grass and stared up at the rusty old weatherboards of our house. There seemed nothing for it, but to lie there in the grass and get stoned. I had no energy to do anything else. All of a sudden even the idea of working seemed impossible — a flash of energy that had just drained out. I had started to feel out of it already.

Moe passed a joint, lying stretched out next to me like a pirate with his red matted hair and the white skin of his burly arms gleaming through the red fuzz. It was a dream moment, the murmuring of the boys among themselves, our two old houses above us, the traffic whining. I could see Rina lying on her back leaning her head on Al's stomach. She was picking at a bit of grass, her eyes dreamy.

As the dope took hold I started to float, softly. Moe's house looked like a parody of one of those innocent white-painted country homesteads you find in the wop-wops. Then when you looked closer you saw that its front verandah was skewed dangerously to one side, loaded down by festoons of drying passion-fruit vines, that there were gaping holes in the walls, and rough boards nailed over the windows. Someone had painted a giant face over the whole of one wall, with jug ears and brick-red cheeks — it had the crude power of a folk-demon, a malevolent effigy. Our two places looked comfortable, both sliding into the earth together. It seemed years that our households had been perched up here, on the edge of the wasteland, with nothing but factories and highways wherever we looked. This afternoon, though, for the first time, none of it seemed familiar.

'Did you say anything to her?' I asked Moe.

'Who?'

'Roxy. When you saw her up there?'

'Nah,' he said.

'Why not? You should have asked her what she was doing.'

'Not me,' said Moe. 'It's your business.' He rolled over on his back, luxurious.

'Well, you certainly seemed to know a lot about it,' I said.

He scratched at me roughly with his long toenail to shut me up. He didn't want the boys to know he'd been talking about anything. Some gang leaders got there by ferocity and sheer violence, others by the fact that they made the boys feel safe. Moe was one of these, and so the balance was more delicate. He needed respect, he had to make decisions about what was good for his boys and what wasn't.

'Gi' us a smoke,' he asked one of them.

'It's good stuff this dope,' Al said. 'Is it Coromandel?'

'Nah,' said Moe. He was still put out by what he saw as a breach of confidence, but I was already too lazy with the dope to do much about it. I tried to patch things up.

I said, 'I mean you certainly seemed to know a lot about her being here,' and burst into laughter. It was so weak. Even Moe had to grin reluctantly.

We lay there in the grass, companionable. The boys were at a slack period anyway, they were nearly all on the dole, and with the bad weather they spent most of their time in the house watching sport on telly or just sitting round. Our household was a bit of light relief for them.

'What are you laughing about?' Al asked, paranoid to the backbone as usual.

'You,' I said. 'You're like a pack of bloody dinosaurs. You're nearly extinct.'

'Oh, Glory's going nutty again,' Rina said resignedly and that made me laugh even more.

'You remember what I said,' Moe said austerely. 'The other day at the pub.'

The dope had addled my responses, and I had no means of knowing what he was really saying. It was hitting me like a soft blow to the stomach. I rolled over, hopelessly stoned. Sometimes at bad moments during a stone, my brain went into fast forward and then got stuck onto a groove at the same time, a revving up with nowhere to go. It felt like that then. It was overload. I was lying there, silent, trying to work it out when I heard a rustling in the grass just a few inches away. I lifted my chin up. There, in front of my nose, was a pair of gleaming leather shoes, a foot away from me. I thought straight away, the dees were coming. A senior detective. They've finally come to take me away. I felt cold and ready for them.

I lifted my chin further to look, and there he was, a little man gazing down at me.

'Excuse me, are you Glory Day?'

I sat up casually. No one moved.

'Yeah, she is.' said Rina. 'Want to make something of it?'

There was a ripple of deep-down enjoyment at this. From then on nothing could be too bad.

'Could I have a word with you?' he asked me. He averted his eyes from all of us as he spoke.

'Sure,' I said. I could see by now he wasn't a cop. He wasn't covering himself enough. He just stood there like a sleepwalker. The expensive suit he was wearing looked slightly too big for him.

'You knew my daughter. Marianne?'

I finally understood. I was being so slow.

'Yes. You're her father?' I felt relieved, at long last I had a chance to explain everything, reassure him, clear the whole thing up.

'I read the story in *Truth*.' He seemed a mild little man with that soft voice, but he had the blank look of a man with certain unalterable opinions about life. I usually kept up a distance around people like that and I should have known by the stillness in him that he didn't like me, but I was dangerously full of euphoria.

I motioned him to sit down, patting at the grass like the lunatic I had temporarily become.

'Have a glass of beer. I reckon it was brave of you to come up here,' I said. I was trying to put him at ease. There was a collective stir among the boys. They were like a herd of deer about to sheer off into the woods, half fascinated, half horrified. They never had contact with people like that usually and they were riveted. He sat down beside me.

'I don't drink, he said.

'I didn't exactly know her,' I said. 'I only met her at Mainstreet. She'd already taken an overdose, so me and another person took her up to hospital. Up to Casualty. We tried to save her life.' I was trying to clear the air.

'Is that right?' His voice was so soft I had to lean forward to catch it.

'Yes.' I said. 'That's what happened. I'm sorry. She was a lovely girl. I wanted to help her. She was like me when I was a kid.' This open admission was so out of character it surprised even me. It was the relief, the simple act of telling the facts to someone like Marianne's father which went to my head.

Looking back on it, it was a stupidly provocative thing to say. Weighed down as he was by grief and anger and righteousness, his worst suspicions confirmed by the sight of us sprawled out on the lawn, it was probably the last straw.

He got back up on his feet. His face was bulging and swelling redly as if his choked-up emotions had all finally burst to the surface. He even had tears in his eyes.

'I won't hear godless scum like you even talking about a

152

daughter of mine!' he spat at me.

'What?' For a moment I was genuinely startled. I had really thought that he believed me, and was as relieved as I was to know the truth. In my hazy state the sudden malevolent change in his face was like a hallucination, a terrifying, inexplicable transformation.

'But I didn't do it,' I said childishly.

'Why is he spitting?' asked Rina. I could tell she genuinely wanted to know. she wasn't just being smart.

I felt a laugh curl up in my stomach and spread. It was a glorious letting sensation — like wetting the bed when I was a kid and feeling the warm urine spreading slowly under my back. I fought it all back, the man had his dignity and his grief, for all his eerie certainties, and I wanted to show respect at least for Marianne's sake.

There was some sort of commotion around the corner of the house, but I was so slow with the dope and trying not to laugh I missed out on the reasons for it. The moments stretched, hung like threads over the grass, and I rolled in them like a great whale. The car engine idling below was like something breathing out bubbles under water, then it took off and went miles up beside me. My body felt huge and comfortable, I didn't even feel like talking to him anymore. Coming from round the corner I could hear a familiar voice.

'Tried to charge me thirty bucks! Newton to Mt Wellington. Prick.'

Teetering over the grass in her high heels, trailing perfume, came Grace all done up to the nines. She looked very angry. I glanced at her face with affection, it was such a relief to see her.

She stopped short, taking it all in.

'Well, who are *you* now?' Such a poisonous purr. I thought she was talking to me, until I realised with a glow of pleasure that she was talking to Marianne's father. I really liked the way she leapt into this new current with such energy. There was nothing neurasthenic about Grace. She had come to have a piece of me, but she knew where her duties lay. Mr Lucas looked at her as if she was a bad dream.

'He thinks I killed his daughter,' I said to help him out. I felt the hysterical laughter rising in my throat.

'Oh God. Are you her father? You poor thing.' Grace was extraordinary. She was the only person there who just took it all for granted. She was all sympathy. She genuinely appeared to have no idea of the antipathy she inspired in him. It made me realise it was no coincidence, her helping with Marianne that night. She was sorry for people in pain. It was like that. Come to give me hell, for all she knew being seen as an accessory to manslaughter or worse, here she was swaying on the damp grass in her high heels, patting him, her grim purpose forgotten. She imagined him stricken with grief, she genuinely wanted to comfort him.

She said gently, 'Glory and I meant nothing but the best for the wee kid. We tried to save her, but she was too far gone.'

The two of them were like people in a play, we didn't really know why they were saying those things but it was lovely to watch.

I lay there entranced by the little epiphanies of life, those charged moments when the great ponderous wheel of it ceased, and hung, in perfect balance, so still I could hear the hum of the universe. They were infinite those flashes, and full of light, and it seemed to me that Grace and I were bathed in the glow of love from the molten core of the world. As I watched, Grace's long flashy skirt with those hippie mirrors in it, spun and caught the light like great glass stars, points of light dancing on my retina. I watched them mesmerised, they were spilling like diamonds over the grass. The dope was shimmering in my brain, I felt it pulling me in all directions as I lay there bathed in ice. It seemed like Grace was trailing the little man for miles across the grass — distances and time hung in the air like great glistening threads, I watched delighted as she followed him and then they went out of frame and I leant back and closed my eyes.

Moe was back again, lying on the grass beside me as if he had never gone away, which was strange. I asked him, 'Did you put something in this dope?'

'Wouldn't you like to know,' he said, still terse with me. We were all so transfixed by the bizarre spectacle in front of us, even gang etiquette went down the drain in unusual times like this. They were usually into more sombre presentations, broken bottles rammed into soft flesh, rumbles in pub car-parks at closing time, vicious fights with secret slashes in the dark, macho storms in teacups. Their sensitivity to less conventional drama had still not been blunted by all the TV, though. I could tell they appreciated the light and shadow of the subtle nuances — there was a general feeling of respect among them once the bizarre couple had disappeared behind the house. Even the fact that they'd all stayed was in itself a sign of involvement. Al was lying in the grass laughing to himself, very very softly, like a child — he just couldn't seem to stop. Rina's head was bobbing up and down on his stomach but he didn't seem to mind. She was still stripping the piece of grass, her stubby little fingers clumsy with it. She looked so peaceful, the little man's words had gone right over her head. After a while though she asked, 'Why do you keep laughing for, Al?'

'Oh it's your mother. She's such a dag. It's funnier than a fight living with her. She calls Roxy nuts.'

I gave him a wide eye-flashing demure smile. I felt as if my eyes were full of light and sparkle, they were reflecting the sun in great shivers of light.

'Well, what do you reckon?' I asked. 'Did I do it?'

It was the most complete stone I'd ever experienced apart from smack. It was Moe's idea of cheering me up, and I was grateful to a point. It was a nice way of dealing with the killer father too as it turned out, but I couldn't even remember what had happened to Grace.

When I woke up in the studio it was cold and six o'clockish, the sky had turned bleak, and I had a terrible taste in my mouth. I got up groggily, I couldn't even remember how I had got into bed. The rush-hour traffic was rocking the house and outside I could see the dwarfish men who owned the factory workshop next door pottering around in the half-dark like two old trolls, creaking at the doors and hammering things in the grass. No one was around at our place, the house was silent and dreary. I felt so blotted out, it was like a bad hangover.

I found my Rina in the kitchen, eating some dry Weetbix and dropping most of it on the floor. She looked so little and defenceless in the dusk, chawing away and rustling. The face she turned up to me was unclouded as a summer day, there was no reproach, only pleasure and relief at seeing me awake. I hugged her and her little body felt chilled through.

'Here, Rina,' I said, 'here,' and hugged her close, her bird bones dear to me as my own. 'How long have I been asleep?'

'Hours and hours,' she said relaxed again now that I was back to take over. 'Can I have them sausages in the fridge for tea?'

I wanted to banish all the shadows and fill the kitchen with light and warmth and fragrant smells of sausages frying. The small mouse shadow in the kitchen had got me on the raw, I knew what that was like — being a kid alone in a cold house. I was still so sensitive from the dope, I couldn't stand it. I perched her up on the bench to watch me cook. We turned the radio on and it blatted cheerfully.

'You were funny,' she said wrinkling her nose at the memory. 'You kept laughing and being silly to Nigel.'

'Nigel?' I stopped peeling the potato appalled. There was a memory tugging at me somewhere like a long ago dream.

'You kept saying to Grace,' and she mimicked perfectly, 'warm him, warm him with your love.' Rina rolled her eyes, pursing up her little mouth. 'Al and me, we moved away. He said Glory's gone bananas, let's get out of here.' Looking at me in her perfect innocence to see if I got the joke.

Warm him with her love? I nearly cut my finger with the vegetable scraper. 'I said that? Hell, Rina, you're sure you're not bullshitting? What were Moe and them doing?'

'They kept laughing,' Rina said reminiscently. 'Moe kept hitting his legs and laughing and laughing.'

'Did that little man go?'

'I dunno,' she said losing interest. 'I'm hungry.'

I gave her a piece of bread and butter. 'No more after that. We'll have tea soon.' We could both go back into our easy roles and she was safe. The smell of the sputtering sausages spread like a promise and sure enough I heard some movement in Al's room. He came in with such a sly grin on his face I was mortified.

'I've never seen you like that,' he said. 'Never.' He sat down at the table absent-mindedly taking Rina's dry little foot in his hand and stroking it. 'You're bloody cold, Rina. Go and put something on your feet for Chrissake.' He sat there smiling to himself drawing it out. I went on poking the sausages, waiting.

'Don't you want to know?' he finally had to ask. I always won in a contest of wills with Al — he was too nice to hold out against me.

'Come on. Rina's already told me the worst.'

'You were such a sloppy old cow,' he said meditatively. 'We were all cracking up, even Nigel in the end. You kept saying how beautiful Grace was. You said she had a pure heart about ten bloody times. She was a bloody dag. She was saying, not that pure deary, and trying to get you to sit down. You kept on smiling, crooked sort of. You wanted Nigel to learn from her. In the end Nigel went home, just to shut you up. You were whacked. Your eyes were all rolling and you were smiling like a weirdo.'

It was one of the longest speeches I'd ever heard him make, but the whole thing had obviously really tickled him.

'Do you want some sausages?' I didn't even want to talk about it. It sounded so gross, quite apart from the vulnerability of it in front of Moe and his mates.

'Yeah. Nigel said to tell you he doesn't bear any grudges. He knows you're under strain.'

'Well, that's bloody big of him,' I said. We all sat down to eat sausages and salad and mashed potato.

'We've got some icecream in the deep-freeze compartment,' Al said.

'I seen your knickers too,' Rina said conversationally, her mouth full.

'Yes. You were lying on the grass.' Al suddenly burst into one of his manic laughs. 'It was bloody funny. Moe and the boys were pissing themselves. They don't like Nigel. You wanted them to hold hands. You was putting his fucking hand on top of hers. Real sly you were. It was a treat, Glory, a bloody treat.'

'Was Grace alright?' I asked, shamefaced.

'Oh, she thought it was gross. She knew what to do. She was really professional. She was much cooler about it than Nigel, but she was making faces.'

'What's a fessional?' asked Rina.

'Someone who gets paid a lot of money for doing fuck-all,' I said real nasty. 'Want some more?'

We ate in silence after that. We were all hungry and the simple meal was delicious. I still felt wiped out, that kind of dreamy faraway feeling you had when you hadn't slept for days.

We finished the meal and I read a story to Rina. It was one of her library books about some wicked witches who lured a little girl into their cave to do all their work for them. I could tell Rina was scared by it. She asked nonchalantly, 'Do those witches live in our land?'

'No, there's no such people in New Zealand,' I said. 'They live somewhere else.'

'Where?' she asked quickly.

'A long way away. Over the other side of the world.'

'You're a bloody witch, Glory,' said Al. He was washing the dishes, he looked homely against the sink.

'No she isn't.' Rina was quite disturbed by the thought. She settled into my lap further, gazing at me with her blank eyes.

'She's a good witch, Rina. There are good witches and bad witches. In fact, very few witches are bad. They're usually just women who want to live on their own.'

'Is Roxy a bad witch?' Rina asked. There was silence in the room.

'No,' I said. 'She's just a bit funny here,' knocking Rina's little head gently with my knuckles, pretending to knock on her door.

'That's what them girls said,' Rina said, satisfied about the witches.

'What did they say?'

'They said — you're a bit funny up there. Up here.' She touched her head with her knuckles in a clumsy imitation of me.

'You tell me who said that and I'll knock their fucking blocks off for them,' Al said, upset for her. He was picking out the globules of fatty food left in the bottom of the sink — bits of potato, sodden lettuce leaves. 'You've got more up there than any of those bastards. Don't let them give you any shit.'

'Nah,' said Rina, picking her nose.

'And the little girl killed the witches and ran home. The end.' I said, suddenly tired.

Rina looked suspicious but didn't say anything, it wasn't in her nature. She got up and went out, and after a while I could hear Bruce Springsteen thundering on in her bedroom.

'She'll fuck that cassette.' I made a cup of tea while Al was cleaning up and we sat at the table to drink it.

'You want to watch out for them kids at school, Glory. Rina's the only one there different. I reckon they pick on her. She's got such a soft heart.'

'She's got to go to school somewhere. They're OK, the teachers. They like her.'

'Nah, she's alright. But I reckon you've just got to watch it.'

'You know what she told me yesterday? She reckons you're as handsome as Prince Charles.'

'Prince Charles? She's a hard case that kid.' Al was genuinely delighted. He drank his tea. Rina was an endless source of surprise to him.

I said, 'You got any money? There's the power bill.'

'I'm getting my dole tomorrow. Plus the back pay. They had to pay for the weeks they stopped it? It was a mistake. Could be a couple of hundred bucks. So we'll be right for a couple of weeks.'

'I hope I sell all those paintings.'

'How much does Nigel make? You know what he said last night? He reckons the artist has to pay for his own booze at the opening. Miserable, eh. That guy makes a killing out of you — he could pay for the booze. It wouldn't hurt him, the prick. He's driving a fucking BMW — he can't be exactly broke. He's the sorta guy who's always saying he's short.'

'I know,' I said. I was surprised at his vehemence. It was

159

obviously one of Al's long-standing grudges.

'Well, Moe and me'll bring the flagons. Fuck him.'

They must have decided on that when I was rolling around pissed and stoned and monstrous. Glory the Grotesque badgering that poor bitch Grace and embarrassing my daughter, lame brain as I was.

'Thanks,' I said. It was a mistake. Al hated being thanked for anything. That kind of intensity threw him off dangerously and with his usual paranoid acuteness he knew I was moved by his clumsy offer. He got up abruptly, his skull flaming.

'Well, I'm just going down to the shed.' Mutter mutter.

I sat at the table drinking my tea and smoking a roll your own. The meal and tea had made me normal again, I felt a physical stillness for the first time in days. Drinking the second cup, looking at the wall, I thought that at least I had located the enemy. I knew who she was, even if I didn't know why she was trying to kill me. I decided to work all day the next day whatever happened, there was nothing more constructive I could do.

Just settling in at the kitchen table, getting used to the idea, relaxing into it was an effort, and when the phone rang again I felt such a rush of adrenalin it scared me. It was Sarah, hyped up to the eyeballs. She'd been at it since I saw her this morning and what she told me only confirmed my own worst scenario. It turned out she'd even interviewed Patrick who had been really scared and said he didn't want to be involved. Neither of us commented on this, it was only a secondary irritation. Sarah had been concentrating on finding out about Marianne, and even though her main source of information was the cops, and they weren't very friendly, what she had was enough.

Apparently she had been a newcomer to the drug world, started hanging around about six months ago when homebake first hit the streets. She was one of those young kids who got hooked straight away, out of a sense of drama or glamour, the heroin being just an excuse. Anyway she'd picked up a good, raging habit. She was involved with the big dealers, doing small-time courier work and having sex with them to get her five hundred bucks a week. She was still fresh and beautiful, it was easy to see why they were prepared to pay for a while, at least until her skin went bad.

The police told Sarah that in Weasel's last session with them, he had mentioned all this in passing, probably to cover himself. He was starting to go so gaga he'd almost outlived his usefulness as a police informer, most of his stuff was suspect. Anyway, his status in the drug world would have been about zilch by then — no one would have told him anything. The cop thought he was still doing a bit of dealing though, and that was why Marianne had hung round, a honey bee for the honey. Weasel had even tut-tutted about her — said it was sad such a young thing from a good family was going down the drain so fast — he had been quite moralistic apparently. The cops in fact knew from another source that he was making her have sex with him when she wanted cheap smack. She was obviously getting desperate dealing with an old derro like that. She probably had no idea of her market value and was being ripped off all the time.

I stayed noncommittal to Sarah, though I was grateful to her for the facts. With her usual tact she stopped talking about it when she heard in my voice that I'd had enough. We said good-night to each other, carefully, like old dear friends — both of us too disturbed to go into it any more.

It was obvious that Marianne must have been there when Roxy and Mitch came over. They'd found out Weasel was informing on them, and they were paying a little visit late at night. No doubt Roxy had had to tread her way through a mine-field keeping her own informing activities from Mitch, but she was in her element with that sort of tricky situation. Marianne was just another problem she had to deal with as well. They didn't expect a witness, it was a simple as that. I could imagine them forcing their way into that horrific room, and witnessing the piteous sight of the child kneeling in front of Weasel, her soft head bent over his cock. They would have started in on him with no mercy. Weasel would have caved in straight away, trying to do deals, whining, offering up Marianne as a diversion. Mitch had always been turned on by whimpering young girls — the air in the room would have been muddy with sex and death, his sweat when he was excited. Roxy, fired up with the power of it all, getting carried away, would have gone too far with her bullying. And then, once Weasel fell over, she would have been the one to think quickly and finish him off with a shot. The packet of smack, lying on the table for Marianne once she'd paid for it, would have been too much of a temptation for Roxy.

I had thought about this every night before I went to sleep since the time I'd seen Roxy's room; and even before when I did my paintings I could see it happening in front of my eyes scene by scene, inexorable, like a video nasty. Sarah had only confirmed the worst scenario.

The four of them milling in the dark room, Weasel's whining, his muddy pathetic death, Roxy taking Marianne's arm and asking her if she wanted a shot too. Marianne terrified to death, still half dressed, putty in their hands. Roxy and Mitch monstrous shadows in the death room, then Marianne's soft white arm gleaming like a flower while she held it ready for Roxy's needle, terrified into submission, half wanting it. All of them shit scared, death all round, Roxy's heavy breathing, like an animal, Weasel's limp body at their feet.

The smell of the room, suffocating in the dark, the three of them jostling, sweating with fear and excitement. I imagined she'd somehow got away, broken free while Roxy and Mitch were whispering together in the dark. And then Roxy was out after her, fast as a tiger, chasing her stumbly woolly little prey through the streets. Up K. Road, down Queen Street — there was never any question for either of them that Marianne would get away, little broken mouse feebly dragging itself away from the cat.

And Roxy had one of her strokes of genius, that brilliant instinct for split-second decisions which always kept her on top. Part impelled by her obsessions, partly by a half-formed plan in her head, she watched Marianne stumble past Mainstreet. She remembered I was singing there, and took Marianne, fumbling and faltering, already dying, with only the hidden Shorty as witness, into Mainstreet, helping her up the passage to bring her home to mother.

162

10

Afterwards, much later, after doing some work on the painting to try and get myself in a relaxed frame of mind, I gave up and just sat in the studio, a glass of wine beside me. My mind was too overloaded with the story of Marianne's life and death to think seriously. Instead, the image of her father's blank face kept coming up like a comic strip. His spiteful rage, Grace's kindness, his tense little body were images which somehow made his daughter's mind clearer to me. I could see that Marianne had had to be pretty extreme just to remain viable in face of his confusions.

The *Truth* article had meshed so perfectly with his official views of the world that he would find it hard to let me go, my manner had only fed his prejudices. It was probable he had treated his own daughter with the same injustice. The tone of the man went a long way towards explaining the sheer desperation of her acts, the childish air she hadn't been able to cut out of her repertoire right up to her death.

Sitting there, weighed down by the knowledge of it all, in the false clarity of late night brooding, with the dope and booze still circulating busily, I suddenly saw a way out. It was a magic idea. I would go and see Marianne's parents. It seemed the obvious thing to do. The picture of Roxy in Weasel's room was too potent for inaction on my part. I had to do something. I could let them know what really happened and stop her father in his tracks. I could sic them on to Roxy, turn all his driving force against her instead of me. It wold be one less fanatic after me, I thought to myself with great reasonableness. It would also help me to lay Marianne's ghost, if I could track her down, find out where she came from. A friendly visit would solve a whole lot of problems in one hit. It was the half-drunken thinking of someone with her back to wall, and I recognised it even then, but it was my old need for action, and I wasn't in the mood to question it.

Putting on my Dominion Road fur, I looked up her address in the phone book and left the house. Within ten minutes of thinking of it, I was back into the car again, toiling along the freeway, awake as a bird, the chill of the pre-dawn nipping at my face as I drove, the all-night rock on Radio Hauraki giving me a false sense of the rightness of things.

By the time I got there of course, serious doubts had already started to creep in. And when I saw the house, one of those monstrous old white two-storeyed Epsom villas, immaculate, I nearly turned and went back. The reality of it was daunting, with the garden clipped down so far it was barely alive, the straight concrete path gleaming white in the shadows so clean you could eat off it. But I went on, although by that time it was out of pride.

The front door was comfortingly crass though, as if they had temporarily forgotten who they were supposed to be. Fake oak panelling, an antique English lamp set in wrought iron brackets and clean brass knocker. In my heightened state I half expected to see snow. It was only when I knocked that it occurred to me it was very late to go visiting people like this.

There was no reaction inside, the great dark tombstone of a house slept on, forbidding. I knocked loudly again and waited. I noticed a white square fitting neatly into a bracket on the door. It was a novelty message pad. When I bent closer I could read the printed heading: 'If we're not home when you call, leave us a message. We'd hate to miss out on you.' There was a picture of a smiling woman in curlers for some reason. Next to the pad there was even a little neatly sharpened pencil in a plastic holder. It looked as if it had never been used. I wanted to write something comforting, but before I had time to pull the little pencil out, the hall light came on behind the frosted-glass panels.

'Who's there?' a trembly female voice called. 'Who's there?'

I said, 'Hello, Mrs Lucas. Don't worry, it's alright. I'm a friend of Marianne's. I just wanted to talk to you.' There was a long silence.

'It's very late. Come back tomorrow. Father's not here.' The voice was so frightened and crushed and tearful I wanted to see her, even for a minute.

'Please. Open the chain and have a look, if you're worried. It's important.'

There was another long silence, and then the sounds of the chain and the door being opened very slowly as she obeyed me. I could only see one eye and a sharp angle of cheek as she peered out, then the door opened unexpectedly further still against the chain and it was Marianne's mother, unmistakable by the huge eyes — the only softness, in a face so eroded and dry it seemed fleshless.

'Who are you?' she asked, still keeping the door only seconds away from a slam.

'I'm Glory Day. I came to tell you how your daughter died.' It was ridiculous talking like that, at that hour of night, but I couldn't back down now.

'You're the one in *Truth*,' she said. 'You're the one who gave her the drugs. How dare you come here?' The door slammed in my face and I could hear her weeping on the other side.

I raised my voice desperate for her to hear me. 'Mrs Lucas, I tried to save your daughter's life. I never even knew her before. I just wanted to tell you she died with someone looking after her.' It came out like that, it was what I had always wanted to tell her. But now that I was here, in the gloomy depths of Epsom, it all seemed completely irrelevant. This woman had other preoccupations, someone telling her that meant nothing beside her grief and shame and dread of the world. It was definitely a miscalculation, the whole expedition. It made me realise I was in another planet from these people, and that I was starting to make serious misjudgements.

She was calling out, her voice muffled, hysterical with malice towards me.

'You tell that to the police! You tell that to the police! I hope they lock you up and throw away the key!' Carried away by her own daring and her own grief, her voice had lost the genteel hush and become a sharp street whine. I recognised the ring of it, it was like home. She'd obviously come up in the world as well as me.

'You'll find out it's true, Mrs Lucas,' I said. 'I don't blame you for not trusting me, but you'll find out it wasn't me.'

'Clear orff,' she called, 'clear orff, or I'll call the police!' You could tell she was the sort of woman who had a very intense mental life inside her four walls, who gave all her energies to guarding it from outside opinion, keeping up appearances, holding back the normal disorders of family life by sheer force of will.

It was hard to imagine a child like Marianne fitting into that mausoleum, the sort of life she had eked out with the father commuting between God and his own earthly temptations, and the mother, crazed by him, turning the air sour with clenched gentility. It was all such a fuck-up I didn't want to leave without somehow retrieving things.

'Good night, Mrs Lucas. I'm sorry to wake you. I hope you remember what I said.'

She laughed, she was half mad with it all.

'Wake me? I never sleep.'

I went down the path heavy-hearted, full of remorse. As I drove away stone sober and clear-headed I cursed myself for even going there. The frozen house and garden were worse than I'd ever imagined, and on top if it I'd just upset Mrs Lucas for nothing. She would never have listened even if she had believed me. People like me didn't even enter her calculations. I was too close to the bone for one thing; for another, she had her own prejudices to conserve. How could anyone believe me anyway?

As I drove home, my mind wandered away from the pain of the situation, in sheer self-defence. I started thinking of a painting by Robin White that I've always liked. It was of her mother standing in front of a suburban house. The tone was very serious, but full of light and painted with such careful love it made me envious.

The Lucases' house was begging for a painting as well — it

would be white and clean, but so full of foreboding it would vibrate off the canvas.

When I finally struggled awake the next morning, there was an acid feeling in my stomach as if the disturbances in my blood had lain there all night. I was aching, and my eyes were stony, I had obviously been fighting off demons all night, or running through gorse over hard ground. My heart was still thudding from the exertions of the night, but opening my eyes gave me no more relief. There they all were around me, those paintings of mine, my sleeping kid, the room where I worked and slept, but even this careful comeliness, the marvels of my life, could not give me the usual protection.

All my surroundings were saturated with a level of anxiety that morning, they were like a jolt of electricity straight to the heart — there was nothing neutral to rest my eyes on. Sometimes in the past when I'd been thrashing myself or taking too much dope I had the same anxious feeling, and when I was a kid life was like that all the time, so it was nothing new. I'd learnt from an early age that this diffused anxiety meant nothing was safe, it was a clear warning to me of new dangers.

I stayed still among the rumpled blankets, staring at the wall and trying to think. For once I didn't even want to get out of bed, my huge old bones felt cumbersome under the sheets, weighed down by the dangers of the day. The bush singlet I was wearing was about the only comfort, it was full of my own smells, the creases of my body, like a second skin. Lying there, blank, I thought of the cuddly I used to carry with me when I was small. I would rub my knuckles so delicately against the cloth that I could feel the soft tips of the threads set up their own little stirring against my skin, a delicious caress. As a kid I sniffed and stroked the softness of it till it fell into rags — my magic talisman against the troubles around me. I hadn't thought of it for years.

It was Roxy of course who was paralysing me like this. It was a bad sign that I was reduced to calling on old passive childhood comforts to magic her away, but I suppose I had to use what was available. There was the same terrible pleasure in thinking of her as I had when I was trying to get a scrap of meat out of my back tooth. She stayed there, stuck, fermenting, out of reach, cushioned in my most intimate recesses, and there I was, a huge old baby, whiffs of fear coming off me like smoke, reduced to sniffing hungrily at my own clothes for solace.

Not only that, but I was allowing a classic paranoid obsession to creep up slowly on me — that it was in fact me who had set the whole thing up, that I had fatally influenced Roxy and set her dancing just by the force of my own personality, my paintings, my past life. It reminded me ominously of a man I knew who said he controlled the weather, and smiled this crazy smile at me once when it was sunny. It was so freaky I hated it at the time. And here I was almost lurching into the same frame. I knew there were limits, that I couldn't lie there and let myself drift into it, or I'd be gone, so with a great effort of will I got out of bed. For a start there was Rina snorting away beside me, a bath was next on the agenda for me to wash away the sweats of it, then maybe a beer. I recognised that I should take things one at a time, my nerves were too stretched for much more stimulation. I went into the bathroom to run the bath and when I came back Rina was awake staring passively at the ceiling.

'Do you want a bath too?' I asked her, but she wrinkled her nose no. I knew there'd been too much for her to take in recently as well; I sometimes saw her slow little brain being bombarded into craters like the moon. I wondered what strange torpid pictures crossed her mind as she lay and thought about things — I gave her a kiss.

'You go back to sleep, Rine,' I told her, 'forget about school.'

The bath was delicious, the water creeping silkily over my skin like a blessing. I just lay there watching the huge white islands of my body, the slop of my belly glimmering magnificently, trying to think of nothing. There was a knock at the door, and just by twisting my head and looking through two lots of frosted glass I could see it was Nigel, wearing sunglasses. Not a good sign.

'Coming!' I bellowed, but Rina had already opened the door to him. Before I could move she'd ushered him into the bathroom. They both looked down at me for a second, Rina loving, Nigel horrified. The female odours, the overpowering mist of water and gunk, my whale body and female hair floating on the greyish water must have been a terrible revelation to the poor man. I just caught one glimpse of his white, terrified face and it passed out of my vision in a blur. I finished soaping luxuriously, but for some reason I felt slightly more cheered up. I took my time because he'd probably fainted outside in the hall anyway. Nigel was the sort of guy who only appreciated human nakedness in paintings.

'Coming!' I yelled, just to observe the courtesies, pulling myself up with a great whoosh. There was no sound outside. There was only Al's dressing-gown shoved under the bath to wear — it was a bit pongy and dusty but I gave it a slash of Jeyes fluid which was all I could find. I even liked my face in the mirror — my colour was high with a feverish flush and my eyes were alive. It was probably sheer adrenalin by now.

Nigel was sitting outside on the verandah with Rina beside him. She was earnestly ear-bashing him about something. Probably school. He was leaning back with his eyes closed trying to avoid Rina's eyes I could tell. She was gazing into his face intensely. She'd put her hair up into a pigtail on the top of her head, and was swathed in a ragged old dress of mine which was her favourite dress-up because of the sequins. Sometimes I could read Nigel's mind — he was thinking dramatically to himself, 'Is it really worth it?' He opened his eyes, caught sight of me and closed them again.

'God you gave me a fright. I thought it was a bloody great slug. You were so white.' He shuddered, genuinely disturbed.

I settled beside him in the weak sun, my hair dripping pleasantly down my warm bare shoulders. I even lit a roll your own. I was prepared to give him a half-hour. There was a couple of bottles of Steinie on the verandah as well.

'Whose are those?'

'Don't inrupt. I was telling Nigel a story,' Rina said.

'I bought them. I swear I don't know why, Glory. Yesterday I was met by an amazing apparition. I'll never forget it as along as I live. You, out of your head on some disgusting substance, wallowing and — forgive me for saying so — revolting, and a hooker you picked up from a massage parlour or something. I mean God, Glory, you could have caught something from her just by inhaling. You kept forcing me on her almost physically. You were soaking wet for some sordid reason, and insane. It was like being greeted by a huge dripping bull. In front of all those men. It was a nightmare. Never in my whole sordid connection with you, Glory, have I ever had to undergo such an ordeal. I don't even know why I'm telling you. You don't even remember do you? Do you?' He was determined to rub it in. Another Glory story to tell his friends. It was hard to tell with Nigel, he was so theatrical, but chances are he probably enjoyed it for all I knew.

'Oh, cut the crap, Nigel. You'd be bored out of your brain without me. I'm your draw card — I'm the only mileage you have in that sheltered little upper-class life you lead. You're so bored with all those snooty dinners and parties.'

'So much stereotyping, Glory. So early in the morning. What a cliché view of my life. Still, what can one expect from a fucking social defective? I might have known I wouldn't get an apology.'

'Alright. I'm sorry,' I said.

We drank some beer. After a while he said, 'Is Al here?'

'I don't know. I haven't seen him.'

'Don't you ask about Al. That's not your business, Mr Nigel,' said Rina. It was so out of the blue even Nigel had to crack a smile.

'Alright, Glory. Enough of these pleasantries. I got a phone call. From your little friend.'

'What little friend?' I had so many of them it was hard to even guess.

'That man who was so charming yesterday. That guy with the druggie kid. The druggie kid's father. You know.'

'Oh him. Not him again. Jesus Christ. How did he find you?'

'Easy. Just rang a few dealers.'

'OK. What did he want?'

'He was trying to get me to cancel the exhibition. He said you were a known drug dealer and a killer. He said it was a moral outrage for me to encourage your vile art. He said he was going to get in touch with the owners of the building who are personal friends of his, and fuck up my gallery lease. He described you as the queen of the underworld with connections right across the board. What else?' He pretended to think, just to string it out. 'Oh yes, he said he was in hourly contact with the police and it was only a matter of time before they swooped and cleaned up the whole network of poofters and druggies you surround yourself with.'

'Is that all?'

'Don't joke, Glory. This has gone well beyond a joke.'

'I can't do anything about him. I've got too many other things to worry about.'

'Well you do attract them, dear. It's your fucking aura. You seem to be attracting every serious psychopath in Auckland. When your agent starts getting threatening calls, it's going over the top.'

'That says something about you,' I said shortly. I was on a very short fuse. 'Did you apologise?'

'No. I said I'd be in touch with the police over what I considered was a threatening call.'

'You what?' I was impressed in spite of myself.

'I rang the cops too,' said Nigel, carried away by the flattery. 'They gave me short shrift, but at least the call will be logged — it would be evidence if it came to it. No flies on me, Glory. Unlike you, I've covered myself.'

'Get off my back, Nigel,' I said. The beer tasted lovely going down. It was the first I'd had for what seemed ages.

'Now listen. I'm not the staunch type. I'm not a gang member or a crim sworn to loyalty with a blood pact or whatever tacky things they do. I've never ever just stuck with someone through thick and thin, and you'd be the last person I'd made an exception for. I do not have the plodding bovine loyalties of the working class. So tell me. Can you just answer me without going into one of your animal rages? Was it really you?'

'Do I look like a murderer? A murderess?'

'Yes,' he said. 'In that bloody bath you looked as if you could swallow a man whole.'

There was a silence. We both sat for a minute to recover for the next round. It was unseasonably warm that morning. The grass was so long now that there were wild daisies in it — a real meadow of irises and onion flowers and paspalum. Al was over on the next-doors' verandah trying to feed the dogs as they snapped and snarled around him. The traffic hummed up a storm with the nine o'clock rush hour in full force.

'As a matter of fact, I don't really think you did it,' he said. 'You have many serious drawbacks, Glory, but there are some things still sacred to you. I know you're a woman of unimpeachable integrity.'

I just grunted. The conversation was the usual precarious balance of insult and ingratiation, and I had a lot of things on my mind already.

'Well, who's trying to frame you then?' he asked.

'Roxy. The one I smacked when you came on one of your innumerable visits.'

'Oh charming. Innumerable are they? Don't imagine for a moment, Glory, these innumerable visits as you call them are a pleasure. I never know what's going to hit me in the face next. It's like — walking into the offal floor at the freezing works.' Nigel always took offence. It was one of the irritating things about him.

'Offal floor?'

'Just an image. An image.' He couldn't resist it. 'You know, earthy, wholesome, vile.' There was a silence.

'Well, what do you want? I've got work to do. I can't do anything about Mr Lucas, he's another nutter. Another loony parent.'

'Fair enough, Glory. I'd be the last to stop you from work. Roxy, eh? A wonderfully poisonous lady.'

I was surprised. I thought he never noticed things like that, he was so busy scoring points off everyone I always had the idea that his immediate environment was a closed book to him. In any case I was sick to the bones of it. All I wanted to do was shut myself in my room and work. I needed hours of sweat just to roll it all off my back. Nettie's death, for instance, was still lying on my heart undigested, I didn't even have time to think about her. I watched Rina mooning away, pushing in amongst the grass, her little pigtail waggling.

A taxi was stopping at the bottom of the drive, and there was Grace getting out, as usual arguing with the driver.

'Oh God,' said Nigel. 'Is that her again? Who is she?'

Grace came up the path. She thrust her chin close to me. I could see the stubble on her cratered skin, her huge bloodshot sad sad eyes. Her teeth were brown, she looked blown, lacquered, tired by the stress of it all. Even her dress under the fake leopard skin coat was dirty. The yellow polish on her nails was cracked.

'Well, are you stoned today, Glory?' She didn't acknowledge Nigel's presence. 'No? OK. Tell me what's goin' on, Glory. I've rung up and visited you and you won't even speak to me.' She faced me, hands on hips, hair glinting in the sun. 'I read the *Truth*. Even my mates are looking at me sideways.'

'It wasn't me,' I said calmly for the second time in an hour. 'Or you.'

She wouldn't even sit down.

'Oh, I know it's not me, dear. No worries. I'm quite clear on that score. That's not the worry. I'd like you to tell me what's going on, because I don't like being taken for a sucker.'

'I'm being framed. By Roxy. I told you before on the phone. You've never met her. She's a junkie. She kidnapped Rina, she's got the ear of the cops, she's out to get me. She's obsessed.'

'I knew it,' she said. 'Trixie told me. She said you were fucking mad. Me and my big mouth. Why did I ever get involved? You come bursting into my life all twenty stone of you, with a face like the back of a bus and a dead kid strapped to your tits — you've involved me up to the eyeballs in fucking ODs and drugs — they've beaten me and arrested me and you leave me to face it all while you piss off on some country jaunt. Look at you. Sitting in the sun up on Vinegar Hill chatting to your boyfriend, never a fucking care in the world. Not to mention sicking me onto that little shit. He looks like he'd take all night to get it up. No money mentioned either.' She was genuinely momentarily scornful as she looked over at Nigel, but her attention shifted back to me almost straight away. 'No explanations either. And then to be met by you yesterday was like a horror movie. I don't trust you, Glory. You're too much into macho for my liking. For a woman. As soon as some arsehole talks to me about being framed I know to get out. Fast. It's the last resort of a maniac. And stoned, you're a monster. A fucking monster. See, I'm starting to doubt the whole thing. You probably roped me in to frame me more like it. Lugging that kid up Queen Street. I'm such a fucking sucker — that's always been my trouble. You wouldn't lug your dying grandmother to the toilet, much less some little tart of a junkie.'

She had completely lost her nerve, and I couldn't think of what to say. Her rage and fear, the smell of her was over-powering.

Nigel said, 'I'm Nigel by the way. If you ladies are interested.' We both turned to stare at him.

'I know, sweetie,' Grace said offensively. 'You gave me a lift and saved me from myself.'

Nigel got up. He was seriously offended. Talk about sex was never to his liking. He had been brought up sheltered.

'Please keep in touch, Glory. We have exactly two days to go,' he said sternly, and stalked off. He looked comical, on his high horse like that. I was relieved to see him go. His busyness and petulance were getting me down. He reminded me of a fox ter-rier yapping and yelping at a wolf — he never knew how far to push the great dim shape in front of him.

The thing about Grace was that I'd gone wrong right from the beginning. I shouldn't have gone over to her place the next day, I probably shouldn't even have got a lift with her on the Friday night. I had intruded into her life in a big way. You could tell Grace liked the peaceful life, she had her own circuit, a bit of dope, a bit of booze, business, gossip, but she kept herself to herself. Even if most of the girls she worked with were using regularly, she didn't want it herself. Maybe some recreational coke, her morning smoke, but nothing more. There was a weary intelligence in the way she'd organised her life. Not only that but you could see by the way she treated Marianne's father that Grace was a classy whore, it was almost a vocation for her. In the face of huge odds she'd carved something out for herself. My intrusion had shaken the precarious balance of her life, her carefully constructed ways of getting through.

I said, 'I'm sorry, Grace. I never meant you to get so involved. It happened.'

'Sorry? Sorry is nothing. That doesn't pay the fucking bills. Taxis, lawyers. Not only that. In the pub they're starting to talk behind my back. Some of them won't believe it was all lucky lucky chance. Funny. The cops don't either. And I'm starting to think the same bloody way about you. Look at all the coincidences. You knew that junkie, you knew the other druggie who was blown away — who don't you fucking know? Then I find out Mitch Nathan is your ex. That shit bucket. Tortures people for information, but goes beyond the line of duty. His thing is blood-stained motel rooms, and blown-out zombies brain damaged by baseball bats. You know? Travelling with him as well the day after. You had a dying aunty? Went 400 k in five hours for some old kuia. Half of these crims are your exes in fact. I mean the only bloody reason I helped you and that kid was because I thought you were a dyke. That's the real reason. And here you are, hetero as all come out and crim into the bargain.'

She was starting to invent grievances in her anxiety, she was almost lamenting, standing there, buckling at the knees under the stress of it. I knew I had insulted her, fucked her over quite inadvertently and she was helpless in face of it — for all her personal power. She was as trapped as I was. She was now half believing she'd seen through me, and the worst of it was that in the beginning we'd taken a liking to each other. I was just hoping she was using this anger adrenalin for keeping her spirits up and that she still recognised deep down I was innocent. It was almost as if she too had been talking to Roxy — but I tried not to stray on that paranoid path.

'We're in the same position,' I said. 'I haven't hidden anything from you. If we start fighting we'll really get into the shit.'

'What shit,' she said very softly.

'Roxy's completely cracked. She could kill us both if she put her mind to it.' It was a relief to say it.

'Oh thanks, Glory. That's very reassuring, that's truly wonderful to hear. Now why the fuck would a druggie want to do away with an old queen like me?'

'You're a witness,' I said. 'She doesn't like them.' I didn't even dare to mention Mitch, after what she said about him.

I was at a loss. As some kind of gesture, I just blurted out, 'Come into my studio, Grace, and I'll show you my work.' It wasn't exactly adequate but it was the only peace offering I could think of at the time. Grace didn't seem to see it as unusual.

'What work? Oh that's right. You're a painter. That jerk told me. He goes, do you realise that creature out there on the lawn is one of New Zealand's most exciting painters?' She had him off exactly.

I said, 'Do you want to see the pictures?'

All the little bonhomies of the morning bath had drained away and I had to face it again whether I liked it or not. There were deaths and violence and uncertainties wherever I turned and nothing was safe. That was the reality, and Grace's emotions were understandable in light of all this. I thought if she saw the pictures she might understand more than she did, but of course that could be another blind alley. I could never predict what people's stance about my paintings was going to be. Anyway it was all I could do.

She was not mollified. 'I'll come and see them if you pay the taxi fare. You owe me a bloody bundle, Glory Day. You owe me an ocean.' At least she'd accepted, although already I knew her well enough to know forgiveness was in her nature, so it didn't take much. As we got up I remembered the Tretchikoff but it was too late by then.

We trailed with dignity and in silence through the meadow, with Rina following dreamily, her kind little face intent on some fantasy she was acting out. She was probably being a princess, I recognised a couple of the signs. She had tuned out completely from me and this Grace, I could tell she was fed up. The door was already open out onto the lawn and I felt a sudden lift of panic. Rina and I had left it shut an hour ago.

'Who's been in there?' I called. We stood at the threshold and once again I looked at the ruin of my life. The studio lay there like a disembowelled animal. The window was cracked right across, there was what looked like mud smeared on the walls, my pictures lay face down on the floor. Dollops of paint from the jars were thrown over every surface — my bed looked as if it had been chopped in half, sheets and blankets were ripped and stained. The malevolence in the air hit us in the chest, none of us could move with the sheer momentum.

'Who done that?' asked Rina, scared. She came and stood close to me and I touched her head soft. After that, she stayed quiet. She didn't want to talk.

'Al!' I yelled. We all jumped. Drops of paints were still dripping every few minutes from the top of a jagged bookcase.

'Al! Get the cops!' He came out of the shed where he was putting the dog food away. He stood frozen, dismayed.

'I'll get her back for this,' I said conversationally.

He went to pick up a painting. It was my favourite, the corpse of the woman on the lino. The one she thought was of her. Blue globs of paint stuck to the canvas — you could only see her bare feet tender on one corner.

'Don't touch. Phone them. Tell them to get out here. I'm sick to death of this now.'

Al went. I sat down in the grass by the glass door, leaning my head against the wall. I couldn't speak with it. I felt as if someone had just thrown me into a lime pit with the bodies still being digested around me.

Grace wordlessly handed me the beer. I drank, not tasting it. Rina sat down beside me petting me with her soft hand. We just stayed there in the warm hum of the day as the shock advanced and receded around me like a heat wave.

'What kind of crazy cunt is she?' Grace was awed, shaken out of her anger by the sheer weight of the malice lingering in the air around us. She picked up a crunched-in bookcase, dislodging showers of dust and rubble absent-mindedly. 'What did you do to her?'

'She didn't do nothing to her. Nothing,' Al said, coming back from the house. 'Get your hands off it,' nodding at the bookcase. 'The cops are coming. They'll find your fingerprints.'

She dropped it as if it was scalded and it crashed at her feet.

'Fuck off, dear. I was talking to Glory. I couldn't of done it.'

'I wouldn't put nothing past those bastards,' he said grimly.

'That could of been your head,' she said, still awed. She looked over at me. 'She certainly don't like you, honey.' We were all silent. 'Hey look. Your bloody stash. Right there for the cops to slam a possession on you and get you for good. You need a fucking trainer.'

'How come you didn't hear it?' I asked Al, keeping my voice conversational.

'How would I know? The dogs were barking, I know that. It must have made a helluva noise all that cracking and breaking.'

'You wonder how she could of done it so bloody fast. She must have gone in there like lightning. Fucking bionic woman,' Grace said. All the accusations in her seemed to have died down, which was one good point. Only one.

I started rolling a joint from the little tinfoil packet Grace handed me. It was something to do with my shaking hands — I couldn't look at my paintings, I couldn't trust myself to say anything. We were all paralysed by the malevolence of it.

When the cops came up silently on cue just as we finished the joint, I was only slightly more ready for them. I was getting jumpy about talking to cops, it was the second time in four days or something. Considering I was so allergic to them at the best of times, it was a record.

'Mrs Day is it?' Young, with red hair and childish freckles, he had come over the grass like a ghost. The other one stayed silent, in the background.

'Yes.'

'Anything of value smashed?' he asked pleasantly. He didn't

seem to know anything about me.

'Paintings. I haven't looked at them closely yet. Around $20,000.'

He whistled. 'Money in art, eh! Insured?'

'I think so.' I wasn't sure. Nigel had probably done it, knowing him. It was the sort of detail he was good at. We all stood in the long grass. I kept looking away from my smashed-up room. Now and then I imagined the expression on her face when she was doing it.

The cops scrabbled around for what seemed hours, dusting off fingerprints, searching for things, sorting around in the shambles. They finally stood up and dusted themselves off.

'We'll find out who did this. Fingerprints all over the place. Any other damage?' The red-haired one was doing all the talking.

Al said out of the blue, 'Damage to mental health. This lady here has worked on those paintings for months. All down the drain.' I was surprised. The cop looked at him. He was obviously out of his depth.

'I just picked this up a few minutes ago,' Grace said, indicating the bookshelf with her foot, 'so it'll have my fingerprints on it.' I noticed her high-heeled jandals were those cheapo plastic ones but they had glitter and little coloured feathers stuck onto them. She'd obviously done it herself. The cops noticed too.

'Fair enough,' he said, looking away. The other one tried not to smile. He made a note about her fingerprints. I could see they were both anxious to get away. The four of us were probably more than they'd bargained for.

'I mean I love visits from you boys, no worries,' Grace said, 'but not at the moment.'

'Could I have a statement from you, Mrs Day?' the red-haired one asked. 'Do you want to go somewhere private?'

'No. They all know,' I said. 'Her name is Roxy Williamson. Her address is Brighton Road, Parnell. She has already kidnapped my kid, and she's harassing my household and me. She's one of yours. She's a junkie. And a police informer.'

He was looking at me incredulously. 'Your full name?'

'Glory Day.'

There was a silence, and he closed the notebook. You could actually see his brain racing. He'd obviously made some kind of fuck-up.

'If your statement is true,' he said formally, choosing his words, 'and it's a big if, then you're dealing with a person of unsound mind. I would advise you to take extra precautions for the safety of yourself and your daughter. And, er, any companions involved.'

'If there's another death,' I said, 'who will you try and pin it on then?' I couldn't help it.

'I have no knowledge of the case you're referring to,' he said austerely, making to go. The other one had already started over to the car.

I said, 'Am I still a suspect for the kid's death or not? The cops haven't been around for at least two days. Surely even they wouldn't believe I'd smash my own place.'

I was going to say more but Al dug me viciously in the back. He was tired of my confrontations with police. He just wanted me to shut up. There were certain requirements Al had which I respected, so I let it go. There were other, more immediate concerns anyway.

The cops made off across the garden and their car started with a huge squeal as if they couldn't get away quick enough.

Moe and Kingi came over, casually, the minute the car went. They always crossed the grass between our two houses as if it was the bloody Berlin wall.

'Trouble again, Glory?' asked Moe, barely hiding his incredulity. At least he had the tact not to mention last night. I'll give him that. He said, 'Shit! Who done that? Roxy?' He was genuinely shaken out of his cool.

We all stood round looking at it in silence. The only person moving was Rina. She was working away like a little dog, pulling and tugging away at the paintings. She was lining them all up on the grass one by one, working in silence with the utmost concentration, her pigtail grey with dust, smudges all over her face.

The pictures lay out on the grass looking bruised and sullied. It was such a heart-rending sight that I felt great tears starting to roll down my face. I didn't even care at the time, but afterwards I realised that it had rocked everyone. No one had ever seen me cry before except for Rina. They stood with frozen half-smiles of embarrassment as I wept.

'I'm going to look for her. Fuck that.' I went down on my knees to touch a painting. Everyone was trying to ignore the tears.

'Well, I'm not fucking coming,' Al said. 'I've had enough.' He was overwrought, genuinely pissed off with me. My tears were the final straw. He had a fragile soul at the best of times did Al, haemorrhaging from contact with the outside world, he was full of secret sensitivities. This terrifying orgy of destructiveness in front of us had set a tic going in his cheek, always a sign of breaking point with him. I mean my own skin was jumping from it, Christ knows what was happening to Al's. His was tightly stretched even when we were peaceful. Cops, the uncertainties, Sue, and now this were all driving him nuts. His eyes were wild and bloodshot. As well as that, he of all people knew what the pictures actually meant, so he was still trying to keep his own panic under control for my sake.

'I'm not coming,' he said again, calmer. The last trip had been a real nightmare for him. I don't think he'd left the house more than twice since the time we found Weasel's corpse.

'Fair enough,' Moe said. 'I'll come. What a bitch. I told you didn't I? I've never seen a chick that poisonous. She shouldn't have done that to your pictures.' He wanted some action. Something to do. He was itchy with boredom. I sat there watching Rina's patient work, my mind rearranging things yet again.

'Jeez you're doing a good job,' Al said to her, to make amends. 'Watch out for them bits of broken glass, will ya?'

Some of the pictures didn't look so frightening once she had lovingly started to dust them off. Roxy's manic whirlwind had spared objects. The sheer speed of the destruction had left some things still untouched — like the houses you saw on American TV left freakily untouched in miles of wreckage. The centre of the whirlwind. She obviously just hadn't had enough time to pay full homage to everything, or give each picture her individual attention. As it was, the sheer force of her madness had given her the strength of three people. It had been risky for her, but then the forces driving her must have cancelled that out. My worst fear was that her face had been blank when she was doing it.

Grace touched one of the pictures delicately with a feathery jandal.

'Well, they're certainly not my bloody cup of tea, your pictures. I mean I can understand why the poor woman went absolutely berserk. Look at this. It even makes me feel funny. Look at all that stuff dripping from her mouth for Christ's sake. My clients tell me *I've* got a diseased mind. They should meet you, dear. You'd go down a treat. If you painted me like that I'd want to slit your throat as well.'

'I'll get Roxy for this,' I said to no one in particular. There was no doubt that the dead woman on the lino had been singled out. There were slashes of paint all over the canvas where it looked as if she had attacked it head on, for minutes at least. It seemed to be the one she'd concentrated on. 'Are you coming?' I asked Moe. I took off the dressing-gown and put on a paint-spattered dress I found under the wreckage. Rina passed me up my old jacket without even looking at me. It was as if I was going to an execution.

I got into the car without speaking. I couldn't say a thing.

'You drive, Moe.' He started the car and we drove in absolute silence down the drive onto the freeway. Moe was silent out of respect and I was just sitting looking out the window, the blood pounding in my temples. I was trying to conserve my energy and my rage before it dissipated, worried that I was getting too demoralised to be effective anymore.

Outside Roxy's house we both sat for a minute. I said, 'You wait outside. I'll give you a yell if I want you. It's better if I go in alone at first. Come in ten minutes or so if I don't come out.

It was down the nightmare passage again — an old gracious house which had probably sheltered generations of innocent sixties students plotting revolution and smoking dope before the androids of the eighties took over. A metallic death-smell hung in the air still. I moved down silently to her door, but it was shut. I put my head against the panels. There was no sound at all, it felt hollow in there, like an empty lair. I tried the handle but it was locked.

'Well,' I said very softly to myself. 'I wonder where she is?' I looked around to check and then leaned hard against the catch. The door just gave, soft as a sigh. I had never felt an atmosphere so strong in a room before. It was the whiff of madness which leapt out at me. It was like a wild animal's lair with that strong bitter stink and the fear of imminent return hanging in the air like something you could taste.

Nothing had changed, and no one was there, only the paper whiffling in the draught set up by the open door. I suddenly felt very physically close to my persecutor, my mad judge. For days now I'd thought only of her, and fought her, and feared her, and now this the second visit sheeted it all home.

Behind me someone switched on the light. I jumped so hard, it was like that high-pitched screaming in *Psycho* when the old woman was revealed and the madman came screaming down the stairs. With that insane jabbering a death-wail in my ears, I turned around pulling out the piece of jagged glass I had in my jacket pocket.

'Hell,' said Moe in awe, looking around, 'It's all about you!'

The relief was so huge my mouth was dry with it. I stood there collecting myself.

'It's not ten minutes,' I said, when I could get my voice back.

He wasn't listening. He was transfixed by the room, awe-struck. He said, 'She reckons here you're the world's greatest living painter. "She could give me some of it. Look how she paints me." Some of what? Whew! Off the air's right. Fucking Jesus.'

We were both inexorably drawn to the walls and the messages she'd left. This time around I saw different things — a copy of the letter she'd sent right up on the ceiling. She had written on one review, 'Glory had better watch this guy. He's got,' but I

183

couldn't read the last word. It looked like 'style'. We read on, Moe horror-struck. I could suddenly feel a draught as the door opened wider. We both looked over at the door, the long thin guy stood there again. It was a replay of last time, he looked exactly the same.

'What are youse doing here?' He was still blank.

Moe stood there, chewing, sizing him up. His honest nightmare gang regalia looked almost wholesome for a change.

'Where is she?' he asked after a silence.

'You one of them Headhunters?' the strange kid asked in the same tone. He was a walking zombie.

'Where is she?' Moe was using his strangled voice. A bad sign. He never liked anyone asking direct questions like that, especially from such obvious weirdos, even though he was probably flattered at being taken for a Headhunter.

'Are you?' Moe started walking over to him. With the ease of practice the kid pulled the knife I'd seen on my last visit. It was hard to tell from his expression whether he was frightened or bored. He just kept it in his hands.

'I don't know where she is,' he said really sulky. 'I'm not her keeper am I? She's going to be real pissed off at you breaking the door.'

Moe said, 'I'm giving you one chance, fuckhead. Tell me.' I knew he always carried a knife. It was a worrying moment for me. Moe just had to ask directions and he ended up in a fight. Very soon he would have to give him a hiding. It was typical of him to leave me in the lurch like that. Luckily the guy made the right decision.

'She works up at that caff in K. Road sometimes. She could be up there.' He backed out of the room, probably to warn someone.

'Don't mention it to anyone,' I said in my softest voice. 'We'll know it was you.' I was old enough to be his mother.

Even Moe had to smile after he left. 'They're all gaga in this house.' There was a creak upstairs and we both moved instinctively to the door. We went up the passage really fast, but everything stayed silent.

When we got inside the car Moe lit up a joint before we started. Even he was feeling the pinch.

He said, 'I've never seen nothing like that. I never realised she was such a nut. She looks like a movie star even when she's smacked out of her head. It's hard to believe. She's dealing with all those big-time crims and you have to keep your bloody wits about you with those bastards. I wonder whether she invites any of them home.' He took a puff. 'I thought you was getting paranoid, Glory,' he said as he started the engine. 'I thought you were really going a bit off yourself.'

We drove up K. Road and parked just up from the pub.

He said to me, 'Do you still want to find her? Roxy?'

We saw her straight away when we looked through the window. She was sitting at the table with two men, and she looked so beautiful I couldn't move. Her hair floated around her like a crimson cloud, she talked and laughed, gesticulating with her cigarette. You could see the paint all over her hands. She was wearing a long pink skirt and a loose soft white blouse — there was such innocence clinging to her, the flowers of the meadow wreathed her hair and her soft face was full of the pleasures of the morning.

I was paralysed for a split second with disbelief. It seemed impossible that this beautiful vision was capable of such doggish cruelty. It was only a second, and I knew Moe was there with me too, but it was long enough for a wild animal like Roxy with all her instincts in full flower. Her face froze, she turned to us with a grimace so ugly we almost fell back and then with a half-turn and a swirl of her skirt she jumped up on the table and disappeared over the back. I didn't even see the point in chasing her. Roxy was fantastically quick, even when she was coked to the eyeballs she could move so fast you wouldn't notice she'd left. And in fact people hardly noticed the whole incident — half of them probably thought they were imagining a beautiful woman streaking past them out the back. They certainly saw us, scarecrows, ragged, ugly with embarrassment.

'Friend of yours?' asked Moe. We sat down at the table with the two men. They both had fleshy, priestly faces — men with inflamed skin and big swollen knuckles, angry flesh against tight fabric. They didn't like us being so physically close. They could have been twins with their red enraged faces, although one was much older. Out of context, I didn't even recognise them at first.

'Got another partner have you?' he said, nodding to Moe. 'You certainly pick 'em. Mind you, you're no oil painting yourself.' They went off into paroxysms of laughter.

'I know you,' I said. 'You're the jerk who picked me up.' It was only a few days ago but it seemed like years.

'Watch it,' he said, still smiling. He turned to his colleague. 'You reckon we should pull them in?'

'Nah. Later,' the other one said, carefully stirring his coffee. They were both ready to jump any minute.

'You've got some pretty fucked informers,' I said. 'They'll lead you up shit creek if you're not careful.'

'Your mate Roxy? Come on, Glory. She's a lovely girl. She's always praising you to the skies. Only wants the best for you.'

'I've been meaning to see you anyway. I'd like to have you for unlawful detainment. Harassment. A few things. You'd probably have to plead guilty with the evidence I've got.' I was reckless with frustration.

'I'd rather bite my bum,' he said lazily, drinking his coffee. Their bodies were so hyped up I could feel the tension drumming off their muscles from where I sat.

'You'd get AIDS,' I said, taking a leaf out of Gracie's book.

He sprang, the false bonhomie gone, his congested face brutal with rage. His mate held him back. He was a real friend, no Judas. He said to him private, urgent, as if he knew his capacities even in public, 'Leave them. It's not worth it. They're scum. We'll get them later.' He turned to us almost conspiratorially. 'Bit unfortunate. Get out now. Get.'

Walking down the street with Moe, I said, 'We're a couple of no-hopers.'

'What's tonight? Friday?' Moe asked. 'You're supposed to be singing tonight.' He didn't want to talk about it. He was going to have to get his own back. It made us equal anyway, which was a blessing in my present fragile state.

'I've got that opening as well,' I said. I didn't feel ready to go home anyway. I wanted to talk to Patrick, though I didn't mention that to Moe. He'd be in there like a shot, and I wanted to do it in my own way.

11

In the end I got Moe to drive up to the little gallery in a back street somewhere off Queen Street.

It was an electric night, huge beat-up machines with their mufflers off, thrashing up and down the main drag, the drivers hanging out the car windows full of spunk, racy with sexual tension. New Zealand mums and dads and kids tormented with fear for the future, shrinking from the menacing edges of city life, only sheer love for their children drawing them past the people they'd rather not know. You could see that muggings in carparks, disease and violent death haunted them as they walked.

The air was so full of urgency you could smell it — babies to be born, people to fall in love with, there was blood on the footpath outside the pub, the shine of sex in the air, and rock music so loud you couldn't think. It was so cheap and flashy and alive we stopped to watch it for a while.

Moe said, 'Shit, there's some class here. Those girls walk past so beautiful.' By common consent we didn't refer to Roxy.

'Well, I've got to go,' I said.

He didn't want to come to Patrick's opening.

'Nah. Is it that kid Patrick? Nah. I might go round and see a mate of mine. Out Sandringham. You going to Mainstreet after?'

'Yes,' I said. I wasn't feeling very enthusiastic.

'I might see you there.'

'You've got my car, mate. You bloody better.'

'Fair enough,' he said, not put out. We were still respectful of each other's weakness.

Walking inside the gallery was like entering another dimension. Queen Street was raucous and seedy in contrast. Graceful kids in light white airy clothes, they looked like sprites in the clean light. It wasn't the sort of place I liked and I felt like leaving the minute I walked in. There were art students, glamorous musos, executives, people like that, confident in their chosen vocation and out to further their careers by a little talk in the right place, something I've never been very good at. They were all wonderfully decadently beautiful, their extravagant skin and mouths and hair touching on a certainty that I knew nothing about. They were good-natured and on the make and the air was full of projects which didn't include me.

My own plans were quite nebulous — I just wanted a couple of quick drinks, a word with Patrick and then off to Mainstreet — but as soon as I got there I could see it wasn't going to be as easy as that. Patrick wasn't there for a start. He'd probably seen me and bolted. His betrayal was only a minor matter to me in the face of everything else, so he was really overdoing things. I knew he was young and scared and I didn't hold it against him that much. I was surprised that he was taking it all so seriously.

I just stood against the wall drinking, waiting for him to come back. Everything looked promising for a first exhibition, there were even a few red stickers. Those cream gallery walls always suck the vitality out of even the best painting and his was no exception, but you could see at a glance that they were good. It pissed me off seeing them hanging there so pristine and cared for when my own pictures back home were lying in a heap of murderous rubble. But that was something I couldn't risk giving my full attention to. It wasn't worth giving way to my instincts in this piss-weak little gallery. There was too much else going on in my life, without making a scene here. I had to keep all my energy for the real performance.

The gallery was student-run by some kind of loose cooperative and you could see the rough edges. They'd put on a huge feast, and there were empty platters everywhere littered with chicken and ham bones and the odd bit of crusty French bread. They'd made the mistake of putting out too much wine as well — you could tell business wasn't their strong point. You could always pick the successful galleries, they doled out wine by the glass and gave you little crackers with bits of parsley. Not only that, but here there was an expectation in the air that you never felt in the high-class galleries. People were still half hoping for a miracle. The style, the expectation, all of it reminded me of the first opening I ever went to, at the Uptown Gallery, for an exhibition called 'Urban Sprawl' or something like that.

I went feeling apprehensive as if there was going to be something very significant about it, but it all turned out quite differently. The pictures were all Gretchen Albrecht clones and not nearly as strong. They were semi-abstract, with no style or conviction to them, dead as mutton. Even at the time I was an uppity bitch and never patient with bad work, and I remember the pictures irritated me from the moment I saw them. Not only that, but some middle-aged jerk attached himself to me before I'd hardly walked in the door.

He was the kind of guy who was hoping everything about him would be remembered and written down, so he was always playing to the invisible biographers. He fully expected future generations to marvel at his light play of wit, his triumphant sexuality. He was frozen in the Henry Miller phase, women being bowled over by his powerhouse intellect and hard-cock type of approach. He'd done it all so many times before his eyes were tired. He talked to me for a few minutes and eyeing me like a dog, he put his arm patronisingly around me and said something like, 'You're very special. I fancy you.' Then he put his lips close to my ear so that I felt the sigh of foul breath and the tickle of his beard and whispered dramatically, 'Do you know, little girl, that I come like a train?'

I found out later he was a writer well known for his silliness. At the time the very thought of that flabby middle-aged body rotted out with wine and pretentious literary endeavour was fairly hard to stomach. I am always the first to admit that my life has been fairly sordid, but at least I'd never had to put up with crap like that.

I knew instinctively at the time that there was no answer to the man except violence so I threw the full glass of wine in his face. The wine dripped off his beard, and he started to lick it,

making a big thing about the taste, going, 'Im, im, delicious.'
But he looked a real arsehole and I was launched in the society
of Auckland artworld as the woman who threw wine over Leon.
Generally, people approved of the action, and a lot of women
came up to me at parties openly envious that they hadn't
thought of doing it. That was the innocent time when women
believed their function was to be handmaidens to the tortured
muses of Grafton. That sort of life was new to me, to say the
least. But even then women were becoming more open to different interpretations.

Watching Patrick's opening, you could see a different tone.
The people carried themselves with less self-consciousness, they
had their own row to hoe and coming like a train was their own
private business. Even the shyest didn't have to prove themselves in such a sad way. There was a harder edge, people here
knew it was all for real. They were more interested in money
than sex anyway by the look of things.

'Are you Glory Day?' A young guy with a soft red mouth
came up to me. He was very pretty, with pale skin, a bit like Al.
'I just wanted to say I love your paintings.' He had a slight
stutter and was obviously suicidally embarrassed, but determined to plough on and get it all out, with some pain to both
of us.

'Thanks.' There was a moment of hideous embarrassment. We
stood poised, the boy looking down at his wine glass, his hand
tremulous, a half-smile fixed horribly on his face. 'Thanks.' I
said again. I had caught sight of Patrick and lost my concentration. In the end I said, 'Excuse me' to him. I wanted to get out
of the place. I moved over to Patrick and grasped his hand really
strongly before he could move.

'How's things, Patrick?' I asked him.

He smiled at me. He'd dyed part of his hair blue since I'd seen
him last and there was sweat on his white-painted face. It made
him look sinister, like a bovver boy.

'Hello, Glory. This friend of mine wants to meet you,' he said.
In seconds we were surrounded by his mates. I realised later that
it was nothing sinister, just that they had all been waiting for a

chance to pounce anyway, but in my paranoid, semi-drunk state it was like being in the middle of a ring of menacing puppies. I could see they were ready to savage me, play with me, show their baby teeth, and fawn. They wanted a performance. Their good nature shone out of their clear eyes, they were such well-fed, soft-faced babies all ready to take on their rightful heritage, a life of wealth and ease and professional status. The aura of Remuera and Epsom still remained in their glitzy Elam clothes. They were only playing decadent. They let you know it was only temporary by a certain clipped authority in the voice, the way their smiles faded quickly once business was completed. But they were admiring in spite of themselves. I was definitely the real thing.

I couldn't hear what they were saying. I said that and they all laughed ingratiatingly. My voice sounded slurred in my own ears. Everywhere I looked I could see their cool skin and the youth of them, the sheer intensity of their attentions. And there was Patrick, edging away, his face a lively mixture of fear and triumphs. I caught his arm back and said to him, 'I've only got a minute,' and pushed him past the ring of kids who watched fascinated. One little punk even moved forward and said, 'Hey, what are you doing?' but was quickly shushed. I must have been rougher than I thought. I stood him against the wall.

'Don't keep running away, Patrick,' I said. 'I haven't got the time.'

'I'm sorry,' he said. 'That chick Roxy came round. She freaked me out, she said she'd tell my parents if I went witness. Anyway I knew you got that other witness. The transsexual.'

'The kid's dead,' I said to him, real quiet.

There was a hush around us. For all the seemingly absorbed attention people were paying to each other, it was a fragile gathering totally aware of my presence and desperate for news. People readjusted their faces and the buzz of conversation became deeper and more frantic. They were like flies. Glory Day, flavour of the month, riding high, suspected of fuck knows what. What a coup for Patrick.

'Please.' He was licking his lips like a soap actor. He didn't want his precious opening going down the drain. 'Listen, Glory, I swear I'll go witness if it comes to it. I know you're innocent. I wouldn't let you down. I just promised her, and then when the cops rang I was too scared.'

'It's a bit late. They still think it's me. You want to help, before it goes to court?' His soft hand felt like jelly as I crushed it between my hand and the wall.

'Of course,' he said, frantic.

For a while now I'd been wondering whether Patrick had actually set me up with Marianne. I was never normally so paranoid, but Roxy had taught me a few things. Talking to him I could see straight away that was wrong. He was too shrewd to get involved in such a seedy deal, people like Mitch were too lower class for him. His potential for trouble as a hostile witness had been recognised, that was all, and they had just got to him before I did. He would have made no trouble, a self-server like him, but I was curious about such a flagrant act of betrayal. Even Cash had still tipped me off about Rina. I wasn't that concerned about it because Sarah would subpoena him anyway, it was just that I didn't want him to think he'd got it all his own way. It was a point of pride with me.

'I'm sorry,' he said. 'I didn't realise. Of course I will.'

He reminded me of Cash — he was so resilient, so hopeful, so wonderfully on the make. But he came from a different strain altogether. His people were from generations of big businessmen, opportunists, pillars of the community who were so quick off the mark at making a buck it was poetry to hear. It was in his blood, robbing people blind, knowing when to smile, when to withhold the power and when to go for the jugular. He didn't have Cash's vulgarity, it was all smooth with him. His instincts were so finely honed they did not desert him even in a tight corner.

He was assuming, and I could see it clearly in his eyes, that he would worm his way into my good graces again. He was prepared to go through a period of apology even, it was that important to him, but it was clear he saw no real lasting obstacle. Things were there for the taking and obstacles, even betrayals were nothing once he'd put his mind to it. It wasn't in his nature to allow anything to be refused him.

'I came round to tell you that if you lie in court I'll see to you personally,' I said. In some ways he could be as dangerous as Roxy if he was saving his own skin.

He said, 'Are you threatening me?' but his voice was shaky with it. It wasn't to my taste, scaring him, but I had to make him see it wasn't worth his while.

'You know what I mean.' I patted him on the arm, real soft. 'Mitch and them will go inside for sure over this, but I'll still be around, so just stay with me.'

'I don't know what you mean,' he said, his eyes wide. I started feeling testy with him then, ready to push him if he tried to approach me with any more of his little boy upper-class bullshit. Not for the first time it was only his paintings which saved him. I walked quietly away from him. I had pins and needles in my legs from the tension. Bloody Moe was nowhere in sight and I just wanted to go. The pale little boy was standing in a corner, pretending to look at a painting. I was drunk enough to go over to him.

'Can you give me a lift?' I wanted to get up to Mainstreet, away from this place and Patrick. Up there seemed like a haven in comparison.

The pale boy said, 'Yes, yes surely. What — where do you want to go? Do you want to go now?' He was not coping well. I began to regret asking him.

I said, 'A woman is trying to kill me,' to put him at ease. He looked around panic-stricken. He was very well mannered, I'd give him that. 'She's not here for God's sake.' I was starting to get testy with him as well. Either he admired me enough to give me a lift or he didn't.

He said, 'Let's go then,' collecting himself. He was scarcely out of his teens, poor little man. I must have looked fearsome to him. He was probably wondering if it was some kind of sexual come-on.

Outside it was starting to drizzle and the early exuberance of the night had faded. Things looked uglier, there was less light, people were more menacing. There was a real edge of violence, a strident brassy hum to the streets with cars screaming past, and a group of street kids openly sniffing glue in front of McDonald's. We found the car just up the alley and I knew I'd asked the right person. It was a Mercedes.

'This is snazzy,' I said, heaving myself in.

'I — I borrowed it.' He was genuinely embarrassed at the display of wealth.

'Top of Queen Street,' I said. He winced at my tone. I suppose I could have been talking to a taxi driver. 'This woman has just smashed a painting of mine. Wrecked it,' I said, just to explain myself. He was so suitably horrified it was worth it all.

'God. Did you get the cops?'

I glanced sideways at him. There was a little shine of moisture on his lower lip, his profile was achingly pure. The car purred over the streets.

'Yes. I'm doing an exhibition called "Senseless Violets". It's a continuation of the last series, but it's much tighter. I'm using enamel instead of oil. Murders. A series of murders. Violence generally.' Booze had unlocked my tongue to a degree that was shocking even to myself.

'Did this woman take exception to the paintings?' he asked. He was very sweet.

'No. I don't think so. She was the model. She's loony. A victim of obsessive identification.'

'Really?'

'Mixed up with all sorts of shit — murders, drugs, big-time crims.'

'Love the title,' he said.

I was boasting, expansive. Suddenly I wanted to talk to him all night, get his clean responses, have it all fixed in my head before I had to sing at Mainstreet. I liked riding in the car as well. It was such a cone of silence after all the heaps I usually travelled in. The seat sat like silk, the windows were slightly tinted so that the world outside there in the sordid streets was irrelevant, not to be thought of. We hummed along in a scented closed capsule.

Riding along in the half-dark with the boy, so sympathetic, so openly admiring, made you wonder what it would be like to be one of his women — with the softness of them, so full of delights, decked out for their owner. To watch the world through tinted windows, swim like a fish past sleek potted plants and musak and the plastic smell of the cage.

'She's way off the air,' I said.

'What are the police doing about it?' he asked, his forehead painful.

'I'm one of the suspects. Because I took the girl to hospital.' I was slightly impatient. He wasn't following quick enough for me.

'Oh,' he said, scared. He wasn't looking at me any more, but he drove faster. 'What girl?' he asked to soothe me.

'A junkie who OD'd at Mainstreet. A young kid. It was heroin. We took her up to Casualty and the cops thought we'd done it. Or they were led to believe.' I felt a grief in my heart when I mentioned Marianne. I could see a glimpse of Mainstreet in the dark as the huge car slid softly into the kerb.

'Thanks for the lift,' I said. There wasn't much more I could say in the circumstances. As I went into the entrance I could see out of the corner of my eye the Mercedes pull crazily out of the kerb and bucket into the traffic — I could just see a blur of a white face before it was all gone. I allowed myself one small secret drunken smile before I pulled myself together. That was one buying fan down the drain. But when I walked up that old dungeon passage with the torn posters of past bands and the soggy feeling in the carpet, it wasn't that funny. I suddenly felt really down. The place reeked of Marianne and her death. It hit me with a smack in the chest as I came in the door.

I'd known that Marianne dying had touched something in me I hadn't felt for years, and that it was to do with reliving my own life as well as being moved by her. Something to do with an unloved child, the fear of a father hell-bent on dismemberment, the uncontrollable terror a small child feels when there is no one to trust — so huge that it never goes away but sits behind your eyes blocking out the light. I knew she was me years ago, she had the same numb disregard for her own safety, the same desperate childishness under the sleaze. We were sisters under the skin. I wasn't prepared for the intimacy of it, and the strength of the grief. With Nettie it was different, her death grew out of her life as the night the day, whole, finished. Marianne had been cut off before she even opened her eyes. Her death remained a warning to me, a reminder, a soft thud to the heart.

Walking into Mainstreet drunk, the impact was as fresh as when I first met her. I'd only known her for the last hours of her life, but I was intimate with all the odds and ends of her living and dying — her house, the face of her mother at the door, her father standing over me on the grass, her dying body as I hoisted it up the street. Clues to her miserable life, the only wisps left.

What I imagined though troubled me most. That picture of her last monstrous attendants in the death room shooting the smack into her tender arm. It was that old fear of mine that I was somehow to blame that still affected me, my connections with the tawdry people who fed her drugs and left her to die were so disturbingly close it still seemed more than a coincidence.

The letter of Roxy's when she called me a spider stuck in my head and in my worst moments seemed to be the truth. If I allowed myself, I could see me, busy, busy spider, huge on the ceiling, dissolving victims with the poison I'd accumulated in a lifetime, acting out some insect urge, a death machine with no compunction. I knew I had to redress that, that Marianne was still there, distressed, waiting for me to avenge and release her.

I wasn't sure what it was I had to do even, but I was in it whether I liked it or not, and her death was mine, justice for her was part of my bones. It made me realise that nothing had been finalised since the night she died, it was all up in limbo. Even the cops had temporarily drawn a blank.

Shorty came out of the box like a rocket when I was only halfway up the passage. He'd seen me stumble against the wall. He pounced on me, his skinny little hand scrabbling at my arm, his breath whisky-sour, spitting great gouts of saliva at my face in his honest indignation. He was shouting in my ear.

'I've got something to tell you, Glory.' He broke off into such a fit of extreme coughing it looked as if his face was inflated with bad air. It seemed impossible that human lungs could take such a bashing. I felt in all decency I should wait there till he recovered himself.

'It was her,' he croaked, scarlet in the face. 'I reckon it was her, that mate of yours. You know your mate, the big good-looking one, you know the one with red hair? Her. Always hanging around waiting for you she is. I seen her. She was leading that kid up — you know when you was singing — she was leading her up and I swear by the bloody Bible, Glory, she was leading her up and muttering sort of. She was coming up the bloody passage her face pale as a ghost. Shaking her head. She gave me the fright of me life. 'Course I didn't like to say nothink when youse come out together. She was like a spider with a fly and that's a fact. I've spoken out, I'm not afraid to speak my mind — I told Bob, I told Dave. I said I'd go witness for Glory, no worries. Disgusting it was pulling you into scum like that. You're rough and ready, Glor, none of us are going to deny that, we'd be stupid, but you're not a scumbag like that sheila. Your mate. Roxy isn't it? Scum of the earth she comes from. I seen her before. So what happened, Glory? With that girl you were taking up to the hospital? Dead, eh? See, I seen it in the papers. The boss was pissed off, but we know someone else done it. Drugs? Not our Glor I sez to him. You was up there singing. I said to Dave — that was no murderer. You ain't into drugs and all that carry-on I said to Dave. You do your pictures and you've got your little kiddy to mind. That's all I said. That's no murderer. I told 'em.' He started coughing horribly again. 'Sit down, dear,' he gasped out between spasms. 'You look knackered. Bob isn't even here yet. Come on sit down. Here, have this.' He pressed some whisky on me, fussed around, trembling, old. It was hard to know whether he really had seen Roxy take Marianne up or not. It sounded ghastly true.

'I don't know what you think, Glory, you've got your own ideas that's for sure. But so have I.'

'You want to be witness?' I asked. It was worth asking, though

I knew from experience how hard it was to pin him down.

'Sure, sure. Glad to. 'Course I'll have to get time off and that's always ticklish. He's that mean, that bastard, he'd charge his grandmother. You know what I mean? He knows where he is with me — I'd stick my fist down his froat soon as he looks at me if he oversteps the mark, you follow me? But you never know with him, he's a moody bugger. Sometimes he's right up your arse, then the next day he just doesn't want to know. Treats you like shit paper. You know what I mean? I've got my job to think of.' He paused majestic. 'Then a course, Glory, there's the cops. I don't have nothing to do with them if I can help it. I've had some run-ins with the demons in my time. I can't be too careful in my position. You got me?'

'Yeah, Shorty.' A subpoena was just as good as long as he didn't shoot his mouth off. Shorty had a penchant for gossip, violence, the life he used to know anyway — and all this might go to his head, it was so long since he'd been anywhere near the centre of things.

'See you want to watch out for them bastards. Look at the Arthur Allan Thomas case. I always reckoned that man was innocent. My mate, his brother-in-law, had the contract for the laundry and that out at Parry. He kept his ear to the ground, and the crims knew long before the bloody cops I can tell you. See they want someone, the cops, they'll go for it. I said to Dave, someone wants her. Whether it's cops or the other, they're out to get you. You want to watch out for your back, Glory. Your ex-hubby was it? Hard to imagine you married, Glory, and with a husband. He sounded a bad lot anyway. You was right to get out of it with the kiddie being the way she is and everythink. You can't be too careful. See they're jealous. When I think of you being written up in the paper over your paintings that many times and your photo all nice. And now this.' He shook his head overcome.

I said, 'Be really careful, Shorty. They don't like witnesses. Don't go and shoot your mouth off, alright?'

'Nah,' he said. 'What do you take me for?' His eyes were shrewd as an old bird's. 'I'll keep my nose out of it till I have to, you know what I mean?'

'I'm just telling you. You're in danger, seeing that.'

He put his finger beside his nose knowingly. I'd never seen anyone do that before.

'I can look after myself. Anyone after me, they'll get a bunch of fives and a swift kick up the arse before they know where they are. He, he, he. Right up the fundament. When I was working down the line down Taupo way and some bastards, Dallies they were, were trying to put one over me, see I was the champion then, just knocked out Woody Fellowes in Napier 1949 —'

'I know, Shorty, I know. Who's Dave?' I said, trying to change the subject. He never seemed to mind being interrupted, he was so used to it.

'Me mate, me mate. He lives in the room with me. Sleeps in the day. In the boarding-house up the road. He comes down here of a night, for a bit of company. You've seen him. Old bugger he is with grey hair. Not like me. He, he, he.' He took a great gulp of whisky.

'I probably know. Can't place him,' I said. I had another pull myself. It was good whisky, quite pleasant as it tickled down the stomach. The whisky cleared the haze, softened the blows again.

Bob stuck his head in through the gap, blocking out the light. We both looked up in surprise.

'Gidday. Who do we have here? Queen of the Underworld?' He gave Shorty a brief considering look. 'You lay off it, eh Shorty. I can smell the booze from the bloody door. You'll be out on your ear. One of those bums sorting through the rubbish on Queen Street if you're not careful.' He winked at me.

'Yes, mate,' Shorty said flustered, his old hands shaking as he tried to hide the bottle. I gave him a squeeze and his little bones felt like a bundle of twigs, but he was too thrown to do anything back.

'Thanks, Shorty,' I said. 'I'll get in touch with you later.'

Bob gave me a look as if to say, 'Jeez, you've sunk, my dear, if you have any serious business with him.' He was one of those private school kids who've taken a downward path because of some stampeding obsession which even high-up parents couldn't cover up for. In Bob's case it was young kids and cocaine.

He told me once he was combining business with pleasure and starting up the first decent massage parlour for young gays, but it was probably only wishful thinking. Bob always seemed on top of things, as if everything was arranged for him personally, a hangover from his Kings College days. Talking to him I always had a distinct picture of some mysterious current of money and status and power running like an endless river above his head. It was as if it was all there on tap for him alone, and none of us groundlings would even get a drop.

'Would you like to come into the office?' I followed him into the room tucked under the stairs. It was more like a broom cupboard than an office, Shorty reckoned he'd seen Bob have it off with one of the young musos in there, but it was probably one of his hallucinations.

'Don't call me that,' I said.

'Just a joke, just a joke. I wouldn't say that if I thought it now would I? I'm not exactly wet behind the ears. I've made enquiries. Strangely enough your activities have increased the take tonight.' He leant back, his feet up. It occurred to me that for some bizarre reason he was trying to impress me.

'Come on, what do you want?'

'Now, Glory, I know you've sung here a fair while. On and off.' He paused but I didn't say anything. 'You've chosen the wrong band. I'm not saying it's you. Your band's kaput, that's what. It hasn't been pulling the crowds. I know it's a dead slot but that's why we give it to new bands. Give them a chance to harden into something or crap out. Yours is crapping out. You're not putting the work into it. The other night it was so loose you could have driven a bulldozer through it.'

'What does the contract say?' He silently pushed the paper towards me. I said, 'OK.' He'd obviously got it all worked out. It's true we weren't working. Bob knew his business quite well and he could pick it, the lack of real commitment. What with Cash's criminal activities and my arrangements with the cops it wasn't a going concern any more. My heart wasn't in it, and even though I was only part-time lead it was my energy which kept people hopeful. There was nothing much to say to Bob so I got up and went out. Shorty was still hidden away in his box.

I went up the stairs still feeling drunk with the whisky. It was already late but the tables were crowded, the big lazy fans spun the cigarette smoke in blue drifts up to the stage lights. People danced and drank and talked, a few people waved to me, very interested. Glory Day the drug queen, eh. I had another lurch about Marianne when I brushed past the seat she'd been sitting in.

A group of women were playing, copping the usual half-hearted flak from the audience, but they were good. I stood and listened to them for a while. They wrote their own lyrics — they had serious decadent faces with crewcuts, sparkly clothes, the white make-up on their skin making them look like pierrots. They looked tough, intelligent — their music was Grace Jones urban blight, almost plaintive. I'd never heard of them, but I recognised a couple of the women from the Gluepot and places like that. Grey Lynn guerrillas.

It made me feel nostalgic suddenly, being here at the old place. I'd been singing there off and on for years with different bands and different managers to earn a bit extra and because I enjoyed it. In my drunken haze it seemed a pleasant, almost sacred thing to do — singing to people. I'd heard somewhere that rock music has been seriously classed as a religion, with all its rituals, the frenzy and the love, and it seemed to me the best sort of religion you could follow. Music, spectacle and sexual grief, the releasing of love.

It was a real treat for me personally to get up there and belt it out after all the tortuous excesses of painting, the feeling of wanking in a closet you get after days of solitary hard brain-work. This was a clean thing — you stood up there and said, here I am, and then sang. A simple transaction or glitzy as you liked. And tonight of course there was Marianne, the need to make her death something more significant than another junkie dead. I went out backstage where the band was sitting around on the split plastic chairs, looking really down.

'You're the bloody culprit,' said Simon, by way of greeting.

'There's no doubt about it. Written up in the papers and all.'

'Oh, come on. Go easy on her. She's been having hassles of her own, man,' said Cash in such a hypocritical tone that we all laughed.

'That's not what you were saying two minutes ago, Cash boy,' said Jeff.

I sat down and rolled up a joint. The air was already thick with the fine stuffy smell. It was what I thought. Recently I hadn't been turning up to rehearsals. Roxy, the exhibition, my preoccupations were killing us as a band. The publicity about the murder probably only attracted jerks anyway.

'I did say I could only work part time,' I said.

'Yeah, sure you did, Glory, sure you did,' Ross said hastily.

'You're not even rehearsing,' Jeff said resentfully, accepting the joint. 'What happened to you on Wednesday night? You've missed two fucking rehearsals.'

I tried for a moment to remember but it was impossible. 'I'm sorry,' I said.

Simon looked over at me disbelievingly. They were all so taken aback no one said anything for a while.

'We'll have to talk about it,' I said, aware I'd gone too far.

'Well, fuck me,' Simon said. 'At least you apologised. I mean that's something.' There was a silence, not a happy one. 'Things must be bad,' he said after a while. 'Are you OK? What's the guts?'

'What do you mean, Simon?' I asked him, hard.

'Look I just assumed you didn't do it. I get all this crap from Cash about what's going on. I'd just like to know. I'm your bloody friend aren't I?'

'It's a long story,' I said. 'Cash knows more about it than I do.'

Cash said, 'That's a lie, Glory.' He was genuinely outraged. 'You don't tell me nothing.'

The band out there finished their set, taking their gear off to the usual late night dribble of applause, a few catcalls, thin cheers from the real fans. They came in backstage.

'What a fuck of an audience,' one of them said. There was a smell of perfume and sweat. They looked like rangy animals as they lugged their gear off. Jeff gave one of them the joint which she took absent-mindedly.

'You poor suckers on next? They're into massacre tonight. Reckon they're all here to see you. You've had some good publicity,' nodding over to me.

'Watch it,' said Cash. He'd been caught out and he wanted to make amends.

She hadn't meant to be insulting. 'Watch it yourself, arsehole. I mean they want to see the real McCoy. That's all. They've been reading about you.' She spoke directly to me. She was sour about it, but not curious.

It was getting restless outside there, like a great beast waiting for its haunches of meat, still nice, but growling in anticipation. I wondered how Bob had billed it tonight. The bouncer was moving around a lot. I could hear him talking to people in that soft sinister undertone of his.

'Who are you calling arsehole?' said Cash half-heartedly.

The women went down the back entrance hauling their gear. They didn't give him any attention at all. It had been a long night for them.

When we went out ourselves, the audience was silent, the white blur of faces still round the tables. I could feel a great deal of interest in me, not nice. You couldn't actually tell by the silence which way they'd jump. The muso had been right though, they were coming for a horror show, the rustle among the waiting bodies was sinister. They were watching me for a sign. Luckily I was drunk and stoned, so as the band was setting up I did the best thing I could do in those difficult circumstances. I grabbed the mike and shouted, 'Yes, roll up, roll up!' My voice was thick with extra stimulants. 'Roll up now, come and see the killer. I'm Glory Day and I'm out to get you!' I hadn't even planned it and I knew it was a gross and unforgivable act for someone like me, but I couldn't stand the thrills they were getting from their secret perving. I wanted to bring it out in the open. There were some scattered cheers, a slight delighted recoil.

Did you do it, Glory?' A brass-voiced punk, a real apocalypse kid with purple hair and a bare moon-face right in the front row. That's why he'd come obviously. He wanted me to say yes, he hungered for heroes, poor little bastard.

'No, mate. Sorry,' I shouted back at him. There was a roar of delighted recognition from the crowd and from then on they were all ours. It was clean emotion at long last. It seemed like years since the night I sang with that child dying in front of me. I'd stored it up blind for a week almost unaware of my own fierce emotions about her. I needed to act out my grief, strutting and thundering over the stage like a make-believe rock star. Something tawdry and flashy to open up my heart. I wanted to tear the memory out, hold it up bleeding to the light, see it razor-sharp for the first time. I wanted to sing directly to her, beg her forgiveness and let her go.

Being here again had set off a shockwave of reaction in me, I wept, drunk on stage, pushing off the tears with my puffy hands. My throat creaked with the intensity of it, the band behind me, dazzled, playing willingly. I felt the tension in my spine lift, turn and go away as I sang. That night I had come backstage down-spirited, drunk, with no interest, and somehow miraculously this lack of desire had opened a channel in my throat.

It was easily the most successful set we'd played yet. I'd been smudged, muddied over by the wicked replay going on in my head, so the cheers of the kids listening to the music, my mates in the band, the tears, were a blessed release. We sang our hearts out, lost in the joy of it, and by the time I came off, sweating heavily, tears in my eyes, my throat almost burnt out, I was exultant. It was that orgasmic burn-out after a class performance.

We were all too whacked to talk coherently, but the four of us jostled around in the room, drinking and passing a joint, full of afterglow. We stayed there for what seemed ages and then once the crowd had left we took the bottle out onto the stage, and sat together in the semi-darkness. Someone had turned off the fans and most of the lights, and it was a tepid, clinging, unhealthy darkness like being in a burial vault.

'They loved us,' Cash kept crowing. 'Bob'll be pissed off. He'll be so pissed off. He'll have to come begging on his hands and knees.'

'Fuck Bob. We can go somewhere else,' Jeff said. 'That was class that set.'

'Glory, you were so heavy,' Cash said. 'You were heavy, man.'

We sat there in the dark, content, the whisky passing like a talisman between us. It set off everything else I'd been drinking all day, the beer with Moe, the wine, the whisky, the whole wreckage of my studio, the dope — and I started to get wonderful, almost hallucinogenic flashes.

I thought of Marianne and Rina and my next idea, the great kites I was going to make — really monstrous ones with tails so highly decorated that they would be like trees or fiestas or masses of spring flowers flying up against the blue sky. As formal and stylised as Chinese kites, with rich, decadent plumage, birds of prey. Savage kites, big enough for a child to cling to and ride.

12

Al was waiting for me in the kitchen when I finally rolled in. I can't remember when Moe turned up at Mainstreet, but he was with me in the car coming home, egging me on to go through red lights and flog the car up to 120 k — not that I needed much encouragement. I got miracles out of the old heap in fact. I knew he was embarrassed riding in an early-model Holden, even at four o'clock in the morning with no one there to see him. It offended his macho gang instincts even though it was hoony, with rust on it and the exhaust pipe was hanging by a thread. He kept saying what a heap it was until in the end I said to him, 'Well, fuck off then, Moe. You can walk,' but he didn't take offence.

He was actually trying to get me to screw him. He was so drunk he kept crooning 'What's love got to do with it?' his favourite Tina Turner, in a very affected way, scrunching up his eyes like James Brown and leaning heavily against me like a big dog. He was not a violent drunk as a rule, though his mate Kingi once told me he really did go off his head and pushed a broken beer bottle in someone's face. I never forgot that, and always took it into account in my knowledge of him. Like all machos, he could be an excellent mate but a wild beast with anyone outside the magic circle. The way Kingi told me, so casual, made me wonder whether it was that unusual, but he was quick to say Moe was a reasonable man usually and a good leader with a lot of mana for a Pakeha. As it was I had enough on my plate without him slobbering all over me. In the end I had to kick him out halfway up the drive.

'You're getting to be a real pisshead,' Al said. He was annoyed with me about something.

'What's wrong with you?' I asked blearily, 'Sue been at you?'

'Rina's been asking where you were. You went off looking for Roxy and that's the last we heard. For all we knew you were lying in a toilet with your throat cut.'

'Oh God,' I said, sitting down holding my head. 'I thought I did ring her. Is she alright?'

'Did you find her? Roxy?'

'No,' I said. 'Bitch got away. I've been at Mainstreet as well.'

He said, 'The cops came here again, as well. Oh go to bed, Glory. Go on. You're so out of it. I'll tell you in the morning.'

I said, 'Al, you've been a real mate to me. I want you to know that.'

He stumped out of the kitchen ignoring me and I must have dozed off in the chair. When I woke again with a start the heater was still on full bore, drying my mouth so I felt like a burns victim. It was a nightmare awakening, I felt so ill and drained out and poisoned. I lurched out into the grey morning to have a look at the world now that I was ready for it, my mind anaesthetised by the booze.

Flies were buzzing around the wreckage as if there was a corpse there; the graunched and wrecked objects had settled into place more solidly. But there were my paintings lying out on the long grass in the shade of the kerosene tree. They must have brought them all out again. Rina was there in a green sundress and piggy, mucking around busily; Sarah in shorts, with the most dazzling white legs I've ever seen, was brushing them with what looked like a hairbrush. Grace was there too, sitting under the grapefruit tree. Al was wiping off the paint from my lino woman with Swarfega of all things. There were big globs of the green cleaner bleeding into the red paint Roxy had used, like kids' birthday jelly melting into the cake. He looked serene, pleased with himself as he turned the painting this way and that. He was even humming. I couldn't face this latest outrage. The painting was ruined anyway but the sight of the Swarfega was so repulsive that I let go with a tide of nausea, vomiting onto the grass till my stomach wrung itself dry.

Rina came and put her arms around me, we hugged

awkwardly, her lovely familiar doggy smell soothing me.

'Pooh! Your breath stinks.' She sniffed me, tickling me. 'You've been to the pub,' she breathed, her little whiskery chops pressed lovingly into my face.

'What happened?' Did you see her or what?' Al asked. I didn't have the heart to tell him it was the Swarfega that made me sick. He hated seeing people vomit. He'd gone inside the minute I started. He sat on the step, his face pale, looking at me with distaste. 'Pooh,' he said. 'It stinks. Can you go and get some water or something? We're trying to work out here.'

'I know what,' I said. 'Get a spade.' Rina went to get a spade and I dug a hole and sprinkled the earth over the vomit. The flies just stopped like magic. I kept piling it on, enjoying the clean smell of the earth. I realised I must have put on more weight in the last few weeks. I so rarely did physical things that I felt really ungainly, as if big piles of fat were set to moving all over me, lolloping — hanging from my arms, my legs, around my neck. They all watched me, fascinated.

'What happened?' repeated Al. I was panting and piling on the earth. 'That's enough,' he said impatiently. 'It wasn't that bloody much.'

'Moe agreed,' I said, throwing away the spade and lying down panting, my eyes shut against the light. 'Roxy is suffering from obsessive identification alright.'

'Whatsat?' Rina asked tenderly, sitting next to me, patting my stomach.

'She kind of thinks she's me,' I said.

'Christ,' said Grace with feeling, from where she was sitting. 'I should have thought she'd be thanking her lucky stars she wasn't.'

'What are you doing here, Grace?' I asked her. I realised straight away it was a tactless question. It was probably safer for her to be in the thick of things with us than go back to her room or be on the street.

'Well, you went off in the car, dear, on your little expedition and I thought I might as well stay the night. So I slept on your couch. I dreamt all night of that vampire. It was horrible. I'm

209

so worn out today, I can only watch all these Good Samaritans.'

I sat up and put Rina on my lap.

Al said, 'Well, don't you want to know about the paintings? Eh?'

I said, 'Of course I do. I was just going to ask.' I could see they were OK anyway.

'They're OK. They're fine. I reckon this is the only one she really damaged.' He held it up, very pleased with himself. It was probably fucked, but he looked so excited, so wonderfully handsome my heart went out to him. It hadn't been easy living with me recently. He had obviously chosen to ignore my drunkenness of the night before as well, which was a relief.

Sarah said, 'I was very sorry to hear about it. But I've enjoyed fixing them. A highly constructive Saturday morning.'

'Jesus,' I said. It was a shock. 'Is it really Saturday morning?'

'Yes,' Sarah said, sorry for me.

'The opening's tonight then,' I said. 'Shit and hell. I'll have two paintings less and Nigel's just going to have to whistle. He'll be pissed off. He'll go on and on about cancelling.' It made me feel tired even to think of his precise little voice.

'Well, we all knew that,' said Rina smugly.

'You told him yet?' I asked. 'About this?'

'He'll soon find out. He's coming at midday with the van. He's pissed off already about leaving the hanging so late.'

'What did you tell him?'

'I just said you've been out on a binge,' he said, sitting back on his heels to look at his work. 'It's fucking good considering.' I could hardly bring myself to look at it again, but in one way he was right. The figure of the corpse, the lino, the air of it was still physically intact, but the faintly sinister swirls of Swarfega gave it an unhealthy bloom of red like the cover of a Pan paperback. The power and tenderness of the corpse had magically gone, and what was left was almost laughable. Roxy's last laugh. I didn't like to say anything to Al — he'd obviously put a lot of work into it — but I could see there was no hope. Months of work down the drain, the curse of Roxy hanging up there.

'Maybe we could sell it at a discount,' Sarah said seriously. 'Once all this comes out it'll have real historical value. It's an extraordinary story. It might even be the best investment of the lot.'

'I'm going to make some kites,' I said, more to myself.

I started dragging all the broken things onto the grass, sorting out the undamaged books, the easel, my brushes. There wasn't a lot left. Rina came out to help me.

'Where was you yesterday? You bloody didn't tell me,' she said.

'I was out chasing Roxy and then I went to Patrick's opening — remember Patrick? And then I went to work.'

'Do you like here?' she asked, nodding her head around the rank garden, the smashed heap of rubble, the old house, the motorway below, Moe's broken castle beside us.

'Yup,' I pulled out a pillow smashed and slashed right through. The little feather bits went floating off, out onto the grass.

Al went into the house and brought out some beer to us.

'The hair of the dog,' he said sitting down beside me. We all sat on the grass looking at the morning's work.

'Well, dear, your paintings have been saved,' Grace said, 'the world can breathe again.' Rina had taken one of her all-consuming crushes on Grace and was snuffling and burrowing around, driving her nuts.

'She's so relentless,' Grace said, nudging Rina's head off her shoulder quite sharply with her elbow. 'I wouldn't mind so much if she didn't have all those festoons of snot hanging off her. Isn't she getting enough love for Christ's sake? I'm in no position. My life's hard enough without having her all over me.'

'She likes your tits,' Al said. Al was looking so relaxed I thought Sue must have finally left him. I asked him where she was.

'She's coming round later,' he said. I'd half hoped it was over, it wasn't so fraught when she was around. I wanted him to stay too. Not that I'd ever admit it to him.

Rina said it for me. 'I don't like Sue,' she said, leaning her pint-sized head against Grace again.

'What's wrong with her?' Grace asked, extricating herself again. 'Doesn't she like being slobbered on either?'

'She's always telling me off and Al off. She's a crabby arsehole.'

Al said, 'You lay off, Rina, or you'll get a thick ear. Show a bit of respect. She's my girlfriend. We might even get married.' He went red as we all turned and stared at him.

'Married?' I couldn't keep the amazement out of my voice.,

'She thinks she's pregnant.' There was another short silence. Even Sarah's kind and polite face, creased as it always was in a professional concern, went blank.

'Congratulations, dear,' Grace said, always quick thinking. 'Can I be your bridesmaid?'

'It'll be at the registry,' Al said seriously.

'Isn't she the lucky one scoring a hunk like you,' Grace said, openly admiring. 'Now remember, if there are any little problems in the marital bed, come to Gracie for the best therapy in town. They don't call me Miss Ecstasy from Te Kuiti for nothing.'

The idea of Al in a marital bed was so embarrassing we all stayed silent. I wondered why he'd told me in front of everyone, so casual. He looked very sheepish. He sat there picking his nails, his sunglasses hiding his face. I noticed he'd started growing his hair as well.

'You growing your hair?' I asked after a decent interval.

'Sue doesn't like it bald.'

Their relationship must have taken an upward turn in the last few days. I'd been away so much recently, and so intensely preoccupied that I hadn't given him a thought. The idea of Al being a father was so strange we all sat there mulling it over. To be fair, he had proved himself with Rina.

I said formally, 'Well, I'm sorry you're going.' I shifted my huge carcass on the grass and reached for another beer. I felt achy, sad, drained with the events of my life. 'I'll miss you.'

'I will too,' he said quickly. The atmosphere of almost hysterical embarrassment intensified. Even Rina was awed.

'Well, you win some you lose some.' I was just thinking aloud, sipping my beer. Banalities came easy when everything was falling around me, it was the most comforting way to deal with all the lunacies. My mother always used verbal rituals in times of stress and for the first time I understood. Life was so hard you fell back to grasping at all comforting straws. Al gone, eh? Can't cry over spilt milk. These things happen. You've got to take the good with the bad. It's six of one and half a dozen of the other. You could go on forever. Al going felt like a death sentence — there was no room for me in their airless relationship. What would life be like without him there? I hated to admit my attachment to anyone, that was the worst thing. I'd prided myself on a few things, attaching myself to someone wasn't one of them. But there it was, and I couldn't get away from it. Nettie, Marianne, Weasel, the band, and now this. Al a working father, locked into battle with his cold Sue, enmeshed, lost from me, gone forever from our free and easy life.

Rina burst into heart-rending sobs. She cried so hard it was almost comical. Her big mouth stretched and heaved, tears rained down so hard that in seconds her whole red blubbery little face was streaming. The strangled sounds were so close to laughing, choking, calling for something. I moved over to hug her and she pushed me away.

'Why did you let him go? I want Al to stay. You get away. She lay on her back drumming her heels. She was in a real size ten tantrum, and she was so loud Moe came to the window. Even from where we were, he looked terrible, puffy, his face pale and drained against the tattooes and clotted hair.

'Tell her to fuck up, will you? She fucking woke me up.' He slammed the window shut with a crash, Rina kept crying and we just sat and watched, there was nothing much else we could do.

Al said, 'I'll come and visit you, Rina. I'll come and see you, eh?' He patted her severely. 'Don't cry, mate, come on, mate. Don't cry.'

'I want you to stay,' wept Rina. 'I want you to stay. I hate Sue. I want you to stay.'

'It's been a good house,' Al said, giving me an appealing

glance. He was thrown by all this, it was the sort of provocation which had him hiding in his room for a week. I couldn't do anything with Rina though. She was really upset about it. Al had been there for two years since she was eight and I suppose it was something we took for granted, her love for him.

Grace said, 'Would you like some lollies? Would that keep you quiet?' But Rina wouldn't look at anyone.

Cash and the rest of the band came over the grass so softly we didn't even hear them. They looked so pleased with themselves. It was a shame none of us were in the mood.

'What's wrong with her?' Cash said.

'Al's getting married,' I said.

'Getting married? Al? Who to? That bird with the blonde hair? Sue?' He was so surprised it was comical. He recovered himself with his usual smoothness. 'Well congratulations, mate. When's it to be?'

Al said to me, 'You bitch. That's not for public bloody knowledge.' He got up and stalked off. It was his way of getting out of the whole thing.

Rina still wept on the grass, but the first sheer impetus of it had subsided. Cash had his mind on other matters anyway.

'Look at this!' he said. He was waving the paper. 'There's a review! In the Scene page.'

'What of?' I asked, my mind on Al.

'Us! You! Listen to this. "Glory Day showed her punchy bluesy style at its raving best at Mainstreet last night. Backing band Starlites were right up there beside her showing a maturity and polish that has been lacking of late. Day has finally put to rest any doubts about her talent with her blistering rendition of Marianne Faithful's classic, 'Broken English'."'

'Well,' I leant back on the grass. 'That's alright. We could get another venue if Bob stays shitty.'

Cash said, 'Listen kid, with a review like that the bloody sky's the limit. I've got a mate, knows the manager at the Gluepot. They have those blues nights up there, all the trendies and that, the *nouveaux riches*. They pay a fortune. That pub pays the best in Auckland. They pay bloody heaps. We can just call the tune.'

'Oh stop being so fucking grandiose,' Jeff said. 'You're always raving on.'

'You see what I mean,' Cash said, taking no notice of Jeff whatsoever. For once he wasn't sucked in, the currents of money were too heady. 'That guy doesn't often give a bloody review like that, because I read those reviews.'

'I didn't know you could,' Jeff said, but he was half-hearted about the insults. They were all in such an unusually good mood, even Simon, sitting on the grass, helping themselves to Al's beer, I didn't have the heart to tell them to piss off. I wasn't concentrating.

'Well ring up your friend then,' I said. 'I need the money now Al's moving out and that.'

'Is he serious?' Cash asked, jerking his head over at the door Al had just slammed.

'I don't know. It's the first I've ever heard of it.'

'Jesus,' Cash said, noticing the wreckage for the first time. 'What are all your pictures doing lying out in the sun for?'

'Who did that?' Simon asked. The backyard was usually such a wreck they hadn't even noticed.

'Roxy,' I said. I felt completely weary.

'Christ. Not again,' Cash said. 'Are they OK?'

'That one isn't,' Grace said touching it with her toe. 'Thank God.'

'Christ,' Cash said. 'I wouldn't like to meet her on a dark night.'

Jeff said, 'Why is she doing this? You been upsetting her?'

'No. True dinks, Jeff,' I said.

'Seems hard to believe. Why would she want to do that?'

'Who knows?' I said. I didn't want him to say anything else.

'It must have been something you did,' he said. He never knew when to shut up that guy.

'Do you want a hand?' Simon asked hastily. He had seen the look on my face.

Sarah said, 'Look, boys, how about leaving her alone? She's had it this morning. She's got her opening tonight, she's had nothing but trouble. I appreciate your kind offer, Simon, and

I'm sure Glory does, but forget it. We're fixing it up ourselves so it'll be ready for the van.'

'OK. Fair enough,' Cash said. 'We were just going anyway. We've got some things to do.'

'What things?' Jeff asked. 'What things, Cash?'

'Business,' he said. 'Stuff about the band.' He made a hideous face at him. The last thing he wanted was to get offside with me now.

'I don't know what you're talking about,' Jeff said. 'You said we were going to the pub. Here's Glory with all her stuff smashed. We could help her. That's what friends are for, Cash, in case you didn't know. You didn't talk about no business when we were coming over.'

'Can you shut your big ugly mouth for one fucking minute?' Cash shouted, 'Sorry, Glory.'

Their bickering was the last straw.

'I don't want you to help, Jeff!' I screeched at him, 'I don't fucking want you to! Why don't you just go!' I was aware of Sarah making faces at them behind my back.

'OK, OK,' Jeff said, sulky. 'Just trying to help.' They all got up.

Cash said to me, very slick, 'Catch you later, Glory. I'll try to make it tonight. Good luck anyway, man.' They stumped off. They looked more like a troupe of circus workers than a band — they had that edge-of-society hard seediness.

I said to no one in particular, still very irritable, 'Cash always sounds like Neil Young when he says man. It sounds like a fucking sheep baaing.'

'Well at least he doesn't sound like a bad-tempered shit,' Grace said languidly, stretching back on the grass. 'He was just wishing you good luck, you fiery great thing you.'

'I don't want his good luck,' I said. 'I wouldn't trust him as far as I could throw him.'

I was in a bad way and Sarah knew it, bless her. She came over to me. She looked so clear and ordinary it was a treat. Her bare legs were like milk.

'I thought afterwards I shouldn't have telephoned you last

night,' she said. 'I realised you've just about had enough anyway.'

'Oh no,' I said. 'I had to know about that.'

It occurred to me from the way she said it that she'd heard from somewhere about my visit to Marianne's parents, but with her usual tact she didn't mention it.

'I've given your statement to the cops, and I suppose we'll just have to wait. Just be careful, Glory, I don't know what they're going to do next. Please ring me if anything happens,' she said. 'And good luck for the opening.' She gave me a little embossed card with good luck on it. In it she'd written in her scholarly handwriting, 'To a brilliant painter, best of luck for the opening, your devoted friend, Sarah.'

I said, 'Thanks, Sarah. And thanks for helping me clean up like that.'

'Well, I think the whole thing's got out of hand. It's disgusting that you should have to go through all this before the opening. It was the least I could do for you, Glory. And please be careful. It's a real rats' nest all this.'

'We'll have to talk about it. Straight after the opening.' My voice sounded tinny in my ears as if weariness had robbed it of any human resonance.

'You go and have a sleep. I don't know how you've survived all this.' She gave me a pat on the arm. It was the first time she'd ever touched me; she with her private school reserve, and me with my jail cool were an undemonstrative pair. I took it in the spirit it was intended, but I couldn't respond, my brain was moving so slowly. She understood as usual.

'Listen, Glory, I've made up the bed in the studio. Well, temporarily. I've propped up the split bit with bricks and the wood from the shelves. Why don't you go and crash? You've got the opening tonight, you need a rest. When's Nigel coming, do you know?' she asked, turning to Grace.

The door of the house suddenly slammed open, Al burst out of it, snatched Rina up and ran inside again. It all happened so suddenly it didn't even seem worth commenting on. Rina didn't seem surprised, poor little bitch.

'Poor Al,' I said absent-mindedly. I was definitely losing my grip. I just wanted to sleep again now that my brief euphoria had dwindled into bleak exhaustion.

'Come on, Glory dear,' Sarah said. She led me into the studio and then left me. I hadn't been near it since Roxy smashed it, but I didn't even care about seeing the malevolence again. If there was a bed there then that was all I wanted, but the room had been transformed. In my state it seemed a complete miracle. Nearly everything had been put together or wiped clean or disguised. The room had Sarah's cool hand on it — there were even curtains at the window for the first time. There was a jar of onion flowers and daisies on the shelf which I knocked over in my collapse on the bed.

Later, at the bottom of a well I heard voices, movements, irritating noises, arguments, but they all passed. It must have been much later again, because it was nearly dark, and I was in the middle of a complicated dream when I heard her.

'I saw you outside the cafe. Why didn't you come in?'

I was asleep, still dead asleep, but the familiar voice nearly sent me through the roof. I woke up like a train, alarm signals flooding my brain, and there she was. She was sitting bolt upright at the end of the bed, her huge eyes wide open staring at me, a knife in her hand. She was utterly still and so pale she could have been dead. I nearly screamed — she looked so horrible. I reached over, groggy as I was, and in a slow-motion dream action I tweaked off the knife. It came away so easily it was like taking something from a corpse. The knife was heavy in my hand and the sharp blade twinkled and shone. It centred me, holding it. It was almost as if I had expected this all along.

'Fuck me,' she said. 'This is like a horror movie. A ton of blubber coming at me in the dark.' She didn't seem to be worrying about the knife. The faint light from the window showed that her face was sunken with exhaustion.

She said again, 'Why didn't you come in?' I could smell her from where I was. She ponged like a polecat, the feral stink coming off her body and her clothes in waves.

'What do you want now?' I asked, struggling to sit up, clear my brain for the emergency. I had to stay absolutely open, receptive, ready to spin off in a second. I made a slight movement.

She said quickly, 'I had to paint over the picture didn't I.' She obviously needed another shot, I could tell by the way her face had collapsed in on itself, Roxy Black Hole sucking in everything around her as she travelled into timeless black space at a million miles an hour.

'What picture?' I asked, keeping my voice conversational.

'The dead woman. On the lino. That was my kitchen. They were my feet.'

'That wasn't you,' I said. 'Come off it, Roxy. I haven't painted you for a while. You know that.' It was like talking to a sick child, trying to soothe her by the rhythm of my voice, the calm of my secretions.

'Yeah? You take me for a sucker don't you? Always have,' she added in a soft whisper. I had to strain to catch it. I had to hear everything she said.

'Have it your own way. It wasn't you. Is that why you did it?' I asked. I couldn't resist, even it it was a danger zone.

She said, 'Give me a cigarette. I've had a lot of things to do today. I'm very strung out.'

'You look it,' I said. I felt ready for her at last. Wrestling with shadows was not my style and I'd been building Roxy up into superhuman proportions. Seeing her perched like a crow at the end of the bed made me realise she had her weaknesses as well. As for me I had Rina, I had that thick skin of mine baked on by years of troubles. I had the cruel stability of a nuclear submarine — while Roxy hunched and desperate was a kamikaze pilot, going down on burning seas.

'Do I?' She brushed back her hair with a trembling hand. 'There are one or two ends I've got to tie up. Your Mitch for instance is a fucking jerko. A real jerko. I told him straight I'm a friend of yours. I've almost become you, I told him, you and I are that close, and I think he's jealous of it.'

'Become me?' I asked. The knife felt so comforting I could have kissed it.

'You eat rat poison, you become the rat,' she said looking at me. 'That's elementary. I learnt it at school. You're so gross, Glory, but you're alive. You give out sparks and then sit back and watch. I look at your hands when you're painting and they're puffy and freckled. So puffy. But you've got other gifts. People look at you, they listen to you, you're God to them. That's why I wanted you to face up to your responsibilities.'

'What?' I asked startled.

'Weasel. I'm talking about Weasel. He was living in poverty and you were flying around being Queen Bee. It's not your fault, Glory, but he looked on you as a mother, you know that? He never mentioned it, but I'd tell him, be patient, she'll come round. I told him we were like that, sisters, and I could talk you into anything. I told him you needed some reality, you were living in a dreamworld.'

I said, 'Yeah?' She scared me the way she was talking. The words she was using were charged with meaning — it was like getting your death warrant in a foreign language.

'It's the same with me. You can't just suck me in and spit me out. You can't get inside me like that and not feel anything yourself.'

'OK,' I said. 'I wish I'd never started those pictures. That's the truth. I wish I've never asked you. It was a mistake. But I'm not going to burn just because you say so. I know what happens when you hit a power-line. I'm not stupid.'

'What do you do,' she jeered, 'when you hit a power-line? No, don't tell me, I can just see you! The fucking Archangel Gabriel, fire streaming off your blubbery back and not a hair singed. Untouchable to the end.' Her voice coiled in on itself in the darkness, spiralled off into dark corners. Then she said, 'How do you think I feel being left behind?'

'I never took you with me in the first place. You did it all on your own. I never even liked you very much.'

There was a silence and then to my horror I heard the soft sound of crying.

'How can you say that? You're lying,' she said. Tears were rolling down her cheeks. 'You were the best thing in my life.'

'I'm trying to tell the truth,' I said, shocked by her crying.

'You can't leave me out there. I've given you my whole life. I know what was between us even if you won't admit it.' She was weeping uncontrollably and I felt the old ache rising in my chest.

'Roxy, why don't you just forget me? I'm a painter. I've got a couple of real friends and a kid. That's all there is for me. Those are the good things in my life and I found them all on my own. The rest is surviving.'

It was a painful statement and too close to the bones of my private existence for my taste, but her tears rocked me. They made me see the other Roxy, not the tinselled, tarted-up, smack-propelled maniac, but a grieving child who had been lying from the day she was born.

'But what about me?' she asked.

'I don't know,' I said. She sat on the bed suddenly quiet. It was almost peaceful. There didn't seem much else to say. It was so still in the room that we both heard someone coming up the hall towards us at the same time. Roxy leant forward so close I could feel her breath on my cheek, and flicked the knife out of my hands.

She whispered, 'I haven't forgotten the opening, Glory. Good luck.' And then she was gone, leaping out the glass doors into the darkness before I could move. The light went on.

'Turn it off,' I croaked. It felt as if a great pressure had been lifted off my heart. I was shaking with the reaction.

'God, this place smells like an abattoir. Had a bad dream have we?' Grace asked, poised in the doorway like an angel. 'Ready for your heart's desire, dear?'

13

When we finally got the show on the road, the only person who seemed innocently excited was Rina. Grace had gone off in a taxi and in the end it was just the three of us in the car. Al was very silent and moody. When I asked him where his fiancée was he made to get out of the car. He hadn't been sleeping I could see, and he was unshaven. As a concession to the opening he'd put his best white jacket on, but there was a motorbike oil stain all over the back where he'd been lying on the carpet. The hair growing out of his skull made him look diseased. He stared ahead, his face so troubled and tight I thought a joint might be a good idea to calm both us down.

'You just fuck up, Glory, or I won't come to this thing. I'm only coming to give you moral support, so don't push it.'

'You're the one who's bloody getting married,' I shrugged and started the car. He and Rina sat in the back seat. She was holding his hand, smiling to herself. She was very smug about her outfit. She had dressed herself up in a startling pink number she must have got out of the dress-ups, and she'd put all her jewellery on. Her narrow little chest glittered and glistened, her hair was shiny with two ribbons, she'd even tipped some glitter onto her hair. Al couldn't get over how pretty she looked, but I secretly thought it was a bit overdone, not that I would have said anything for the world.

We were all pretty quiet on the way in. Al was obviously brooding about Sue, and I was in a seasick state with my nerves fraying out over the opening, my biggest yet, not to mention my fraught conversation with Roxy.

I wasn't prepared for the crowd that surged through when we went in the door. The gallery was wall to wall with people. I've never seen it so packed. We squeezed in, just, and stood there all three of us bewildered and taken aback. Our finery was only a pathetic gesture in face of this shining array. They all seemed so sure of themselves.

The diseased paintings hummed off the immaculate white walls at this copybook crowd. A whole mishmash of Auckland's *crème de la crème* — the sort of people who had connections and lived lives that were so above reproach they were works of art themselves. None of them were fools — you could tell that a mile off. Their brains were all buzzing like computers, you could feel the hit of it in the air. They liked the paintings. The air was thick with appreciation, with self-conscious approval, everyone knew the paintings touched the spot — they were so right it was a pleasure for everyone to be here, liking them.

There was a real greedy buzz going on all around us and I could see Al and Rina felt uneasy too. The tinkle of real glasses, the tables with paté and crackers, the smell of good carpet and perfume didn't seem to have anything to do with me or them. In the ordinary course of events we wouldn't have been tolerated for a minute in a gathering like this. We stuck out like sore toes.

I said to Al, 'You don't have to stay.'

He scowled at me. 'Listen, if your mates can't bloody come.' I went and got some wine for him while he waited there against the door, uneasy, holding Rina's hand. It was true of course. I wanted them there — they were a talisman against those glittering people who wanted my blood, they were a sign that I came from somewhere different. It was no empty gesture either, the way I lived my life, it was the fruit of years of toil, a conscious decision from the day my paintings started selling. I'd always known instinctively where my strength came from and that if I betrayed that, then I'd dry up at the source. That had always been at the back of my mind. So it was a relief to me, at this the biggest moment of my career so far, to be able to smell the fear sweat from my talk with Roxy still clinging to me, to have Al and Rina and my mates there. It was like being rewashed in the blood of the lamb, so to speak, and proof positive to me that I was still potent.

———

223

I'd passed the test with flying colours. Even a glimpse of Shorty, already drunk, dressed in some kind of checked sports jacket and what looked like a stained bowling hat, was a treat, though I wasn't prepared to go so far as catch his eye.

'How long do you reckon Moe and them will be? They reckoned they were coming up after the pub,' Al asked.

I couldn't believe the sheer numbers and I felt a wave of panic as the dope struggled with my paranoia. People were actually looking at the paintings too, examining them closely, a staggering fact in itself, because most people at openings stood in elegant little groups laughing maliciously, ignoring the work and drinking wine. It was usually paranoid territory for a cross-grained socially hick painter like myself. There were red stickers already on most of them.

Seeing them all up on the walls, it hit me again how strange and intense the pictures really were. It amazed me that all those together, polished people seriously tolerated such disease, such rampant sickness to stay unchallenged. It was hard to avoid the fact that the murky struggles of my life were bled into them, scratched into them with a knife, they were squeezed out of my own sufferings and most personal essences. It was like my own skin and bone tacked up on the wall, and glump they were swallowing them whole, bones and all, peering, smiling, boozing, happy as sandboys, full of delight.

That's not to say I didn't get a charge from all those pluty people so respectful. When I was a kid I used to imagine people like that lived in glass towers high above me. The rooms in the towers were sparkling with light, massed bright flowers, and white carpets, and the people were wearing clothes of magical softness. Their flesh was aglow with the good food they'd just eaten. They looked down on us with a smile of indifference — they were up there under the eye of God, they were taller and whiter than us, and glowed with the holy light of money. When I saw the film *Metropolis* and that private image of mine translated into black and white right there in front of me, it was an invasion, a trick move right into the heart of my childhood.

And here they all were again in the flesh, feeding off my

fantasies, absorbing them. I had always suspected that silvery people like that needed other deeper roots to feed them. Out of our mean lives, from furnaces which never scorched them, people like me forged the artefacts which they took as their own, embalming them in art galleries and museums, safely locking them away for their own delectation. The creations of outsiders like myself were the food of the rich, without them the beauty, the sheer flamboyance of their lives would wither and die. They fed on the black muck of our lives, their petals grew sheeny on the stink. It was happening right in front of me, you could almost see it oozing off the walls. It wasn't that I felt superior or anything. Far from it. Those people out there were tigers. I was no match for them on nearly every level.

'Well, you reckon they'll come?' asked Al impatiently. He was definitely out of his depth and wanted some moral support. I didn't even have time to answer because Nigel came sweeping up. He was in full sail, dressed in an impeccably cut grey suit. He was as excited as a small boy — smiling at everyone, rubbing his hands, his newly washed hair shining under the lights. I hoped for his sake everything went well — it was such a big deal for him. It was very important for me too, but Nigel definitely seemed to be taking it all the way over the top. It made me nervous to see him so hopeful.

'I see your entourage is here,' he said. 'Glory, dear, come and meet —

I said to Al, 'See you soon. We won't stay. You OK, Rina?' She nodded, struck dumb. I had given her a whole packet of biscuits and she stood there, guzzling them, clods of brown sog all over her face and down her jewel-bedecked dress. She was deep in just looking.

Nigel whispered to me, 'They love them. Love them. It's a killing. For the love of God Almighty why did you have to wear that? You look like a New York bagwoman.'

I said, 'At least I don't look like a sixties stock-broker greasing up the chairman.' It was the injustice of him that got me nasty, when I wasn't even in the mood for a fight. We really were a bitchy couple. He was quite stunned for a minute when I said that, the image had obviously touched off some painful memory.

'A stock-broker?' He had always respected my opinion deep down. But Nigel never stayed introspective for long. His face and voice picked up, and he switched his smile on for a tall middle-aged man squashed into designer blue jeans and white denim jacket edging his way over to us, smiling widely.

'Glory, This is Bob Newman. Just the man I wanted you to meet. He's the gallery agent from Sydney. He's just been telling me how interested he is in your work.' Nigel was smiling so hard, the saliva was cracking round his teeth.

'I certainly am, Glory. May I call you Glory? These paintings are really remarkable. Remarkable.' He added, more to himself, 'You can see people are going for them in a very big way.' A quick covetous, calculating blue flick over the crowd and then back to me. A very smooth man full of little calculations. He was almost strangling on his vowels.

'Thank you,' I said, knocking back the wine.

There was a slight disturbance at the door and I saw out of the corner of my eye the next-doors filing in. They looked as if they were attending a funeral. They were very self-conscious, eyes to the floor, a suppressed air of unease. All of them had come. That was nice of them. I missed the thread of what Bob was saying. Gang patches, the lot, the full regalia. I was touched.

'My God,' the man called Bob said involuntarily as he followed my glance.

'Her neighbours,' said Nigel, looking at me with hatred.

'Oh? They look tough customers.' He laughed uneasily. 'Anyway, that's the deal. A few Sydney painters I know would like to be in your shoes. We give slightly lower percentages, but we're talking huge markets here and a pool of talent —' He sighed, letting his hands push back those armies of painters. It looked as if the comparison with Auckland was too much for words, even his.

The joint I'd smoked in the car finally hit me properly. It always took me a while and then I started off. His voice kept fading away as if someone was turning the volume up and down. I missed something, and then his voice went on full blast.

'Yes, of course. Hopeless trying to discuss anything serious in this crowd. Would you like to meet for lunch? Nut the whole thing out? Nigel? Can we organise a day now?'

I suddenly heard Rina crying, so I said to him, 'Can you get in touch with me? Nigel's got the details. I've got to go.' I nodded at Nigel. I didn't want to be rude because of the money he was offering, but his whole bearing was giving me a terrible pain in the back. I could feel it coming on the minute he came over and started talking and it was taking me all my time to be halfway polite to him. He was taking such saccharine liberties with me that it made my teeth gritty, I felt as if he wanted me to agree on something unspoken, that there was some kind of hidden understanding between the two of us. He wanted me to admit laughingly that the room was full of suckers, and that only he and I really understood the real reason behind the whole charade. Dough, bucks, you know what I mean? As I pushed off with great difficulty through the crowd I heard Nigel laughing in that false way of his when he was trying to impress someone.

'Eccentric. Absolutely eccentric, but lovely,' he was saying.

Bob was looking after me, startled, calculating, bemused. 'Well, I see what you mean about her size.' It was obvious that they'd already come to some understanding, with Nigel selling me down the river left, right and centre. Men's talk it was, I could tell by the faintly contemptuous expression. I'd see to it all later.

Rina, bless her, was crying because someone had stood on her toe and bruised it. Tears and biscuit trails were mixed in a paste all over her face, her hair ribbons were sticking out like rats' tails. Al was trying to comfort her, Moe and the boys were sticking together. I noticed there was a ring of space around the lot of them as people kept a prudent distance — there were a lot of nonchalant stares, half-smiles, dangerous acceptances going on from people who didn't know their own weakness. They were a big menacing dirty enclave. Moe had obviously decided to stick it out, partly out of loyalty, and partly because he was fascinated by the whole set-up. He was riveted. It was like two gangs of children staring at each other. They'd brought a whole lot of casks and were passing them around grimly, stacking them up on a table, a lot of them were just drinking from the little plastic tap.

Moe said, 'Gidday, Glory. What are them red stickers all over?'

'Those are the ones she's sold,' Al said. 'She's made bloody thousands tonight, mate. Thousands.' He had obviously been getting stuck into the wine as well, he had that loose bloodshot look about his eyes, and he was in a better mood. Moe and the boys were quietly drunk anyway, some of them were getting restive already. They had only turned up because of Moe, and they weren't really enjoying it. They didn't like the attention.

'Well, you're doing alright,' he said. 'It's good this wine, not bad for cask.' He was being very formal. There was a certain amount of awkwardness in the group as we all stood there, shifting a bit. None of us were accustomed to social niceties in our own life. I held Rina in my arms, even after she stopped crying. She kept wriggling to get down and in the end I had to let her.

Al said admiringly, 'Look at her. She's alright. She's talking like a bloody adult to them.'

We all watched her weaving her way through the forest of adults, her little head perky as a bird, down among the legs. Someone touched me on the arm. It was Patrick, relentless to the end.

'Glory, congratulations. You know they've all gone? Everyone's here — every step I go I recognise someone famous. It's a beautiful show, Glory. God bless you.'

'What?' I said startled, but already another painter I knew slightly had come up to congratulate me. I wondered briefly whether Patrick had turned to God since his brush with the underworld, but before I had time to ask, he was sucked back into the swamp of well-wishers. Moe and Al had receded behind me in the momentum of the crowd and I was surrounded by strangers.

There was a camera flash right in my eyes and in the after-image I caught sight of Grace and Rina, walking past like princesses. They looked so elegant, I tried to struggle over to talk to them, but the crowd hemmed me in. The two of them moved away, out of my sight before I could even walk a few steps. Part of the problem was my size of course, the sheer momentum of my bulk produced air pockets which trapped me. The room had become claustrophobic. I tried as a last resort to avoid eye contact, I had this paranoid feeling that everyone there wanted to say something significant to me. In the end I forced myself to stand there, trying to relax, drinking the last shot of wine in the glass and keeping my head well down. I was trying to figure how to get out with the least amount of disturbance, but the room seemed even more dense than when I first came in.

In the distance I saw another familiar head. The woman turned slightly and I saw with a thudding heart that it was Roxy. Of course. The opening. Jesus. It hadn't crossed my mind in the last half-hour, but of course she'd warned me and everything. She was on the run but I could see she intended to go down in flames. I'd never seen anyone who was so active on smack, it seemed to act as a stimulant. She'd got herself up beautifully as well — she was no longer the haunted woman perching like a crow on my bed of a few hours before. She was resplendent, shining in some diaphanous thirties dress. She'd obviously got a fix from somewhere and timed it right. It was as if she'd slipped on another skin, moved into another psyche. She was talking to someone, very animated, seemingly serene and unaware of anyone else. Her hair flamed around her like gold, she stood there so beautiful even I, with my secret facts, had to blink. She was a heroic vision, back from the dead for another visitation. I'd thought it was almost over between her and me, surely the fire between us had burnt out, but her persistences and her obsessions were obviously eternal. I was frightened seeing her stand there. As soon as it happened I knew I had to get out at all costs.

As I turned to dodge her, there was Mitch right beside me with his back to me. He hadn't even noticed me, he was so busy stalking her. Of course, he'd have known with his weasel cunning that she wouldn't be able to keep away so he'd come to have a few words with her. I could see it was urgent business. The two of them stalking each other at my opening pissed me off. I leaned over and said in his ear, very soft, 'Do it outside. Not here.' He jumped and spun so sharply that I knew he had a lot on his mind.

'Well, long time no see, Mitch. Then bang, twice in a week,' I said, still very quiet.

'Hello, Glory.' He was so guilty, he was actually smiling at me before his eyes went hard again.

'Hey, you in trouble? Want some help?' I said. I felt cold with anger when I saw him.

'What are you talking about?' He looked as if he was going to jump out of his skin.

'Working with Roxy, eh? Don't you know she puts a spell on people? Especially cops.'

He actually shuddered. 'I don't know what you're talking about.'

'You better watch it,' I said. 'She might get you first.'

'Some friends you have,' he sneered, but he looked seriously disturbed. He didn't like the drift of the conversation. His big bull head was cocked for danger.

'Don't bullshit me, Mitch. I'm not interested. I've never liked informers.' He was beside me in a second, his face close, like a lover. His breath was rank, the pores of his dirty skin like craters shining with sweat.

'Who told you that?' His voice was cracked with the stress of it.

'You were the last to know,' I said, choosing my words. 'It's been her trade for years. You didn't used to be such a sucker.'

'That's crap,' he said, gabbling his words. He knew he was gone. 'I'll tell you why. See Roxy's got connections someone like you wouldn't dream of. Biggest names in the business. She couldn't afford it, get it? They'd blow her away for the price of a beer.'

I could tell he'd been hearing rumours, and that was why

he'd come to the opening, but he didn't want his suspicions confirmed, especially by me.

'Nah. You've been taken for a ride. The cops know everything. They're just waiting.'

He didn't want to hear. He was still trying to convince himself. People milled around us, the noise was deafening, but we were in a private bubble, both of us totally intent. We had a fair few hatreds to hiss out, and there wasn't a lot of time.

'I'll give you an example. She was giving information to a gang. I won't mention names. In Avondale. She's got a cousin or something working at the bank there. I don't mean she done it, but she got some of the take. Now you can't tell me she'd throw away a sweet little arrangement like that? It wouldn't be worth her while. She knows that. They'd do her.'

'She's an informer,' I said, and moved away. I wanted to turn him inside out.

'Can you prove it?' He even grabbed me in his desperation to know. 'You're just trying to make trouble. That's your fucking trick isn't it? I haven't forgotten you ringing my boss that time. It's always been at the back of my mind. You and Nettie always on my back.'

'Your luck's run out,' I said coldly. 'You're dealing with a complete crazy. She wanted to bring her prey home to Mum. You were her protection, that's all, and you've been blown.'

'No one fucks around with me,' he said.

'I wouldn't be in your shoes for anything. If she doesn't get you and the cops don't, I will. I owe you for Marianne.'

'You? You haven't got the guts,' he said, real soft. 'I'd stick this fucking knife right through your throat and out the other side.'

'You'd have to move quick,' I whispered back, coming close. 'But you know all about guts, don't you? It must have taken guts to rape a fourteen-year-old and kill her. Wow. Guts.' The rape part was a guess, but I could see it was inspired.

'What are you raving on about?' His face had gone like stone and I could taste his hatred. He was ready to kill me.

'You know, baby. You know,' I said.

231

My attention was momentarily distracted by someone pulling at my arm and for the second I looked away Mitch melted into the crowd. I said to the guy, a painter I knew slightly, 'Can't you see I was talking?'

He said, 'Sorry, Glory. It's just that I thought you'd better know. There are some nuts outside the gallery. They're picketing you.'

The adrenalin in my veins propelled me like magic to the window, Mitch forgotten instantly, and sure enough, there they were, waiting for me.

They were a small group, only three or four of them, all dressed in sports clothes, and their faces, drained of all colour by the street light, were murderous with the glory of their cause. They looked like androids, unstoppable. Roxy would have been at home with them. Already people were gathering to watch and read the professionally printed placards. Even two storeys up I could make out the stern messages they carried for me. 'The Wages of Sin are Death' and 'Death Penalty for Drug Dealers'.

They were obviously fundamentalists, deeply preoccupied with the sins of other lesser beings — they had that well-dressed righteous look of the chosen. This was no scruffy, sincere band of desperadoes wrestling with the consciences of the world, this was money and slick PR, the complete ease of righteousness.

I had no doubt that Marianne's father was the brains and the money behind those careful, careful signs. He was probably hiding out somewhere directing operations, or even waiting in the gallery, mingling discreetly. Nothing as direct as street protest for him. He was on a mission from God, that guy, and nothing would stop him. He even looked slightly like an aging John Belushi when I thought about it.

I could feel the ache in my back rising to my head as I stood there, riveted, looking down at my persecutors. They wanted me dead, their placards made no bones about it. It was hard to know how to react to such respectable bloodlust.

Even as I watched, a TV van drew up. I thought wildly of sicking Moe on to them, even if my reputation got another battering. The idea of those people getting a smack in the mouth from the cream of the street gangs had a lot of appeal. It was as if Nigel was reading my thoughts from the other end of the room. He materialised behind me, breathing heavily in my ear. He must have even torn himself away from Bob. He acted as if he was trying to calm a horse.

'Don't do it, Glory. Don't you even tell your mates. This is horrendous enough without all that scum getting involved.' He was white with rage, apoplectic — whether at me or the pro-testors was hard to tell. With a visible effort he tried to take a hold of himself. 'They'll go away,' he said in my ear, as if he was praying.

Already the crowds in the gallery were beginning to scent a drama and there was a blind surge towards the window. Down in the street a TV man was interviewing one of the Christians. It was like seeing a dumb show behind glass. We both watched the silent scene intently, in total disbelief.

Before our eyes a tiny bright clown-like figure suddenly erupted in front of the group. It was my Rina. Seconds later, Grace, in high heels and a scarlet sheath dress, ran out behind her. They were gesticulating, screwing up their faces like monkeys, giving them the finger. One of the Christians pushed at Grace. I roared, 'Fuck that! They're not getting away with that. They must be crazy!' I threw my shoulder against the jammed window with all my strength. It looked as if it hadn't been opened for years. The sounds from below rushed in as I slammed it open with a wrench. I shouted down to them, but I couldn't be heard above the din. I thought desperately of crawling out onto the flower-pot ledge to abuse them from there. At least it would be quicker than running down the stairs — I would lose valuable minutes getting through the wall of people. Certainly, the sight of me — huge, awkward, teetering and flapping like a nightmare bird on that tinny little ledge — would attract instant attention. I started pulling up my skirt, and felt a hand grasp my arm. It was Nigel of course.

'Don't you climb up there or I'll strangle you,' he said, quite decently for him.

Get your hands off,' I said very quietly.

233

There was a look of manic determination on his face as he tried to grapple me down. He was fearsome with adrenalin, at all costs he was going to keep the lid on things, even if it meant knocking me unconscious. The tussle would have become quite ugly because I was pretty overwrought myself, but new strife erupting outside stopped us both in our tracks, as if by magic. We both heard the sudden screams and let go of each other in sheer panic. I ran to look out the window.

Down below the small crowd had started swaying back and forth like a rugby audience when there's a fight on, and the white squares of the banners disappeared with startling suddenness. It was Moe and a couple of his mates — I could see their sombre gang-patches and jackets against the bright clothes of the protestors. They must have sized up the situation in minutes and raced out like a pack of commandos.

A TV light arced and keeled over, shooting sparks, there was a chorus of screams as it hit the ground, plunging all the arrangements into darkness. Someone, probably a protestor, was whingeing into a megaphone before the sound was cut off suddenly.

'Thanks, Glory,' Nigel said. He sounded almost resigned. 'This is a masterstroke of course.' He was so calm it was thrilling.

I said, 'Don't blame me. Don't even speak to me,' and moved with great dignity towards the door. They all stood back respectfully for me, I felt like a queen sailing through the crowd.

Just as I was getting to the top of the stairs, a crowd of people burst in and started surging up the stairs towards me. They looked as if they were getting away from the cops — with a few innocent by-standers caught up in the press. They were all there, Moe and his two mates, the protestors, onlookers and TV people — all scuffling into the gallery, shoved into the room by the people behind them, arguing, punching, like a gang of schoolkids. As they forced their way in, everyone inside was pushed against each other and the wall, in a mass of seething bodies.

Fights started to break out in front of my eyes. It was hard to know who was fighting who, but it didn't seem to be just the protestors and Moe's gang.

The air was thick with old scores and new ones as each little scuffle set off a chain reaction. There was an unmistakable feeling of madness in the room. It was the first punch-up in a gallery I'd ever seen, and in another situation I might have enjoyed it. But all I wanted to do was get Rina out. There were groups of people thumping each other in every corner of the room, glasses breaking, shouted abuse, an occasional panicky scream. A couple of pictures were knocked off the walls and cowering art lovers crouched down in corners as missiles flew through the air. The old wooden building was vibrating like an earthquake. The mass of people shifted for a second and I could see Cash and Jeff in the far corner of the room standing behind one of the tables still drinking. They seemed to be arguing. Even while I was watching in disbelief, in that brief instant what looked like a full flagon of wine sailed through the air and smashed against the wall behind them in a great bleeding mass of glass and red plonk. Their survival reflexes were fantastically fast, they were both under the table before it hit the wall. There was no sign of Simon. Before I could tear my horrified gaze away, the crowd had moved and massed again and they were lost from sight.

I thought I saw Mitch lying out cold, but everything was so unreal it was hard to separate fact from fiction. Al loomed up beside me with his strange spikey head trickling with blood.

One of them bastards hit me with his sign,' he said to me. It was like a dream.

I said, 'Where's Rina?' He just shrugged. I thought much later that he was probably concussed or something, he was acting so strangely.

He said, 'Sue's here somewhere. She's looking for me. And you. She's ropeable, man. Some jerk's just told her about you and me. She thinks I'm a pervert.'

'Pervert?' I repeated dazed, and he disappeared again, just as a big bearded painter I knew slightly shoved into me so violently I was graunched against the table and winded.

'Call themselves Christian, those mealy-mouthed pricks. I'll get that bastard if it's the last thing I do!' he was screaming. He was either drunk or mad — he punched at the air with his huge freckled fist as if he was going to do someone.

I kept trying to push through the crowd in search of Rina. Someone screamed so loud in my ear my head was ringing. I was frantic about her, she was so small amongst that mass of maniacs — she could easily get trodden on. She didn't know how to think fast and protect herself either, the noise alone was enough to terrify her.

It was only a matter of time before the cops got there, so it was high time for me to get out of the place, but I couldn't go without her. I piled recklessly through the flailing bodies, shouting for her. The boys and Moe had suddenly disappeared, they had obviously gone within minutes. It was a typical gang run — a lightning strike, then off before the cops arrived, leaving the other poor suckers still slogging it out in the aftermath.

They were experts, they could turn over a pub in sixty seconds flat and then piss off so quickly you wouldn't even know. Someone careered into me, throwing me against the wall and my side was bruised and aching from the thump. I started to call out for her.

'Has anyone seen a kid? Rina!' I called out so loud it roared above the noise of the crowd. There was a confused babble of voices and suddenly Roxy was there in front of me — her eyes dilated, unseeing, mad. She had been drawn by my voice and come straight as an arrow. Before I had time to move or even react I saw the glitter of her knife as she thrust it deep into my side.

We fell against each other and the knife came out in my hand. With a huge effort, in slow motion I plunged it into her shoulder. It made a creaking noise like an old iron gate being opened slowly. She staggered against me, her eyes so huge they looked as if they would burst out of her head. She sighed and gasped and bled and crumpled like a sagging doll in front of me. I felt my own fierce wound tearing at my guts — we did a slow dance the two of us, like giant dolls dripping sawdust blood.

The last thing I remember is falling onto her soft haunch which lay open to receive me, half mad with the pain, and glorious night settling down around my ears, her perfumed body tender against me.

14

After that I surfaced only very occasionally into dream scenes — a glimmer of white, an icy-blue screen, the mound of my body tightly swathed and bandaged in cold hospital sheets, nurses moving like ghosts through my delirium — then I was back down again, lost. I was in a fog, floating through a sea of drugs and pain with only my gashed-out side throbbing and heating like an engine to keep me going. It often seemed easier to go under, give way to the fog which was so softly nudging me, always ready to enfold me in its love.

The only thing I knew for sure in all that time was that I had to contain the spirit which was daily leaking out of my side, from some primitive part in me I knew I had to direct all my energies there with absolute accuracy, because there was no second chance. Even lost in the fog I learnt the gestures which could save me, like an obsessive woman washing her hands fifty times a day or a kid terrified to stand on a crack. I had to keep myself inviolate, stay in certain positions, keep very still to preserve my life. In the short waking times I gave all my attention to certain areas of the room which did not disturb me — the peeling paint on the bed-ends, a panel of cool green just beside the window, my own huge stranded sea-lion shape under the blankets. Each of them had some significance, each of them anchored me to life.

Other sights, like one particular nurse's face and a nightmarish painting of Venetian canals hanging above the locker, filled me with dread, started the gorge rising in my throat, set all the feverish images dancing in my blood. Then faces tilted up, went black and swollen in front of my eyes, and menacing shapeless dreams when my eyes went dark and I would start to float, took over. I was never even sure whether they were dreams or not. There seemed to be no barrier between life or death, dream or reality, and I floated in the fog like a child waiting to be born. Even Rina was only a distant point of light somewhere far away.

The first time I woke outright and saw my room clearly it was like the slow awakening after drunkenness — first the real details of the room and then of my own body, then the pain, in vivid technicolour.

I called experimentally, 'Rina! Rina,' to the sort of silence which could go on for years. 'Rina,' I called. My head was thumping. For the first time since it happened the entire remembrance of the opening hit me as I half turned in the bed, and I saw Roxy's dog-eyes as she lunged for me with the knife. I groaned out loud. I could see her walking purposefully up the corridor in the ward, looking for my name on the door, muttering to herself, determined to knock me off for once and for all.

I felt as if there would be no end to her, she would pursue me to my death, even the ferocious wound in my side was not enough for her purposes. It was such a holocaust of a vision my brain closed down again. It seemed like hours that I lay there semi-conscious, trying to clear my head and get my courage back.

It wasn't just the fear. The knowledge that Roxy had stabbed me in public, the intimacy of the act— the knife, the panting, my own heart's blood — was so obscene in front of strangers. And Rina seeing her poor lumbering cow of a mother being stabbed — the image she'd carry in her muddled, loving mind troubled me badly. I called for her again, hours later. I wanted to touch her and see her friendly little pug-face. Finally a nurse wearing some kind of weird flowery cap must have heard me. She came in and bent low over me. I could hear the creaking of her uniform and smell her faint sweat. I was like a camera sharply pulled into focus, and the nurse's human smell was so comforting I wanted to grasp her hand.

'So you're awake, eh?' she said. You could see she was pleased, she took it personally in a comfortable sort of way.

'Your wound got infected as well, Mrs Day, and you were away with the fairies for a while. Nice to have you back. You don't even recognise me, do you?'

'Fairies?' I croaked.

'You're alright now, love. Don't worry. We've been giving you something to put you out as well, not to mention all the antibiotics they've been pumping into you. You're going to be OK.' It was a very pleasant thing to say but I had my doubts.

I said, 'Where's Rina?'

'That your daughter, dear?' the nurse asked.

'Yes.'

'She's fine. She's with that chap with no — hair. I could ring them and tell them you're awake.'

'The phone's cut off.' I said in my new harsh voice. 'I forgot to pay it.' I was light-headed with relief. Al would be looking after her.

She smiled at me. She was really young, but she treated me motherly.

'You're not allowed visitors for a wee while,' she said.

'Is Roxy dead?' I asked, fearing the worst.

The nurse said, 'Oh you poor thing. We've got a lot on our mind haven't we? It was only a flesh wound they said. She's in Oakley. Her lawyer's pleading insanity,' she added as delicately as she could.

'Thank God,' I said, lying stone still with the relief. 'Thank Christ.'

There were so many things to catch up on. I hadn't even realised I had been worried about it. I'd stabbed her to kill in the heat of the moment. The instinct had risen up as easy as falling; the quick reaction, the creak of the knife, the pain given and received was no problem then. But now it was a relief she wasn't dead. Killing Roxy would have lain undigested on my heart all my life.

The nurse said, sitting comfortably on the white bed, 'Well, you've been in the papers as well. You're quite a celebrity. There's a photo of you on the front page.'

I groaned. The very thought of it all made me feel like hiding for years. I must have been mad that night. Poor Rina. The nurse had even kept the cutting for me. She reached across in the locker drawer and there I was — a madwoman, huge black mouth open in a scream, cascades of flesh and dress billowing around me. It looked as if it had been taken beside the window when I was looking down on the protestors. It was blurry but startling. It was front-page news, with a big headline. The nurse wanted to read it all out, she was enjoying her role of news-bringer.

'Thanks,' I said. 'I'll read it later.'

The relief was so strong I felt the tears pouring down my cheeks, and I didn't even mind that the nurse could see.

'Now don't get upset,' the nurse said, hastily getting off the bed. She was the sort who obviously only liked her drama vicarious.

The whole thing was over then, blown over like a great black cloud. I just had to get my suffering old hump of a body out of here, and there would be no more Roxy stalking me. The relent-lessness of the past few weeks would have disappeared like a nightmare. That whirlwind of deaths and dying and old vio-lences, old pains, was going to blow out of my life again, when I had started to believe it would go on for ever. I'd grown so accustomed to the stress of it, it was hard to imagine life out there bare and fresh as a clean-swept room. I had a lot of work to catch up on. I wanted to laugh with the joy of it.

'I'd like to go home,' I said.

The nurse laughed. 'Now come on, Glory Day. You've got a pretty nasty wound. Not to mention complications. You've turned the corner, but it was touch and go, you know.'

'Touch and go? How long have I been in this place?' I asked.

'Two weeks,' she said. 'To the day, in actual fact.'

'Two weeks.' I thought of the great crack in my side, all those layers of fat sliced through by the force of Roxy's craziness. It was hard to believe that I had been wandering all those days in and out of death, because of the wound she'd wanted to give me.

The nurse said as if reading my thoughts, 'You could have been killed. Another inch. Not to mention the infection. Doctor was just saying on ward round this morning that he reckons you've got the constitution of a horse. So don't get any funny ideas about getting out soon. We've got to keep you here for a while.'

After that, of course, I had a lot of time to think, lying in the icy hospital bed, hour after hour with the smell of disinfectant and the humming of the machine beside me. I felt resigned in there, completely peaceful, just waiting to see Rina and Al, not able to read or do anything except lie blinking like a great stranded animal watching the day move across the wall.

I still had burning obsessive dreams — Rina with a parrot on her head, Al dancing by my bed, his hair falling in curls around his beautiful face, Roxy muttering inside a little box under the table in the kitchen.

I even had a very quiet dream about Marianne, almost a vision in fact. She sat beside my bed like a flower, slightly reproachful, patting my cheeks with the soft hand of a child. I knew in the dream she'd finally let me go. It was because of the way she'd gone out, almost by accident, that had made her spirit so restless and regretful. She had been like a kid threatening to jump just for attention, then tipping, pulling back too late and falling to her death with only a second of regret by way of preparation. There was nothing clean to her end, there was no real readiness in her for such a muddy death. Schoolgirlish playing with fire had gone way out of control and destroyed her. The love between us in the hour of her dying had only confused the process, but now we were equals, a life for a death. I'd come through it with a lot of excess burnt away, but I'd paid my dues to both her and Roxy, not to mention laying a few ghosts of my own in the process. It felt as if the healing had spread further into the skin than the original wound, I was stripped clear of festering memories, lighter than I'd ever been.

For the first time in my life there was some forgiveness in my bones for old injustices. It made me realise the difference between me and them — I'd always known that death was there for the taking any time you cared to name, so I never took it lightly, even at my most destructive. I had never been interested in playing to an imaginary audience, my paintings were a lucky combination of survival, excellent technique and my own secret joy, not a circus on wheels for the curious.

It was a moment of vindication for me when I woke up after the dream. I was, after all, as strong as the women I'd been brought up with — women who had been beaten up all their lives by their husbands and fathers and sons. That regular bruising, that crushing of their tired skin and bones had left their poor old flesh like iron. Women like them could go through the fire and out the other end, they could carry the world on their shoulders and not even feel it. It was something I knew for sure, lying there in the hospital, dredging through my life's events with my brand new tender brain cells, as the wound healed under the ice-clean sheets.

But I needed a few other things besides the healing to carry me through. The white walls and machines and my physical passivity sometimes engulfed me. So it was a relief when a new nurse came on — a real godsend. She was a squat evil-tempered woman who nagged me about my weight and talked to all the patients as if they were retarded. Her face was fiery with pimples. She was sure she had me taped, and prided herself on never mincing words. Her presence definitely helped me to sharpen my focus. I didn't feel so insulated when she was around. She'd come in preoccupied with her own life, busy about her job, trying to lift me, her face glistening with malice.

'A famous painter,' she'd say in her flat weary voice. 'What would you know about life?' She'd had it in for artists anyway, she told me once. Her sister married a commercial artist. An absolute bastard. AC-DC — used to bring them home in front of the kids. A little shit. She got out of it quick smart and no access. 'They're all mad, it's a known fact. Well look at that blimmin' photo of you in the paper. Anyone who carried on like that should be put away '

Whenever she touched me she'd say, 'It wouldn't hurt you to lose some poundage. Bloody hell, woman.'

I said once, 'Fuck that. It saved my life. I like my fat.' I had a clear image of my small pink glistening organs nestled safely away under the yellow layers of fat, the slice of Roxy's cruel knife, laying them bare in one blow, the slow red seepage of a serious wound.

She didn't blink. 'Language. You shouldn't be so pretentious. It's a health risk that blubber. A famous painter like you should know better,' but she gave a little grunt of a laugh in spite of herself. She was a professional dag, it was the way she got through life — and she wasn't having her position usurped by a common bitch like me.

'Well, what did she stab you for? You must have done something,' she said one afternoon. We were as easy and bitchy as a married couple, there were no holds barred. There was the same careful wearing away of someone else's private structures, the slow acid drip.

'I don't know,' I said easily, gathering myself for the attack. I didn't feel like going into the complexities of it with her, and there were a fair few points I wasn't clear about myself.

She was washing me as she talked, swishing warm water over the great expanse of my back, her skilled healing hands belying the sharpness of her tongue. Netty once washed me like that years ago when I was a child, very pregnant to her death's-head son, and I have never forgotten the warm soapy water and her gnarled hands soaping their way into my starveling soul. Every luxurious caress stayed tattooed on my heart, a rare benediction, and it was the same this afternoon. The intimacy of it made my heart liquid with wanting Rina around, the human warmth of her after the coldness of my hospital bed.

'There's never any smoke without fire,' the nurse said absently. She was thinking of something else already. There were long silences with just the swish of the water, her hands slapping softly on my flesh, her labouring breath. The water trickled over my bare skin like a blessing, a warm rain of mercy. I lay there peaceful, redeemed, ready for the world.

About the author

Rosie Scott is a writer and political activist who has been involved in civil rights protests, peace issues and the women's movement. In addition to *Glory Days*, her first novel, she is the author of several stories and a prize-winning play entitled *Say Thank You to the Lady*. She is currently living in Australia with her husband and two daughters.